What You Call Free

Flora Johnston

Ringwood Publishing

Glasgow

First published in Great Britain in 2021 by

Ringwood Publishing

www.ringwoodpublishing.com

mail@ringwoodpublishing.com

ISBN: 978-1-901514-96-4

British Library Cataloguing-in-Publication Data

A catalogue record for this book is available from the

British library

Typeset in Times New Roman 11

Printed and bound in the UK

by

Lonsdale Direct Solutions

Praise for What You Call Free

'In this wonderful debut novel, Flora Johnston prises open a forgotten window to give a rare view onto the lives of women in one of the darkest periods in Scotland's history.

A sullen atmosphere of unrelentingly wintry weather and impending personal disaster looms over *What You Call Free*, which is set mainly in the lee of the Pentland Hills and Edinburgh in 1687-8, a time when Scotland was riven by religious and political differences. The two principal characters, Helen Alexander and Jonet Gothskirk, were real women, but little is known of the detail of their lives, and the novel's triumph is to make them whole in flesh and blood. They could have remained passive victims of the times in which they existed, but Flora Johnston's acute and sensitive writing reveals their intelligence and courage as they face hypocrisy and cruelty masquerading as righteousness and honour. Yet Helen and Jonet are not saints but whole human beings, full of faith, doubt, hope and fear, and so are the sisters, mothers, daughters, husbands, brothers and suitors who surround them.

The story also features a remarkable portrait of James Renwick, the last of the Covenanter martyrs, whose arrest and trial lead to the novel's stunning climax. *What You Call Free* is historical fiction of the highest quality.'

James Robertson, novelist, poet and short story writer

'Flora Johnston has written a literary page turner about one of Scotland's most turbulent and least talked about periods. It opens in 1687, the time of the Covenant. There are those, like Helen – principled widow with three young children – who bravely offer shelter to religious refugees, whose only crime might be worshipping in a field instead of a Kirk. And there are those like Jonet – pregnant unmarried teenager who wear the sackcloth every Sunday in the Kirk, and suffer the scourge of a community for the sin of falling for a scoundrel.

The novel follows these two women in alternating chapters, their fates interwoven in a tight-paced progression through perilous adventures.

Johnston has created a highly convincing narrative not just of an historic time in Scotland, but of specific individuals with all their quirks and weaknesses and unexpected flashes of both inspiration and despair. Jonet and Helen are memorable, not because they are perfect heroines with just causes, but because they are utterly recognisable as people. It's a bleak story because it's a bleak time, but the characters retain their warmth and humanity.

All in all, a compulsive read. As addictive as chocolate, and as nourishing as a bowl of Scotch broth.'

Cynthia Rogerson, award-winning novelist

'Flora Johnston has created a gripping narrative with engaging, often conflicted characters, and evoked time and place with great skill. I often find myself critical of historical fiction that labours historical detail and over-explains, but Flora has achieved the right balance between big picture and fine detail – not easy when dealing with such a tangled period. I particularly enjoyed the descriptions of the Pentland slopes and Edinburgh itself and the pictures painted of interiors and the life within them. Flora has told a powerful story, steering a sure-footed path through perhaps the most complex and divided period in Scotland's history, in a way that resonates with many issues today.'

Jenni Calder, novelist, poet and literary historian

Dedication

For David, my love. Thank you for believing.

The Covenanters

Hugh MacDiarmid

The waves of their purposefulness go flooding through me.
This religion is simple, naked. Its values stand out
In black and white. It is the wind of God;
Like standing on a mountain top in a gale
Binding, compelling, yet gloriously freeing.
It contains nothing tawdry or trivial.
Its very ugliness is compelling,
Its bleakness uplifting.
It holds me in a fastness of security.

Kirk Session Records of West Calder, 1687

Compeared Jonet Gothskirk, and in Sackcloth confessed before the Session her sin of Adultery with William Murdoch, professing upon her knees her sorrow for the same. She was ordained the next Lord's day to enter to the place of public repentance, and to appear there in Sackcloth.

Foreword

Ink and blood

This novel begins in 1687 but the story stretches back nearly fifty years earlier, long before Helen and Jonet, who were both real women, were born.

On a short February day in 1638, the National Covenant was first signed in Greyfriars Kirkyard in Edinburgh. Many Scots would go on to add their names to this document, pledging to defend their reformed faith against crown interference and control. Those who supported this and subsequent declarations were soon on a collision course with the Stuart kings, who believed their absolute right to rule as they chose came directly from God.

Decades of conflict followed. When Charles II was restored to the throne in 1660, Helen Alexander was a little girl of six, unaware that the hopes of the Covenanters had just been shattered. Charles rejected the Covenants and reintroduced crown-appointed bishops to rule the Scottish kirk. Those who resisted – about a quarter of all ministers – were removed from their parishes. Some fled abroad, while others took part in a campaign of theological persuasion, open-air worship and armed resistance.

Christ, not the king, must be head of the kirk in Scotland.

A series of flashpoints came in 1679. A group of Covenanters murdered the Archbishop of St Andrews, and amid the turmoil that followed, the Covenanting army was heavily defeated at the battle of Bothwell Brig.

By this time, Helen was twenty-five and had become convinced of the Covenanting cause. Her husband did not share her views.

The government of Charles II was determined to crush the rebels completely and used extreme force on the

Covenanters and their sympathisers. In 1683 the 'persecuted remnant', as they saw themselves, gained a new leader in twenty-one-year-old preacher James Renwick. Two years later, Charles II died and his brother James VII and II succeeded to the throne. The new king wanted to protect and promote his own Roman Catholic faith and so offered some limited freedoms to worship. Many who had previously supported the Covenants complied, but James Renwick and his followers refused to compromise. Known as the Society People, they were hunted more fiercely than ever.

By 1687 much ink had been spilled, much blood had been shed, and the struggle continued.

James Renwick was on the run, hiding in the hills and preaching at illegal gatherings. He was the most wanted man in the kingdom.

Helen Alexander, now a widow of thirty-three, was one of his most committed supporters.

As for Jonet Gothskirk, eighteen years old and pregnant, the affairs of kirk and state couldn't have been further from her mind.

Chapter One

This day Jonet Gothskirk entered into the place of public repentance, appearing there in Sackcloth for her Adultery with William Murdoch.

Sackcloth on skin. Harsh and unforgiving, it scoured the softness of her body. The coarse material was uncomfortable, aye, but far worse were the things living in it. Biting. Vicious beasts. But she would not move. She would not twitch or scratch or shift on the stool – or no more than was necessary. They would never know how raw this felt.

And yet, far worse than the feel of the thing was the smell. She could pick out the most pungent odours. Sweat. Piss. Maybe even vomit. And the persistent trace of Libby Kerr, that ill-famed woman who was known to wear this sackcloth gown most often.

It stank of shame.

But Jonet wouldn't think that. If she thought about shame, she might open her ears, and let that monotonous drone become a series of words, directed at her. She might start to see features, well-kent faces, in the formless, shifting cloud just beyond the horizon of her unfocused gaze.

Just dinna let them in.

She was learning fast. It was a different story a fortnight syne, when they summoned her here to the kirk to appear before them in private. She'd been sure of herself then, and sure too of him. She still had solid ground beneath her, then. Aye, she was feart, but her crime wasn't so unusual. She'd opened herself too early to him, that was all. Many another had done the same. There would be a rebuke, and maybe

1

a Sabbath of humiliation before them, Will at her side. It would be something to laugh over later as they lay in each other's arms.

Oh, how wrong she had been. She had stood before them that night in the hollow dark of the empty kirk. Light flickered up into their faces from the tallow candles standing tall on the table, and not one glimmer of kindness or sympathy could she find amid the restless shadows.

'Jonet Gothskirk, you are summoned here to answer a charge of adultery with William Murdoch.'

Adultery?

'Do you admit your guilt?'

In the name of all that was good, what did they mean by adultery?

Then he was leaning forward, the minister, Mr Mackenzie, his eyes glinting in the light of those candles. 'You're a Jezebel and a blight on godly society, Jonet Gothskirk, in your fornication with another woman's husband. And what's more, you're carrying his bastard, are you no?'

Another woman's *husband*?

He got to his feet so fast the table near overturned, and came round close beside her, too close beside her, his black gown brushing the earthen floor. He thrust a heap of rough, clarty material into her arms. 'Put this on and get down on your knees, woman.'

And she was looking round them, bewildered, these men she'd kent all her life. Surely someone would say this was wrong. Will was nobody's husband, not yet, and soon he would be hers. A whispered promise.

'On your knees!'

And the bairn. How could they possibly ken about the bairn?

Then someone had hold of her, gripping her arm with strong fingers, and the gown was hauled over her head. She was choking at the stour on it as another set of hands pushed down on her shoulders, pushing her down until she was huddled on the floor, knees and hands both pressed hard into the damp earth, hair trailing loose and brushing the ground.

Dear God, what is this, what is this?

'Jonet Gothskirk, do you admit your guilt in adultery with William Murdoch, and your sorrow for the same?'

And in the echoing darkness she heard her own voice agree, repeating what they wanted her to say, the dust sticking to the roof of her mouth, nausea rising. All the while struggling to believe what they were telling her about Will and his woman, and yet knowing somewhere right in the pit of her stomach that it must be true. She admitted her guilt and she begged for mercy. On her knees. Exposed. Defenceless.

And she felt the shame.

But Mam was waiting for her afterwards, with the scent and the touch of eighteen years of brusque kindness. Jonet crumpled then, still reeling at what they'd told her about Will, and just beginning to discern through her splintering dreams that those moments in the dark kirk had recast her life. She clung to her mother, terrified at the thought of all that had already been and all that was still to come. And it was Mam who showed her the way to get through it, who lifted up all the broken pieces of her, and let her see that they were still worth something. Who told her how to survive this first horror. *You're no the first and you'll no be the last. Just dinna let them in.*

So now here she was, paraded before them all, this Sabbath and everlasting Sabbaths stretching out before her. She would shelter within herself, and within this old heap of sackcloth. For it was just a rag, rough perhaps, but unable to hurt her. Pain screamed through her soul, but it came from a different place entirely.

Do nothing but breathe. Little clouds of mist formed in front of her lips. *Who* made this garment of humiliation anyway? Who sat, with an old piece – or was it a fresh piece – of sacking, and cut and stitched it into this hideous shape? Probably some poor cow desperate to earn a couple of bawbees from the Kirk Session. Did she try it on when she had finished? Did she twirl for her husband, laughing at the thought of the misery it would bring to the women and men of the parish?

Or did she shiver, maybe, brushed by a memory, unsettled by a foreboding? For who, really, was safe?

There was a movement there, just on the edge of Jonet's vision. Dark eyes and a hostile glare. Her brother Davy, so cold. If only Kirstie could be here among the faces that she was trying not to see, or Mam. But notwithstanding her mother's strength, that was too much for her. Mam would be at home, taking out her anger on the washing, for all it was the Sabbath. Pounding the clothes, and trying not to mind the tears that might fall now she was alone. Jonet could still feel the pressure of Mam's clasp on her arms before she left that morning. 'I'll no be there, Jonet,' she'd said. 'I'd never be able to hold my tongue and let that minister rail at you. I'd only make things worse for you. Be strong, my lass, and you'll get through it.'

You'll get through it. There was a burning behind her eyes, a tightness in her chest. Weeks of this humiliation stretched out ahead of her, and she had no notion at all how she would get through it, but somehow she must. She must.

*

On the other side of the lumpy spine of the Pentland Hills, Helen Alexander pressed a small parcel of food into the fair young man's hands, bade him Godspeed, and watched until he was just another shifting shadow amid the early morning mist that cloaked the lower slopes. She pushed the door as quietly as possible, holding her breath as it grated on the floor. Her hands were trembling, so she pressed them into her apron and turned towards the fireplace, ready to get the oatmeal on.

4

But for all her attempts at stealth it seemed her daughter had been roused, though the lads slept on unaware. Beatrix had slipped from behind the curtain and now stood; a white, silent figure, dark eyes fixed on her mother.

'Get dressed then or you'll catch your death,' snapped Helen. 'And hurry about it, for I need you to fetch some water.'

There was a quick, quizzical glance from those watchful eyes, nothing more, and Beatrix turned and retreated to the boxbed. Thirteen years old, and she didn't miss a thing. Helen set the pot above the fire; her heightened nerves soothed by familiar movements. No harm done, and God willing he would be safely away by now. She would tell them her news today, and that should chase other thoughts from Beatrix's mind.

She waited until they were all gathered round the table, and she had prayed God's blessing on their food, their home, and on all those who were persecuted but remained faithful. It was the Sabbath, but they would be going nowhere near any kirk. Once they'd eaten, they would spend time together in family worship, where they could be free. Sometimes Sandy and Kirstie over by would join them, but today it would just be the four of them. Her wee family: Beatrix, Jamie, Charlie.

They might be bairns, Charlie but nine, yet they understood the dangers of these wicked times. How could they not, when every unexpected knock on the door brought with it an echo of her capture and imprisonment? Surely they too would see that her decision was for the best. She laid down her spoon. 'You ken Mr Currie. Well, he and I are to wed.'

The words, spoken aloud, seemed to summon the presence of the kindly merchant right into their home at once – but of course, he had already eaten many a meal alongside them. Perhaps that's why the bairns were none too startled by the news. The lads had their questions – would they go to live with him, or would he come here to Pentland? Would he bring Moss the packhorse, and where would she sleep? Helen answered, then looked to her daughter. 'Beatrix?'

There was something fleeting in those dark eyes once more, and Helen took in a quick breath, but then the look was gone. Beatrix smiled. 'I'm glad,' she said.

Chapter Two

Sunday 30th October 1687

Sunday 30th October 1687

This is the second Sabbath of Jonet Gothskirk's appearance in Sackcloth in the place of public repentance.

The next week they made her stand by the door before the service. It was a heavy, dreich morning, with a persistent dampness which clung to her bare head and seeped into the rough cloth of the gown. It was so much harder to shut them out, those folks she knew, when they were walking right past her, some staring, others looking away. Murmured comments, just loud enough for her to hear. Foul language they'd do well to keep from the ears of the elders. Och, and she'd often enough done the very same thing herself. Whispering and giggling with Kirstie at some poor soul on show, never thinking that one day it might be her. But here was Davy coming past now, glowering with mortified fury. Self-righteous gowk that he was. Looking away from him, she found herself face to face with a man she didn't know, an older man with thinning curly hair and a belly that hung over his breeks. The look he gave her was laden with lust, and she dropped her eyes at once. She would see no more.

When they were all in, the beadle jerked his head and she tried to walk through the centre of the kirk. But the chilling dampness of the ground had stolen into her bare soles, and she'd have been as well trying to lift the weight of the flagstone threshold as lift her own feet. Her frozen fingers wouldn't grip the material of the gown, and it dragged along the ground. Small shuffling steps, that was the only way to do it. Even so, she trod on the edge of the material, stumbled, nearly fell. No one helped her. Of course.

And then she was at the front once more, below his pulpit, perched awkwardly on the stool. She could feel him, Mr Mackenzie, glaring down at her, and she fixed her eyes instead on the sandglass screwed into the pulpit, supposed to regulate his time – though he would just turn it over once all the grains had drained through. The service opened with a reading from Scripture, and they mumbled through a psalm. And when the minister cleared his throat, she waited for it to begin again. Her feet were so cold. Her hands were even colder. She curled her fingers, half-closed her eyes, and prepared to slide back into emptiness.

But no. This week, it seemed, Mr Mackenzie had something else on his mind. It wasn't her sin at all. His voice boomed out a warning, spit flying dangerously close to her. 'Do you believe it's just a wee thing to go hear those so-called preachers in the fields? You foolish, sinful folk, I have heard of the gatherings near to this very place.' His voice rose in indignation. 'Dinna think you can dabble light in fanaticism. This wickedness is the scourge of Scotland and it will bring you to the scaffold, aye, and to the eternal fire of judgement. But,' his voice softened, and she wondered what was coming next. 'If you have any knowledge of these scandalous gatherings, and most particular of the whereabouts of that damned traitor, James Renwick, it is your solemn duty to reveal it. King James has this week offered a very generous reward of 100 pounds for his capture. Folks like you canna go straight to the justices, mind. Tell me what you ken and I'll make sure you get your share. There will soon be no place in Scotland safe for that dog Renwick to hide.'

Jonet risked a glance at the huddle of faces before her. Bored, mostly. He was wasting his breath. Those of the Society, those of whom he spoke, they would not hear his warnings, for they had refused to enter the kirk ever since their own preacher had been thrown out and Mr Mackenzie had been appointed. As for families like her own, they appeared in the kirk each Sabbath to keep on the right side of the Lord and of the laird, but they cared little for the religious factions which divided their land, or for extremes on either side.

She shifted a little. She was so cold, so weary. She'd barely slept since last time she sat here, a week past. Night after night, as wee Mary's warm body pressed in against her, she tried to rest, tried to welcome the mercy of a few hours of comforting darkness, with no eyes to follow her, no lips to speak against her. But the voices inside her own head were loud enough to keep her awake. And it felt so strange to be back here, back home in bed with her sister, instead of sleeping alongside the girls in the dairy loft, where all was whispered conversations and petty quarrels. But Mistress Dalguise on the farm, she'd summoned her in just as soon as she'd heard the rumours. Yet another accusing conversation. 'What's this I'm hearing from Mr Dalguise, Jonet?'

Aye, it was the night after she'd appeared before the elders. He was one of *them*, her husband, the tenant farmer.

She'd stood, fingers twisting the cord of her apron, not knowing what to say but knowing what was surely coming.

'He tells me you'll be appearing afore the kirk on the Sabbath morn.'

'Aye, mistress.'

'Will Murdoch, eh? Yon groom who was with us ower the summer?'

'Aye, mistress.' But the sound of his name was the vicious slash of a knife through her flesh.

'And him a married man with bairns of his ain.'

She'd looked up at that, quick and fierce. 'I didna ken.'

The mistress had made a sound of disgust. Jonet couldn't tell if she thought her a fool or a liar, or maybe both. Then she'd continued, her eyes narrowed.

'And you are with child?'

A beat. 'Aye, mistress.'

'Well Jonet, you must collect your belongings and be gone. I'll see you get what's owed.'

She'd tried to argue then, to plead for another few weeks even, just until she started to show. And it was then that Mistress Dalguise laughed. 'To show? What's the difference of that, lass? All the world kens of this bairn. No, I willna have your shame brought upon a godly household. You'll gather your gear and go.'

'Godly!' Mam said when she told her. And then not another word. But Jonet knew her wage was a sore loss, for part of their rent these days was due in coin. So hard, to come trailing home to Mam's tight face and Davy's scorn and wee Mary's huge eyes. And so much harder, to find herself alone next day as they all went about their business, even Mary out gathering in the field. She could hear Mam humming at the far end of the cottage as she worked the spindle. Unable to bear the idea of sitting inside doing nothing, she stepped into the sharp October air. It was a dry day, for all it was overcast, and the wind that whipped down from the hill stung her cheeks, but she welcomed that. Welcomed the feel of it, the struggle against it, as she made her way past the small cluster of cottages, following the path that would take her up the gentle incline towards the common grazing.

She had not come this way since she started working at the farm three year syne, yet she knew every tree, every ditch, every leaf. And as she walked along the track in the footsteps of her girlish self, she was able, just fleetingly, to catch a sense of that lass again. The lass who had not yet met Will Murdoch.

But it was fleeting right enough. Round the next corner she met Mamie and her daughters from one of the cottages. And she kent them well, one lass being about her own age, and she made to greet them. But the younger one gave a giggle and the mother actually stretched out both her arms and pulled one daughter into each side, as if to shield her precious children from the harlot in their midst.

As if pregnancy might be as contagious as the plague.

And she stopped and watched as they hurried past, round the corner and out of sight. And then, alone again, she reached out blind and leant all her weight against a tree trunk, sinking slowly downwards until she was huddled at its roots. This was the way it would be from now on, then. Shunned. Unable to find work or a husband, forever a burden to her family. Shamed.

All because she fell for a man who brushed the hair from her face, and spoke as softly to her as he did to his beloved horses.

Another woman's husband.

She didn't doubt it now. Each night as she lay in her bed amid restless and fitful dreams, she heard snatches of Will's conversation echoing round her head. Phrases and stories which hadn't quite made sense. The laughter in his eyes had chased away any worries at the time, masking his betrayal.

She could scarcely comprehend it, but it was quite obviously true.

They were looking for him, of course, to bring him to justice too, and she tried to picture him, the laughter gone, bareheaded and draped in sackcloth at the front of the kirk. What would his *wife* say then? Aye, that would be a sweet moment.

Yet somehow, in the chill, she couldn't quite summon the heat for revenge. He was false, and she was broken. Did it really matter what happened to him now?

She wasn't sure how long she sat there amid the damp fallen leaves, the rough bark digging into her spine, but eventually she pulled herself to her feet and began to walk down, life creeping painfully back into her numb legs. And as she passed along the path near the houses, everyone she met seemed to confirm her fears. Two folk with heads close together, whispering quietly. A child laughing, someone else pointing. It was right, what Mistress Dalguise had said: 'all the world kens of this bairn.' For all the world had seen her, shrouded in shame before the kirk.

And with no Will to be found, that same world saw and judged a wicked, wanton woman.

So she returned to the cottage and she took to the boxbed and lay facing the wall. All that day and all the next. And the week inched forward, and the prospect of the Sabbath drew closer, when she would yet again be paraded as an object of sin and shame.

For a day or two her family let her be, though wee Mary's thin arms would slip around her as she lay there wakeful in the night, and she was grateful for it. But she knew that Mam wouldn't live with such idleness and self-pity for long. She heard her mother muttering as she went about her work, the words never quite distinct enough to worm under Jonet's blanket of grief, but aimed at her, without a doubt.

And right enough the day soon came when her mother was before her, berating her, ordering her to get to her feet and come ben. So she did. She dressed herself and slipped through the curtain into the room where Mam was leaning over the fire, her face flushed. There was a bowl of porridge waiting on the old wooden table, and Jonet sat herself down. She waited. A lifetime's experience told her Mam would speak when she was ready and not a moment before. When she did, it was the last thing Jonet expected.

'Right, my lass. Sandy's coming for you Monday forenoon.'

Her head felt stupid. She didn't understand. She opened her mouth but said nothing.

'You'll bide with Kirstie. It's all arranged.'

Still she could only stare, her thoughts slow. 'But–'

Mam glared at her then. 'Do you no want to go? You'll no be lying in your bed there, mind. You're to help your sister with her bairn.'

Of course she wanted to go, but surely Mam understood it was impossible. 'When will I come back?'

Mam shrugged. 'I'll send someone for you when I want you back.'

'But – I must be here on the Sabbath. The minister…'

'You leave the minister to me,' Mam said, and it was that voice of iron that had undergirded her entire childhood. *You leave the minister to me.* And then Jonet's face was in her hands and she was greeting in sheer relief. And Mam's hand was on her shoulder, and her voice was gentle. 'Och, my love. It willna aye be this way. These are the hardest days. But I'm thinking you could do with a wee bit respite from the long-tongued gossips of this place. For you, and for the wee one that's coming too. By the time you return, God willing, they'll have found something else to mutter about.'

And the prospect sustained her now, as she sat before them all and longed for the service to end. Tomorrow she would hap herself in her cloak and walk out to meet her sister's man, who would take her to Pentland. She'd be gone from here, gone from the cruel words and the lowered glances, and it would just be her and Kirstie again, just as it used to be.

Amid the looming shadows there was the first flicker of light.

*

No fugitives stayed in Helen's house that night.

Nevertheless, she found herself wakeful. She shifted in her bed, aware of the space at her side, space that had been empty six years now, but would soon be filled by the solid form of James Currie. A different man in her bed, with different ways. She'd been but a lass when she wed her first husband, and she'd taken many long months to become accustomed to the way his hard body seized its pleasure from hers. She remembered him now, heavy and urgent, tender sometimes – but not always. He'd given her the bairns and

13

she'd come to accept and even, occasionally, to welcome his lovemaking. But though she grieved his passing she did not grieve his attentions. For long enough that space in her bed was a refuge. Everyone expected her to take a new man, but she simply thanked God that her first husband's modest wealth allowed her to remain Widow Alexander.

And then, somewhere in this last turbulent year or so, a new idea had formed in her mind. Could it be that the Lord wanted her to marry again? And if so, to whom? She turned it over and over as she watched her children playing at the front of the house, her cloak held tight against the snell wind. What would happen if she were no longer here to look after them? Who would be able to protect them?

James Currie the merchant was a fine, godly man who had made it clear he cared for her, visiting more and more frequently and hesitantly speaking of marriage. Helen knew she could care for him too. She looked up at the sky, watching clouds rush by, and let any other dreams she might have had drift away on the breeze. She and James Currie would have a good marriage, serving the Lord together and raising the children as best they could in these wicked times.

Perhaps there would even be more children. She was thirty-three. It was not impossible. And meantime he would care for Beatrix, Jamie and Charlie as if they were his own.

For they all knew there would be no mercy for Helen a second time.

It was on nights like this, when the house was empty but sleep kept its distance, that the darkest time in her life hovered close. Any unexpected noise outside the cottage caused her to stop still, to listen carefully. Last time it had seemed barely a breath from the moment the men arrived at her door till she landed in a dark and crowded room in the Canongate Tolbooth, where the air hung heavy with the stench of human filth and foul water streamed down the walls, drowning hope in its feculence.

On that day four years earlier, she had been alone in the house with her three bairns, all gathered round the table for family worship. There were already whispers against her, so when she heard the horses stamping outside she guessed they had come for her. 'Look to the boys!' she said quickly to Beatrix, grasping for the faint chance they would think her from home, and leave the bairns alone. She dived under the bed, lying as still as she could amid the straw that was scattered over the damp earth, and trying not to breathe. She listened to shouts, curses, Charlie whimpering – he was just a wee thing who might yet give her away – and she prayed and prayed that the Lord would protect her bairns.

'My mam isna here,' came Beatrix's thin voice. The brave lass. And maybe if it had just been some soldiers who didn't know them, she would have been safe. But then Helen heard the voice of Sir Alexander Gibson and realised that the laird himself had come to seize her.

Dear God, he must truly want her locked up, and would surely not go home without her.

As she lay under the bed holding her breath, the flickering light of a candle was thrust into the darkness, and there was a shout of triumph. Sanders Brown, who had once been a friend of her husband, reached in and hauled her out by her hair.

She barely noticed the pain. Beatrix was against the wall with her arms around the two lads. Her wide dark eyes sought her mother's with such panic and fear. It was a sight that would never leave Helen, her daughter's terror. She called on the strength of the Lord to steady her voice as she told Beatrix to find her uncle and tell him what had happened. The lass clasped each of her brothers tight by the hand and hurried with them from the house.

That was the last she saw of her bairns for ten long weeks.

The laird told his men to wait outside and sat himself down on the carved armchair that had belonged to her husband. 'Widow Alexander, will you no just make life easier for all of us and attend the kirk?'

'I would rather beg bread for mysel and my bairns than take such a sinful way,' she said at once. Strangely, the expression on his face was more sorrowful than angry. She thought he must fear the fines he would face for keeping a tenant who refused to attend the kirk. 'I will leave your land if you like,' she added.

He shook his head. 'It is too late for that,' he said, and still, he said it sadly. He was quiet for a moment, looking down at the floor, and then he lifted his head. 'You will ruin my family.'

'Sir, you yoursel are going the right way about bringing eternal ruin on your family through this path you are now taking.' Well, it was only her duty to tell him.

He got to his feet then. 'You leave me no choice,' he said, and called for his men. They placed her on horseback, tying her wrists with heavy rope, and set off for Edinburgh town. They seemed uncomfortable about their duty, these men she knew from Pentland, and she sought to make them more so. 'The Lord will have vengeance on you all,' she warned them. They paid her no heed, so she persisted. 'The Lord is watching the part you play today. A curse on those–'

'Ah, shut the fuck up,' snarled Sanders Brown.

'You'll come to regret this day, you and your family both, for–'

'Regret is it?' another asked. 'You're the one with much to regret, Widow Alexander, like the day you let that damned Andrew Guillon bide in your hame.'

She was quiet then. Andrew Guillon? Her stomach churned with fear. Was that what lay behind her arrest, and the strange sorrow of the laird too? She had heard that Andrew Guillon had been sentenced to death. If they knew she had sheltered him, that sentence would surely be hers also. To harbour a so-called traitor was to invite the scaffold.

When he sent her to Edinburgh, Sir Alexander Gibson knew he was sending her to her death.

Andrew Guillon. Safe now in her home, Helen shifted in bed and remembered the day he came to her. The death of her husband was a sharp sorrow, but from that time on she could offer shelter to any of the persecuted who were in need. For why did the Lord leave her with a house, if not to share with the faithful remnant?

Andrew seemed a simple man of middle years, a weaver from Fife, and he told her only that he had been driven from his home and must hide a while. She took him in, as she had sheltered many others. In the evenings he sat with her by the fire, and they spoke of the terrible days in which they lived, and the godly men and women who had gone before.

It was on the fifth evening, as they sat together in the shadows, that there seemed something restless, something distracted about him. He began to apologise, as he had done many times before, for placing her wee family in danger by his presence. Helen told him that he was not the first she had sheltered, and nor, if the Lord desired it, would he be the last.

'No, but I am the worst,' he said.

Helen thought she recognised the melancholy, for she had struggled under the same cloud herself. Abandoned as they were by almost all good and godly teachers, many of whom were too feart to take to the fields while others had fled overseas to save their skins, the remnant received no instruction and no encouragement. It was easy to heed the whispers of the devil which would have them question their very salvation. She sought to reassure Andrew Guillon, thinking this was what troubled him. His face was turned towards the fire, the only light in the room.

'You are kind, mistress, but there is something you dinna ken. They will pursue me unto death, and I dinna ken what will meet me then, for I am hunted for the killing of

Archbishop Sharp.'

He told her the story then, a story she knew well – although never before from one who was part of the deed itself. His voice was hoarse and so low that she had to strain to listen, though she sat within touching distance of the man. His rough hands, nicked and scarred with years at the loom, shook and trembled uncontrollably as he spoke.

'I fell in with some Fife men I kent on that fateful evening. I was ready to accompany them for I was convinced of the rightness of our cause. There was a man we were to confront. He didna appear, and it seemed we would just go our separate ways, but then this young lad came running and he telt us that the hated Archbishop himsel was approaching in his coach.'

'Well, some of our party were certain at once that the Lord Himsel was delivering that scourge of the faithful into our hands. They said it was no more than our duty to avenge our brothers and sisters. And who's to say, perhaps they were right? They were more learned and more godly men than I. But I didna like the notion of killing, Widow Alexander, and it was killing that they were set on.'

'There wasna time to get away, time to think even. The coach was upon us almost at once, and John Balfour, he leapt from his horse with the light of vengeance in his eyes and he thrust the reins into my hands. One or two others did the same. Well, I thought I could do that, I could hold the horses – and hold my breath too, and pray. And all was dark, you understand, and then the horses were rising up and the men were shouting, and there was the swoop of blades in the night air. And amid all the shouts and the confusion I heard the screams of a young lass. Well, the Lord may have given us the Prelate but to harm his daughter could be nothing but murder, yet these men were caught in a frenzy of blood and revenge. So I dropped the reins and I jumped forward and caught her round the waist. She was a slim thing, but och,

18

she fought like a wildcat to be free of me and to go to the aid of her faither.'

'But there was no aid for her faither. I can see him yet, Widow Alexander, the cause of so much suffering in our land, his body just a crumpled rag, his blood dripping out on that Fife moor.' He covered his face with his hands. 'Waking or sleeping, that is the image afore my eyes. I will see it until the day I die, and I fear I will see it for eternity also. I ran from those men as soon as I could, and I have been running ever since.'

He finished his story and the house was silent again, but for the steady breathing of the sleeping bairns. Dear God, but the stains of that bloody night had soaked the landscape throughout all Scotland and brought a terrible retribution on the people of the Covenant. Helen looked at him across the flicker of the flames and saw a broken and tormented man. On the run for four years, haunted by the deeds he'd witnessed, and hearing of the terrible torture inflicted on his comrades from that night who had been captured. She reached out and laid her hand on his trembling one. 'You didna kill him, Andrew.'

'That is true,' he said.

'And he was an evil man, a turncoat, bent upon destroying Christ's kirk here on earth.'

'That also is true.'

And yet, and yet. The silence lay between them. He raised his head, looked at her. 'I'll be gone the morn, mistress.'

'You dinna need to.'

'That is kind of you, but I willna risk your lives any further. I'll be gone.'

He kept to his word and slipped away before dawn. She thought of him often, somehow unable to shake the dreadful sadness and weariness of him. What wickedness now raged over this land, that such a man – no doubt happiest in his home working his loom – should be driven to deeds so dark

19

that he feared for his own redemption. It was no surprise to hear just a few weeks later that he'd been captured. Now the danger had caught up with her too, and God alone knew what fate awaited her in Edinburgh town.

Helen pulled the blanket closer round her and tried to control the waves of panic which these festering memories always caused in her. She was here in Pentland; she was safe for now. True, Andrew Guillon had been a haunted wretch of a man who brought her great trouble, but she had sheltered many others who brought warmth and comfort and strength. Think instead on them. James Currie himself, he who would soon lie beside her, was one, and the hunted James Renwick was another. She sometimes smiled that those two dear men shared a name – then shivered, for it was the name borne too by the brutal tyrant King James, who would grind them into dust with his heel. *James*, the name favoured over long centuries by the Stuart kings – but these most recent rulers had forgotten the source of their power.

Aye, they had forgotten that they ruled Scotland only under the law of God and by the consent of the people.

There was a reckoning coming soon.

Chapter Three

Sunday 13th November 1687

Jonet Gothskirk being two Sabbaths together absent from the place of public repentance, the Session ordained their Officer to enquire what is the reason thereof.

On the day after her second appearance at the front of the kirk, Jonet set off from Calder to Pentland alone, crossing gentle countryside first, and then reaching the foot of the hills. It was fine to be away from Calder, away from folk who knew her and folk who thought they knew her, striding out under the clouded October sky. The last of the leaves still clung with an impossible fragility to the trees above her. She looked up at those delicate leaves, the dried yellows and browns of them, the vivid scarlet of the rowan berries, and thought for a while of nothing but the trees falling back and the moorland opening out, the hillsides sloping upwards, their gaudy colours disappearing into winter browns. These were the same hillsides she and Kirstie had explored when they were younger, when Faither was alive. She remembered how he took them both, it must have been when Mary was just a new bairn, and he walked with them and showed them where to find the exact shoots and berries Mam needed for her cures.

Or another time when he called to the three of them, unexpected like, Davy and Kirstie and her, and he led them through to the burn for fish. She minded Davy striding out beside their faither, thinking himself the big man as always. She and Kirstie danced along – or, if truth were told, she was the one who did most of the dancing, and the scrambling and the leaping and splashing. Kirstie was there to caution, as she had been throughout Jonet's life, and to hold out her hand when her wee sister couldn't quite reach the next stane in the rushing burn. Aye, and then they'd come to the spot and Faither had shown each of them how to guddle for fish, and oh, how she crowed because she caught the first one. Davy the big man didna much like that, but Faither, he roared with laughter.

Aye, it was grand to walk up in the expanse of the hills, to nod in greeting at an anonymous traveller, and to look down on wee clusters of houses close by, the far horizon stretching out in the distance. It was grand too though to meet Sandy, her sister's man, near the summer shielings that stood perhaps halfway along the track. Much as she'd relished the solitude of her walk, she tired more easily because of the bairn, and her steps had become slower and heavier the last mile or two. It was with relief that she clambered onto his solid farm horse and allowed him to lead her the remainder of the way to his home.

Sandy never had much to say for himself, but it seemed to Jonet he was quieter than usual. What did he think of having his wife's shamed sister bide with them? What did Kirstie think, come to that? Not Kirstie the lass of her memories, but the woman she was now. For Kirstie had done it all the right way, the kirk way. Jonet minded her sister's wedding to Sandy, the grand day of it, with all the folk round about putting in their coin to make a real feast day for them all. Faither was still living – the bleak despair of his death lay just six weeks ahead of them, had they known it – and she could smile now to think of him drinking with Sandy's brother. The two men leaned into one another, droning out something that was meant to be a ballad but sounded more like a dirge. And then there was her mother, that proud and trying no to greet, and the reel leaping from Wat's fiddle, leaping round the walls of the byre with the candlelight and the shadows of the dancing couples. She'd danced and she'd watched and she'd danced some more, and one old besom after another had leaned her way and speired if she would be next to wed.

'Auld Wat?' she'd suggested, with a wicked desire to shock. 'Or maybe Sir Hugh needs me to warm his bed?' And then they'd tutted and shaken their heads at her boldness, and she'd laughed, not caring at all for talk of men and marriage.

Aye, but she'd known nothing then. Not a thing.

And she wondered how it would be, being with Kirstie now she held that new secret knowledge within her. Look at Sandy, her sister's man, walking down there beside the mare and saying nothing. There were things she'd seen, done, *tasted*, since last she was with her sister. Could it be that way, she wondered, between Kirstie and her man? Sandy, with his broad shoulders and the wave in his hair that rested on his jerkin there. Was it that way between them? Did his hands rise upwards, so tender on her smooth skin? Did his mouth come down, fervent and searching? Did he leave her gasping and arching and wild as he thrust himself urgently between her legs? Was it ever that way between them?

Somehow, she thought not. Kirstie did it the kirk way, and Jonet was gey sure the first time she lay with Sandy was on that same wedding night. And now she had her man, a bit of land on Sir Alexander Gibson's estate, and her bairns born within wedlock. Not that everything had been easy for Kirstie, mind. Wee Bel, their first bairn, was still oftimes sickly, and the lad that was born after her had died before Jonet ever got to see him. Her hand slipped under her cloak and rested on the barely discernable swelling there for a moment. *Let not my sin.*

But such things were the way of the world. Kirstie was the one who'd done it the right way, and here was Jonet, pregnant and shamed, and no good man would ever look at her now.

But her sister. Would her sister look at her now?

Gradually the forenoon slipped into midday, and soon they would be there. The closer they came, the tighter that knot in her stomach twisted. She wasn't sure if she could bear it, after all that had been, if there was even a hint of disdain in her sister's eyes. She was tired now, and the constant jolting of the horse was making her feel as sick as she felt most mornings. She wanted only to clamber down onto the firm earth once more and – please God – to take her sister in her arms, to smell the mint in her hair. And here at last was Kirstie's cottage, long and low, built by Sandy and his brothers to coorie right into the hillside. Smoke rose not from a hole in the roof in the centre of the house, as at home, but from the little chimney Sandy had built rising from a hearth at one end of the room. There was a small bit of ground beyond for growing vegetables and keeping the hens. Two or three other homes formed part of the same little cluster, and beyond them lay the common land where the work of bringing in the hairst was newly complete.

As they approached, Jonet looked down eagerly into the darkness of the open doorway, hoping to see her sister appear. But the figure who stepped out, shielding her eyes against the brightness of the daylight, was slight, and even smaller than Kirstie. A girl, maybe twelve or thirteen, with smooth dark hair peeping out beneath her headscarf, and, when she dropped her hand, dark eyes in a waxen face. But the child on the girl's hip was surely Bel.

'This here is Beatrix,' said Sandy, as though that explained everything. He stepped forward and caught up his wee daughter. 'The lads?'

The girl turned her head slightly. 'Charlie!' she called, and a small boy who looked very like her emerged from the house. Sandy placed Bel gently on the ground, whereupon she rushed back to Beatrix and clung to her. Jonet watched, mesmerised. But here – Sandy was waiting for her to dismount. Blushing, she caught his hand and let him ease her to the ground. 'Thank you,' she said, uncertain. He nodded, and then he and the boy led the weary horse beyond the house, and Jonet and the dark-eyed girl were left, watching each other.

And even as one part of her mind told her she was being foolish, she felt a panic rise within her. Who was this dark-eyed lass, standing on her sister's threshold and holding her sister's child? What faithlessness was this? Why did the girl not speak?

And then someone called, 'Jonet!' And she turned, and there was Kirstie running up the hill towards them, breathless and laughing. Her sister, her best friend. The other part of her. Kirstie caught hold of her, hugged her and then pulled away, still holding her hand, to look at her.

Jonet might be the younger of the two, but by the time she was twelve she had grown taller than Kirstie. She looked down now into her sister's eyes, the same soft blue as her own, and saw that they were shining with tears. 'You're here,' was all Kirstie said, however.

'I'm here.'

And there was much to be said, but none of it could be spoken out here in the open, with wee Bel and the silent Beatrix as onlookers. But it was enough for now to look down into Kirstie's heart-shaped face and see the dear love and acceptance that had aye been there. All else could wait.

Kirstie lifted her daughter and thanked the girl. 'Jonet, this is Beatrix, my friend Helen's lass. Helen's been awa a wee bit lately, and Beatrix has been helping me with Bel. Her brothers give a hand to Sandy too.'

The dark-eyed girl smiled shyly, and Jonet knew shame. She was just a child. Will Murdoch might have turned out to be as false as a cloudless morn, but Sandy was a good man. 'Good day, Beatrix,' she said, and the girl smiled and nodded.

Helen came by that evening. Beatrix had already gone

home with her brothers, but Helen put her head in the door to thank Kirstie for minding them. She was a wee bit older than Jonet had expected, her hair laced with grey, and lines surrounding her eyes which were as dark as her daughter's. Her gown was spattered with mud and she had the weary look of someone who had been travelling for too long. Although her greeting was warm enough, Jonet saw that her smile didn't quite extend to her watchful eyes. 'You must all come over the morn,' she said. 'My James is coming, Kirstie – we think we will be able to wed very soon. Come and sup with us.'

'To wed?' Jonet asked, when Helen had left.

'Aye, Helen has been a widow long syne, since Charlie was just two or three, I believe. I'm gey pleased she's to wed again. She's been a guid friend to me, Jonet, especially with Bel and when my wee Robert was born. We'll go and sup with her the morn right willingly. You'll meet some of the other folks too.'

Jonet hesitated. 'Does Helen ken about the kirk?'

'No. Not yet. But don't worry about that for now, Jonet. Trust me. These are guid people.'

Good people despised her back home in Calder. But with Sandy nearby there was no chance to say more, not just then. It wasn't until later, when Sandy went out to see to the beasts and Bel was safely tucked up in the cot bed, that the two sisters sat together before the fire and Jonet knew the moment had come. Kirstie reached over and took her hand. 'Ach, Jonet.'

Just two wee words containing a lifetime of love and grief and regret.

There was so much Jonet needed to say. She longed for the words to spill out, longed to tell her sister everything that had been raging within her these past weeks. The physical feel of it, for one. The uncomfortable hardness in her breasts, the dragging tiredness in her limbs, the need to cough each morning until there were tears in her eyes and she was retching.

Or maybe the strangeness of it, the secret knowledge, the slight mound she could feel in her belly already, but no sense, no real sense at all of the bairn she knew was growing there. The bairn that had to come out, sometime. There was that too, that insidious fear. Mam coming back, exhausted, from another birthing, blood on her clothes and a grim shake of the head.

But more than that, there was the chill that never left her now, the chill of their brother Davy's resentment and her own heavy knowledge of the burden she had become. The chill in the whispers of the neighbours, the eyes in the kirk, aye, even the ones that were lowered in some sort of sympathy.

The chill of the flagstone step under her bare feet.

All of that was part of her world now, but it wasna the heart of it. The chill, the strangeness, the sickness, those were just withered leaves that swirled around the path, blown by the wind. Autumn debris, like the dreams she'd had of love and marriage with Will, dried up and discarded just as he'd discarded her. Discarded her and left her huddled at the foot of a dark and dangerous pit from which there was no way out.

Ach, Jonet.

But the words wouldn't come. She reached out her hand and covered her sister's fingers with her own. Kirstie laid her other hand on top, like the game they'd played as bairns. 'Tell me about him,' she said.

Jonet shook her head. 'What does it matter? He's gone. He's a liar and he's gone.' She paused. She had tried so hard to push thoughts of Will to the back of her mind, but now she was with her sister, and all at once the story came tumbling out. 'He was taken on by the farm in the spring, and all the girls noticed him. You ken how it is with someone new, and

27

he was right fine to look at and aye had a kind word for us all. But I was the one he singled out; I was the one he walked with in the evenings. I thought I was so special. I thought he loved me. We would sit in the evenings watching the sun go down, and then we would take oursels into the stable when it was dark. I ken it was foolish, Kirstie, I ken I should have waited, but he promised me. He promised.' She looked up then, fierce. 'And I loved it, God forgive me, I loved every moment of it.'

Kirstie was silent for a moment. 'How did you find out he was already married?' she asked eventually.

'I didna ken until they called me to the kirk. Even then I thought he would be there too. But then they telt me he'd gone hame to his wife. His *wife*.'

'Are they looking for him?'

'They are – but how hard, I wonder? They have their sinner. And after all, it's much easier for a man to hide himsel away than a woman with a bairn on the way.' She shook her head. 'But for all I miss him, Kirstie, I'm no sure it's about him anymore. There's so much more I must survive.'

'Is it so dreadful?' Kirstie asked. 'The kirk I mean. I couldna face it.'

Jonet laughed. 'Aye, it's dreadful right enough. It stinks, for one thing. But Mam helped me with that. Did you know she's done the same?'

'No!' Kirstie was truly shocked. 'You mean –?'

'Och, no for the same fault as me! No, she says it was in the Commonwealth days when she was a lass, and the minister Mr Kennedy, he was a hard man. And she and another lass were made to repent for cursing on the Sabbath.' The sisters shared a laugh. 'Not that it's done much guid, would you say? But it was Mam who telt me to use my mind, to take mysel into another place through all that's being said about me, and no to hear a word of it. They canna get inside you then. And I can do that. But ach, it's right guid to be here, to be free of it all, just for a week or two.'

Next evening, they stepped out with Sandy and wee Bel into the darkness to make their way along to Helen's cottage. Even a day away from home had worked its balm into her soul. She'd met a few of Kirstie's neighbours, and everyone had been friendly and welcoming. No one knew her shame. She could believe, just for a while, that it could aye be this way. And who knew, maybe it could? She could run away, never go back to Calder, to Davy's scorn and the minister's spittle. She could start afresh, just her and the bairn some place new. She could make a new life for herself; she could be free.

Yet even as she thought it, she knew it wasn't true. The kirk, controlling everything, they would prevent that. With their wee bits of paper flitting from one parish to another, written by one group of disapproving men and examined by the next, there was no hope, no hope at all, of leaving your sin behind you. She'd aye be carrying it alongside. For no kirk would accept her without the testimonial she could only receive by enduring her sentence, and no place would shelter her if she were not first accepted by the kirk.

But never mind that tonight. They arrived at Helen's door, and there was one of the lads out front looking for them. He hurried them in from the bitter cold to the thick warmth of the cottage and pushed the door behind them. Helen was on her feet, greeting them, and Beatrix appeared at her side to carry Bel away. Helen's manner seemed to have lightened since yesterday. The weariness that had clung to her was gone, and she was laughing and sparkling as she introduced Jonet to her friends.

It was only as Jonet shook loose her cloak and sat down on a stool that she noticed movement a little way behind her, half in shadow. Helen's younger son, wee Charlie, was crouched on the floor playing some sort of game with a slight, fair-haired man who was barely discernible in his dark clothes. This must be him then, James Currie, the man Helen was to wed. As he turned his head the light caught his features, and her first thought was that he looked none too well. There was a pallor on his skin, and wearied lines on his face. He was laughing with the lad, though, arguing in jest about who had captured the counters. Jonet kept glancing back at him as Kirstie chatted on to her right. He must be a fair bit younger than Helen, for he could be no more than in his mid-twenties, whereas she was surely thirty and more to have a lass the age of Beatrix. But Kirstie had told her that James Currie was loved by the bairns, and had a thriving merchant's business too. And if he happened to be a bonny looker with the appetites of the young – well, Helen had had a cold bed long syne.

Helen came over then with ale and oatcake and cheese for them all. Beatrix was at her mother's side, helping to hand out drinks, but Jonet watched as Helen carried the young man's pewter mug over for herself. 'Take this,' she said to him quietly. 'I'm sure you have need of it.'

And that was all it was, just a murmured *I'm sure you have need of it*. There wasn't even a touch between the two of them, no more than a look, and yet it stirred something within Jonet at once. Just in the way she looked at him, Helen, the tenderness and care in her glance, you couldn't miss the love she had for him. And Jonet felt the chill once more, for oh, she'd looked at Will like that, aye, and he'd looked at her that way too. And that should have been her, handing him his ale of an evening when he came in weary from the horses, with a quick *I'm sure you have need of it*. A smile full of promise in return.

But no use to think that way. No use. For Helen will marry her James, but for Jonet there will be no wedding.

She took her gaze away from him then, and looked about her. There weren't so many here after all. There would have been more at home for a gathering like this. Beyond Helen's family and Kirstie's, there were just two or three others. No music either. But there was chat and laughter and they spoke of the hairst that had so recently been brought in, a good one, with praise to God Almighty and stories to swap and share. And it was not until they'd been there some time that someone chapped the door.

And later, when she looked back on the evening, Jonet realised how much she'd missed during those first conversations in the house, for it was only when the knock came that she noticed something was wrong. Like a bairn, slow to pick up on the mood among the adults, but suddenly aware that everyone else knows something it doesn't. She watched, startled, as several people leapt to their feet. Sandy moved to the door, placing his huge bulk against it as he called out cautiously, 'Who's there?' The young man pulled his cloak tight around himself and disappeared without a word beyond the thick curtain into the boxbed. And as for Helen, she just stood in the centre of the room, motionless, hands clasped tight and eyes fixed on the doorway. 'It will be James,' she said, but her voice was hoarse.

Bewildered, Jonet turned to her sister. And Kirstie's face, she saw, was white, her eyes fearful. Little Bel had crept to her side, and Kirstie held her very close.

A log shifted in the fire, creating sparks, but even the bairns were silent as Sandy spoke through the smallest crack in the door. And then he laughed, and his laugh rippled round the room, dispelling that unaccountable stillness. He pulled the door open to let the newcomer in, then closed it quickly as a rush of cold air made the cruisie lamp flicker. The man who entered was well wrapped in his cloak and walked with a limp. Helen, still standing in the centre of the room, let her hands fall to her sides. 'Praise be to God,' she said. 'James. At last.' And she stepped forward to receive his embrace.

James?

Jonet was utterly confused.

31

If this was Helen's man – and it clearly was – then *who* in the name of all that was good, had she been looking at with such unmistakable tenderness earlier? Why was everyone so fearful? As conversation rose once more, Jonet turned back to her sister. 'Kirstie, what is going on in this house?'

Kirstie looked distressed. 'Hush, Jonet. You must say nothing. I should never have brought you. Only I didna ken he would be here. But you must say nothing. We'll go, shortly.'

'But who–'

'No. Hush. Later.'

And with that Jonet had to be satisfied, for now. She could say no more, but she could watch and she could listen and she could think. The young man slipped back through the curtain to greet the newcomer, and the laughter and eating and drinking resumed, although perhaps with less freedom than before. Or was it just that she herself was now uneasy, whereas earlier she'd been too caught up in her own sorrow to notice what was going on around her? Well, she was noticing now. And soon a thought came to her mind, a thought at once so unlikely and yet so obvious that she had no sooner entertained it than she knew it was true.

And then Helen asked the young man to pray.

Jonet had to cover her mouth to stop herself from crying out in protest. But he prayed aloud in a soft clear voice with a lilt which was not of these parts. And Jonet heard not a word he said, as she looked in terror and disbelief around them all, their heads bowed, even her sister. And Helen and her man, fingers intertwined, heads bent in prayer. Even the bairns, silent and listening.

Oh Kirstie, you fool. What have you done?

This is treason.

Jonet didn't see Helen again until the end of that week. The boys appeared to work alongside Sandy, but Helen and the watchful Beatrix stayed away. Jonet held her tongue for the time being about that strange evening, about the tenderness in Helen's eyes, about the sudden change of atmosphere when the door chapped, about the low, passionate tones of the young man at prayer.

Could she maybe have been mistaken?

And so she waited and said nothing as the days passed. Friday came. Kirstie, who had aye been a good seamstress, had worked some table linens for the housekeeper to the Sinclair family at Roslin Castle, and wanted to deliver them. 'Let's walk that way this afternoon,' she suggested. 'It's cold, but it's a bonny day and a grand walk by the river. It's too far for Bel, but I'll see if Helen can watch her.'

Jonet looked quickly at her sister. 'Is that wise?'

Kirstie was stirring the stew in the pot that hung from a hook over the fire. She paused, looked up. 'Wise? In what way?'

Jonet took a breath. 'It seems to me that's a gey dangerous household to be mixed up in.'

For a while Kirstie said nothing. She looked down into the mixture she was stirring, the heat bringing a flush to her cheeks. Then she raised her head. 'Helen's prayers and her care brought wee Bel back to us, Jonet, when I thought I had lost them both.'

'Aye. But Kirstie, for the love of all that's guid, she's sheltering a hunted man, is she no? A traitor to the king. No one spoke his name that night, but I believe I am right.'

Kirstie lifted the pot from its hook, moved it carefully to the hearthside, then turned and looked up at her sister. 'Aye, you are right. He is Mr James Renwick, and I never met a godlier man in all my life. And if speaking the truth makes him a traitor, then you must wonder at the laws there are in Scotland this day.'

Frightened now, Jonet glanced towards the door, which stood ajar. Kirstie saw her look and laughed. 'Ach, dinna fear, we're mostly friends around here. We must tak tent of course – well, you saw that yoursel the other night. But have no fear, Mr Renwick will be long gone. It doesna do for him to bide more than a night or two in the one place.'

'When the troopers come, it will make no difference if he's there or no,' said Jonet bluntly. 'You must ken that. To give shelter to such a man – even to ken his whereabouts and no let on – they'll hang you soon as look at you. He has called for the murder of the king! I canna think what you're doing in the company of such a man.'

'What would you have me do?' her sister demanded. 'The guid Lord gave me back my wee lass – do I turn my back on Him?'

'Ach, dinna be daft. How is it turning your back on the Lord to obey the laws of this land? If you care anything for Bel, you'll have nothing to do with those traitors.'

Kirstie glared at her. 'You're my ain sister, you need never question that I care for her. But I care too that she is raised in a land where the Lord's name is honoured and no trampled in glaur, and where His servants are free to preach truth.' She sat down. 'Och, I canna explain it well. But if you could once hear Mr Renwick for yoursel, you would understand.'

'*Hear him?* Kirstie, I'm starting to think they've bewitched you. Do you mean to tell me you've been to their gatherings, their field meetings?'

'Aye, that I have,' she said defiantly. 'Och, we attend the kirk, though Helen rebukes me for it. Sandy willna risk our hame. But when I can get away, I go with her and listen to the true gospel. Sandy too, when he can. Helen and I travelled together to the Braid Hills outside Edinburgh to hear him just a week ago, and such crowds there were! And once you've heard his words, the sweetness and the dreadfulness of the way he explains the Scriptures, you'll never want to listen to those curates again. It's like …' She paused, and then quietly said, 'It's like the Lord Jesus Christ is right there with us, on the hillside. We might be small in number, but there's a blessing in our meetings, Jonet, that you will never find in the kirk.'

Jonet looked at her sister in bewilderment, a dull pain beginning to throb behind her eyes. How could such unfamiliar words be coming from the one she knew best in all the world? She felt a growing sense of panic, an urge to reach across this new distance between them and wrench Kirstie free of the fanatics. 'There's no blessing for the likes of me in any preaching, in kirk or in field,' she reminded her sister. 'But are you no feart to tell me all this? What's to stop me going to the laird or the minister?'

Kirstie looked up quickly. 'You wouldna.'

'No?' asked Jonet. 'Think what it could mean for me. If I tell Mr Mackenzie the whereabouts of the hunted Mr Renwick, they're sure to release me. I'll be free.'

'Free? Your hands would be stained with the blood of the Lord's servant for the rest of your days.'

Jonet stood for a moment, looking right down into her sister's angry gaze, then she sighed and turned towards the table, reaching for a pile of wooden bowls. 'Aye, you're right. I willna do it. But I dinna like it, Kirstie. Can you no just keep your distance? I mean, we aye kent our ain folks didna like the curates, but they held their peace, else we'd have gone hungry.'

Kirstie shook her head. 'I thought that way too, until the night the bairns were ill. I scarce kent Helen then. Och, I'd heard rumours about folks she let bide in her house, and that she near lost her life in the Tolbooth as a result. Like you, I thought it best to keep my distance. And then the bairns were so ill, the both of them, the wee lad just a few days old, and my dear Bel … And Sandy was awa to fetch help, and Helen came by, and she was sent by the Lord, Jonet. She was sent by the Lord. And she sat with me all through that night, and she prayed and she nursed them and she held me. And the Lord took my son into his blessed presence, but he gave me back my wee lass.' Kirstie was crying now. 'After all that, who am I to turn away?'

Jonet was silent. What could she say? In childhood Kirstie had aye been the gentle, law-abiding one, while Jonet was ever seeking after something fresh, and to hell with the consequences. She had realised the other night that her sister was acquainted with the rebels, but had never expected to hear her proclaim her allegiance to their cause. Surely this scheming Helen Alexander had taken advantage of her good and trusting nature. Dear God, Kirstie was risking not just her own life, but the lives of her whole family.

Jonet's crime with Will suddenly seemed hardly a crime at all.

In the end, Bel was left with Beatrix while Helen joined them on their walk to Roslin Castle. 'It's a fine day for it,' she said as she joined the two sisters. Jonet glanced quickly at her, then looked away. She knew that Kirstie had told Helen about the kirk discipline case, but her sister refused to reveal the older woman's reaction. 'You need to become acquainted,' was all she would say.

It was a beautiful late autumn afternoon. The low sun which shone through the last of the leaves on the trees provided little warmth, and the three women were well wrapped against the bitter air. Fallen leaves on the track crunched beneath their boots, and uneven imprints of feet and hooves which had travelled here before them were preserved in the frozen mud. Their way took them first across open moorland, brown and faded as winter encroached, with the first slopes of the Pentland Hills rising above them. Jonet had walked between those hills at the start of the week, welcoming the remoteness and the emptiness of this bleak landscape which promised to surround and shelter her. Now, she glanced up uneasily. Who else was hidden in the sweep and the shade of the green and brown hillsides? In hut, in cave, in glen. The hunted, and the hunter. Someone could be watching them even now, three women making their way along a track, heads close together and talking treason. *Treason.* She shivered. The hunter or the hunted, she and Kirstie should be having nothing to do with either of them.

Yet what was the alternative? To cower beneath the shroud of misery in her mother's house? To return meekly to the sting of Mr Mackenzie's scorn? No. She didn't much fancy striding out across the countryside in the company of the woman who sheltered James Renwick, but perhaps this was her opportunity to persuade Helen to leave Kirstie alone. And so she walked along beside the women, and listened to the chat which flowed between them.

'He's a godly man, and it's the Lord's will that we should wed,' Helen was saying. 'But it will be gey strange, for all that.'

'To share your hame again,' mused Kirstie. Helen laughed, a rich, free laugh, and Jonet, still glancing uneasily about her, wondered at such apparent carelessness from someone living so hazardous a life.

'Aye, there is that – though there are few weeks in the year when the bairns and I have the house to oursels. There's aye some poor soul needing a place of refuge. For why do I have a house if not to shelter the people of the Lord? That willna cease because there's another man about the place.'

'But will James permit it?'

'It's how I met James, giving him refuge, so he can scarce object!' She paused, and the laughter faded from her voice. 'James shares my sympathy for the persecuted remnant, else I couldna think on marrying him. And it will be a comfort to me. Beatrix is a guid lass, but these are such dark days. There are evenings when I sit by the fire, and I long for someone to talk it over with, someone who understands. You'll laugh, no doubt, but it's my greatest hope for the days ahead that James and I will soon be able to discuss these matters of religion when we are awake in our beds.'

Jonet coughed, and risked a quick glance at her sister, whose arm was slipped through her own. Kirstie's expression was demure and only Jonet, well accustomed to unspoken sisterly communication, would ever have detected the gleam of laughter in her eyes, the quiver in her arm. All was not lost after all.

Her skin tingled as she remembered the hunger of her times with Will. *Aye Will, if we could lie together again, it wouldna be matters of religion on our minds in our bed, right enough.*

'Did your first husband not sympathise, then?' Kirstie asked.

Helen hesitated, readjusting the heavy shawl around her shoulders. The track swung round, taking them away from the hills now and down, down, down, towards the river. 'I was just a lass when I wed, Kirstie. I scarce kent him who was to be my man. I was biding with my sister at the time, down near Haddington. My mother was a guid woman; it was she who taught me to read and write, who taught me the Scriptures. But she died. That would have been sorrow enough for a young lass, but my faither took another wife and she had no room for me in her hame.' She paused. 'If anything could persuade me no to take another man, it's the thought of those first weeks after that woman arrived in my faither's house. I mind her malice to this day. I tried to please, for all I missed my ain mother, but I could do no right in her eyes. She would tell my faither false tales against me, passing off her ain faults or carelessness as mine, bid him beat me. It was a hard time, and I couldna begin to think of my ain bairns being treated in that way.'

'But they're fond of him,' said Kirstie softly. 'And he'll be kind to them, I'm sure.'

Helen nodded. 'He will. There's no a scrap of meanness in him, not like that woman. But my sister was kind enough to take me in, for though she was wed and awa from hame, she kent the sairness of my days. But there was never much to go round, and so when Charles Umpherstone came speiring if I would be his wife, I was pleased to say yes. He brought me here to Pentland, to the house I live in this day. And it was here in Pentland that the Lord led me into the company of those who hear the persecuted preachers, and brought me into a true knowledge of Himsel. I heard some of the finest, most godly servants of the Lord at that time, saints like Mr Donald Cargill, whose words were honey to my soul. But although I was drawn to hear those preachers, I still sometimes went to hear the curates too, for I was inclined to follow my husband. And Charles didna feel the same.'

'In what way?' Kirstie asked. But Jonet was no longer listening. They had rounded a corner, and the way before them, which had previously been hidden by the tall birch trees on the curve of the track, now opened out. And in full view climbing the track away from the riverside and towards them were two men on horseback. Soldiers.

Soldiers were no uncommon sight in these turbulent days. Parties of them roamed the countryside, searching for fugitives. Jonet had long since learned to be wary of them, for they were unpredictable and could be foul-mouthed and violent. But never before had she felt such an upsurge in fear, so much so that the rising dread within her left little room for breath, never mind speech.

'Keep talking,' said Helen quietly, as though she knew exactly how Jonet was feeling. 'It willna do to fall silent. Speak of the cloths you are carrying, Kirstie.'

The soldiers were nearly upon them now. The three women moved to one side of the narrow track to allow them to pass, and Jonet lowered her eyes. Perhaps they would press on. But the beat of the hooves stopped, and one of the horses gave a snort and shook its head. The soldier brushed his hand soothingly down its long neck, and even amid the tension Jonet felt a stab of pain at the familiar movement. *Will*.

The nearest soldier was a large man with dark eyes beneath thick, heavy eyebrows. When he spoke, his voice carried strong accents of the west. 'Where are youse travelling to then?'

It was Kirstie who answered, her voice quiet but steady. 'We carry some needlework to Roslin Castle, sir.'

The man surveyed them, and perhaps his eyes lingered a little longer on Helen than on the other two. 'Come you frae Pentland?'

'Aye, sir.'

The other soldier spat on the ground. 'A den of rebels and vipers. Show us this *needlework* you say you carry.'

Kirstie's hands were trembling as she laid down her basket, picked out the package and unwrapped it, holding it up to the soldier. He separated the cloths then held out his hand for the basket. A quick glance told him it was empty, and he spat again, a great thick green gob right at Jonet's feet. He dropped both basket and linens to the ground. Kirstie gave a quick suppressed cry and bent at once to pick them up, brushing clinging earth from the material as the soldier watched her. Jonet's fingernails dug fiercely into her palms, but she said nothing.

The first soldier, the one with the bushy eyebrows, lifted his reins. 'Waste nae mair time, we have business ahead of us. Hurry you on then, you women, or it will be dark afore you return.' He set off, and the surly one behind him followed with a final curse. Jonet watched them go, and, as the tension eased from her body, her legs were suddenly weak. She breathed deeply. Kirstie arranged her cloths in the basket once more, and the three women linked arms and set off, silent at first as they listened to the sound of the horses growing ever fainter.

'What were they looking for?' Jonet asked at last, when the path had followed the curve of the river through the deep gorge and taken them well beyond the soldiers. 'They were scarce going to find a fugitive hidden in Kirstie's basket.'

'There is a paper,' Helen said slowly. 'It's no matter, we had nothing to hide. But I wonder why they are headed to Pentland.' Her tone was troubled, and Kirstie turned to her in alarm.

'Why, do you think they are headed for your house? Where the bairns are?'

Helen shook her head. 'I think not, but I canna be sure. But dinna fear, Kirstie, Bel will be fine. Beatrix will take care of her, she's a wise lass.'

'She canna do much against grown men, and troopers at that,' Kirstie protested. But Jonet was thinking of something else Helen had said.

'Is this *paper* at your hame, then?'

'The Lord will protect them,' Helen said quietly. 'But see, we're near the entrance to the house. Deliver your cloths quick, Kirstie, and we can set off for hame at once to be sure all is well. Jonet and I will wait here while you take your basket to the housekeeper.'

Jonet glared at Helen, resenting her calm authority, wanting to know more of the paper she had mentioned. But all at once she realised how weary she felt. She had been so troubled by the encounter with the soldiers that she had paid little attention to the scenery, but now she saw that they had been climbing steeply, and that a stone bridge would lead them into what appeared to be a ruined castle. 'Does someone really live here?' she asked.

Kirstie laughed. 'Aye indeed. Much of the castle was destroyed by Cromwell's men, but there is a fine house through by. It's where the Sinclair family bide, and I'm thankful for the opening provided to me by my acquaintance with their housekeeper.' She moved away from them, crossed the bridge, and disappeared into the tumbledown courtyard. Jonet leaned against the low wall and looked about her. She had not realised that they had climbed so high, but looking down on the treetops in the gorge below made her feel dizzy. She shifted her gaze upwards, to the broken remains of the once proud castle, the red stone glowing softly against the backdrop of the glen. It was not yet dark, but the sun was fading, and golden light streaked across the sky above them. Something stirred in her memory, something her father had once told her.

'I've heard tell of a chapel at Roslin,' she said.

Helen pursed her lips. 'There is one right enough, just a step the other way, but it's a godless, idolatrous site which has no place in a covenanted land.'

Jonet had had enough of this self-righteousness. 'My faither was taken there as a lad,' she countered. 'He described it as a mystical place, full of wonder and beauty. I should like to see it.'

'Did your faither incline towards the Popish religion, then?'

Ach, this woman, with her certainties and her fiery zeal. She would never understand a man like Faither, the free and easy, all encompassing openness of him. Aye, he had faith, but his was a faith which easily held the words of a psalm together with the charm laid over the door to protect the cattle. Both were soaked right into his bones and revealed themselves in a goodness which never once failed to help a neighbour in need. 'No, he wasna a papist,' she said shortly. 'But Helen, I'm right troubled by those who take shelter in your hame. It's no concern of mine what you choose to do, but I'd like you to stay awa frae Kirstie and her bairns. She's that guid natured, she doesna see the harm all this could cause. But I do.'

Helen was looking out over the glen. The sun had

disappeared below the castle walls and the air was a little bit chillier. 'I ken you're feart for your sister, and I dinna blame you for it,' she replied quietly. 'But there's a greater call on all our lives, and Kirstie has heard it. I have learned that it's a far worse thing to lose the favour of God than to lose the favour of men. The Lord gives strength to withstand all things to those who honour him.'

Lord save us, did this woman never let off preaching? 'I think I ken my sister better than you do,' Jonet said. 'And all this religious strife has never been for her.'

Helen turned to look at her then. 'Do you mind Bothwell Brig, or are you too young?'

Bothwell Brig. Dear Lord, Marion. 'I mind.'

'Aye, all who were alive at that dreadful time remember it, no doubt. I certainly willna forget it, for my husband gave our silver to help those who would oppress the honest, God-fearing people. And the Lord turned his face from me then.'

'This has naught to do with Kirstie or with me!'

A dog howled far below in the glen somewhere. An omen of death, she had aye been told. Meantime, Helen shook her head in the fading light, lost in a memory, seemingly heedless of Jonet's frustration. 'I could find no rest about that silver. When news came of the slaughter of the Lord's people at the battle of Bothwell Brig, I thought my heart would break in two. I took my bairns, wee though they were – Charlie just a babe in arms – and we walked until we were a mile west of Edinburgh. There we came across the whole long broken line of persecuted prisoners being driven towards the town and their deaths. A sorry sight. They were made to walk, though their wounds were open and their backs naked, and the crowds of people mocking and laughing. Never will I forget it.' She broke off, raised a hand to her eyes, then carried on in a tone so quiet Jonet had to strain to listen.

'There was one in particular, no much more than a wee lad he was. He stumbled as he came near to me, fell right at

43

my feet, and one of the soldiers smashed him from behind with the end of his gun. He was there afore me and there was blood running down from a cut to his head, and he reached up his hand to me, dazed. "Mammy," he said. Just that – *Mammy*. Can you imagine? And I wanted so to help him, but they thrust me away, me and my wee ones who were greeting around me. And then there were more of them, more and more, some stark naked but for their shirts, their dirty limbs all blackened and bloodied. So I turned right around and hurried hame to Pentland, and I gathered some silver and some shirts of my ain, and I walked back to Edinburgh and gave them to be passed to those in most need. But I never did tell my man.'

There was the crunch of footsteps nearby as Kirstie returned, her face flushed. She had been running. 'Come now,' she said to them. 'We must get back to Pentland as fast as we're able.'

No leisurely saunter in sharp winter sunlight this time. They hurried along in the gloom, keeping close together, little breath for talk. Jonet didn't mind. She heard once more Helen's voice breaking – *can you imagine?* – saw the wretched line of defeated prisoners stumbling relentlessly towards torture and death. Bothwell Brig. Aye, she minded that time right enough, Kirstie surely would too. They had been just bairns, as Helen had rightly said, she herself maybe eight or nine years old. But there was talk in the fields, there was fear when the soldiers came, and there was Marion …

Mam had been right grieved when she heard of the killing of the Archbishop of St Andrews. He was hated by most folk on account of his treachery and his cruelty, but his murder in front of his daughter was, Mam declared, a deed of folly which would bring trouble down on the heads of all who just wanted to work their land in peace. And so it transpired. There had followed a terrible persecution throughout the land. Soldiers had come to their own community in Calder, rampaging from house to house, obliging everyone to swear an oath to the king and renounce the Covenants or suffer the consequences. She, Kirstie, and Davy had huddled together in the boxbed, watching wide-eyed as first mother and then father knelt to say words they could not possibly mean.

Dear God, what if the soldiers had harmed Bel?

But then not everyone took as pragmatic an approach as their parents. Jonet hadn't given much thought to Marion in near ten years, but when Helen asked her about Bothwell Brig, it was Marion's haunted eyes and her gaunt face which came to mind with unexpected clarity. Marion was a lass of her own age living close by, and her father was one who supported the Covenanters. He disappeared one day, and they said he'd left to join the army of the Covenant in its decisive battle against the king's troops at Bothwell Brig. He never came home. A skinny man with lank dark hair, maybe he was in that line of prisoners who stumbled past Helen on their way to the town. He'd not been executed, they said, but had been herded onto one of their ships and carried off to the Plantations – though not before they'd crushed his fingers to a pulp. Marion's mother smiled bravely, holding his Bible on her lap, told them it was warm where he was living now. He'd have to get used to singing his psalms in the sunshine.

Jonet had no idea whether the woman believed that or not, but in the end it couldn't have mattered less. Marion and her mother and her wee brother were soon singing their praises not in the cold kirk, nor in the hot sunshine, but in glory.

It was hopeless for them from the time the winter came in, and it was a harsh winter that year. The neighbours did what they could, but with no man to work the land in the hairst months, the family had little food stored. And the kirk, provider for the widow and the fatherless, looked askance at them as traitors and rebels. Hurrying along now between her sister and this dangerous woman, Jonet tried to fill her lungs

45

deeply with the clean cold air, but could taste only the stench of a house blighted by sickness and starvation. She'd gone one day with some broth from Mam and found Marion's mother huddled in a blanket on the floor – they'd burned all the furniture by then – her arms tight around the stiff body of the wee lad. Terrified, Jonet had tried to press the food on her, but the woman just turned her face away with an unearthly moan. Jonet minded setting the pot down carefully with trembling fingers, for Mam would not countenance the waste of good food whatever the circumstance, and running, running as fast as she could to pour out the story at home. Mam had dropped what she was doing, calling Jonet to follow in case she might be needed. But there was nothing to be done, not for the wee boy, nor for Marion or her mother, who both passed over within a week. 'All so one man could indulge his principles,' Mam had said. 'It's a shame his faith didna extend to his family.'

Aye, and what would Mam say if she could see them now? Jonet had given up trying to keep pace with Kirstie. The bairn within slowed her down, where Kirstie's fear spurred her on. They were nearing home now, away from the trees and heading back towards the hills. Helen had spoken of Bothwell Brig to show Jonet why she acted as she did, but for Jonet it only emphasised the sheer folly of becoming mixed up in any of these endless struggles over religion. Surely now Kirstie would see that too.

Kirstie had broken into a run, paying no heed to Helen's sharp call to wait. Jonet quickened her own pace and reached the cottage just as Kirstie emerged from within, unable to speak, but with Bel's tiny fair head pressed against her shoulder.

No soldiers had come calling this time.

*

Helen watched them go, Jonet and Kirstie and wee Bel. She was fond of her bonny neighbour. Aye, she had been

46

troubled when Kirstie first told her Jonet was under discipline for adultery, yet she found her heart strangely drawn to the younger lass. There was a spirit about her. It set her apart from her gentle sister but found its echo in Helen's own heart. Timidity would never have brought her to the place she was today. And what was the lass but a sinner who might be redeemed?

But today she had seen the fear on their faces, and she knew they were counting the cost.

She entered the cottage, glad all at once to have her three bairns around her. Talk of Bothwell Brig had clearly unsettled Jonet. It had unsettled Helen too and, as she had done so often before, she whispered a prayer for the lad who had called her *Mammy*. If he wasn't dead, he had most likely been shipped to the Plantations, but wherever he was, she prayed he was still faithful.

There was a moment when the Plantations had seemed a possibility for her too. As she moved about the house, preparing for their meal, her mind pulled her back to the place it so often lingered. Perhaps once she had her man to talk to, these memories would recede a little. Not that she wanted to forget that strange mingling of darkness and light entirely. It was in this the bleakest time of her life that the Lord had drawn most near to her. For when Sir Alexander Gibson had sent his men off with her, they had brought her to Edinburgh and cast her into prison where she had remained for ten interminable weeks. Yet in her torment the Lord led her again and again to the words of Revelation chapter six:

I saw under the altar the souls of them that were slain for the Word of God, and for the testimony which they held.

And white robes were given unto every one of them.

She left the prison only once in those ten weeks, when they took her to Holyrood Abbey to be interrogated. And oh, for all she was fearful of what they might do to her, how happy she was to breathe the outside air as they dragged her down the Canongate to the Chancellor's Lodging in the grounds of the Abbey.

'Today you have the Chancellor and other great men to go afore,' said one of the guards, trying to frighten her.

She tried to stand tall. 'I have a greater Judge to go afore, the Judge of all the earth.' It was hard, though, not to be afraid, and she prayed for strength to face whatever might come her way. *And white robes were given unto every one of them.*

They pushed her into a grand room, and she was faced with a row of men all dressed in wigs and fine robes. Her hair, she knew, was filthy and matted and her face smeared with the grime of the prison, while she had been wearing this same gown since the day they seized her. No matter. God looks upon the heart.

From the guards and her fellow prisoners, she had gained a fair idea of who would be awaiting her. The Chancellor, him they cried the Earl of Aberdeen, was the ugliest man Helen had ever seen. All the finery of his wig and his robes couldn't hide the misshapen features with which God had endowed him. She knew that he held great resentment toward the people of the Covenant on account of the death of his father, and he was said to be thick with the papist Duke of York. Alongside him were John Paterson, the immoral and loose-living Bishop of Edinburgh nicknamed Bishop Band-Strings, and his brother Sir William Paterson, clerk to the Privy Council. Pity the mother who spawned such progeny. There were others too, whose names she could not remember.

It was Sir William Paterson who spoke first. He had a paper before him, and he looked down at it then scowled across at her, no doubt seeking to frighten her. He asked first if she went to the kirk. Thanking God for such a simple question to answer, she told them she would not go to the kirk though they took her life from her.

Then, just as she expected, they asked about Andrew Guillon. 'Did he come to your house?'

'He did,' she said, for they knew that already. Thank God her voice did not shake.

'Why did you give him cloth to work?' asked Sir William. 'He seemed honest.'

They murmured among themselves at that, and then the Chancellor asked her, in that slow voice of his, 'Do you make a habit of allowing vagabonds into your house?'

'I do not.' It crossed her mind to add that she had seen no greater vagabonds than the men sat before her that day, but wisdom for once restrained her.

Sir William Paterson then took up the questioning. 'Do you admit that the killing of Archbishop Sharp was no less than a wicked act of murder?'

She knew then that her test had come, just like the disciple Peter warming himself before a fire in a darkened courtyard. She was unsure what to say, so she said nothing. She could see in his scornful expression that he thought her hesitation was prelude to fearful crumbling. He continued.

'Moreover, do you own that the authority of King Charles II over church and state is lawful?'

She did not plan to say it, but when she opened her mouth the words that she spoke to those proud men were, 'You should not ask these things of a woman.'

Well, they were not expecting that! They looked at one another. There was colour rising in Sir William's face and Helen could see he was flustered. But then the Chancellor laughed and brought his hand down on the table with a bang which made her jump. 'So, she willna answer because she is a woman! Very well. Take this *woman* back to the Tolbooth and see what some more time in prison will do for her. We will see her again.'

We will see her again.

But they did not. Ten weeks passed, ten long weeks of

49

lying on the hard floor of the foul Canongate Tolbooth, twisting this way and that as barbed stomach cramps ripped through her. At first she was sure they would hang her. Then she was sure they would torture her.

Eventually she came to fear that they would just leave her to rot in this darkness for evermore.

Alongside her in prison were a few others who had also been locked up for their faith, and they did their best to support one another. High on the wall, the barred window offered just a hint of the outside world, of brightness, of the Edinburgh air which, though not fresh like the winds over Pentland, sparkled clean compared to this fetid pit. Helen and her friends dragged auld Rab under the window, for if these rattling breaths were to be his last, best make them as pure as they could. Helen sat beside him and read to him from Scripture. He didn't speak, but as she repeated the familiar words, tears dripped slowly over the deep lines of grime embedded in his old, withered face. Rab was one of the faithful.

There was the Lord's work for them to do, even here in prison. They told one another that they had been set apart from all other distractions to contend in prayer for the Lord's will to be done here in Scotland. And that was what they did, despite the provocation of those known as the Sweet Singers who were locked up alongside them. John Gib of the Sweet Singers had taken to roaring like a lion to disturb their worship, while Ann Stewart screamed and cursed. They lay together too, like beasts, and all Helen could do was stop her ears, turn away, and weep.

Occasionally someone visited from the outside world, bringing news, and it was on one of these visits that Helen first heard of James Renwick's return to Scotland. Her friend Hannah came from Pentland with a basket of food which the guards allowed them to share once payment had been made. They sat to one side of the room, together with auld

Rab and one or two others who had remained faithful. Many of those held captive, even those who had been brought in for attending field preachings, had fallen over one another in their eagerness to take the Test, that loathsome oath which betrayed their Lord and Master.

They prayed and broke bread together, ignoring the shrill abuse shouted by Ann Stewart. Hannah's voice was low. 'We are feart for you,' she said bluntly. 'They say you are to die next week for sheltering Andrew Guillon, unless you will take the Test.'

Helen took a breath. So, it was approaching. Well, if it was the Lord's will, the scaffold would be preferable to this unending living hell. She reached out a hand – so clawlike and skeletal after these long weeks that it did not seem to be her own – and clasped Hannah's. 'Will you prepare my winding sheet, then?'

Hannah shook her head, and there were tears in her eyes. 'Dinna say it, Helen. We will pray for your release. The bairns – your Beatrix and the other children of the Covenant – they pray together each day for you.'

Beatrix. Her sweet Beatrix. Beatrix, Jamie and Charlie. If anything could tempt her to speak the words which would drag open the yett, it would not be the stink nor the dark nor the hunger, nor even the savagery of those lying beside her. No, it would be the last picture seared into her soul of her three fatherless bairns, motherless too these last weeks. Aye, but that same thought was the one that held her steadfast. If she were to forsake her Lord, how could she ask Him to preserve those she loved so dearly?

Hannah brushed tears aside. 'Och, here am I come to succour you, and I am the one who greets! But I think I will go out of my wit, Helen, if you are to die.'

'And what use will that be!' she said at once. 'Pray for my release, aye, but if the Lord means me to suffer for his name, then pray, oh, pray that I have the strength to stand

51

firm, whatever they do to me. And watch over my wee ones.'

Whatever they do to me. You heard such stories in here. The guard who came back from watching them hang Andrew Guillon, he told with relish how first they cut off his hands – only it took eight blows of the axe to hack one hand from his body. Helen thought on the man, seated by her fireside, those same rough hands trembling uncontrollably as he told his story. What agony he must have suffered at the last. And now they said his corpse was rotting in chains on the Magus Muir, at the spot where Sharp was killed. Lord have mercy.

Perhaps Hannah was thinking of this too, for she changed the subject. 'Do you mind those young students the Society sent to Holland last year to be trained for the ministry?'

'Aye.' It was the one truly hopeful thing that had happened in the last year or two.

Hannah glanced round quickly and lowered her voice, so that no one else would hear. Auld Rab had drifted off to sleep, and the others had moved away. 'Young James Renwick has been ordained by the church in Holland and has returned to Scotland.'

Helen was astonished. 'Already?'

'I ken. There's much talk, including that there was strife between him and the other lads out there. Mysel, I thought Johnnie Flint was the promising one. There are those who say his ordination isna valid. My Donald was full of it the other week. But then Donald's sister came by our house last night, and she has heard Mr Renwick for hersel.'

'Heard him? Is he preaching already, then?'

'Aye, well Donald's sister at Kirk o' Shotts said when the people kent he was passing their way they gathered around him, and he spoke to them, and his words were very sustaining. She seemed quite taken with him. Mysel, I dinna ken. Lord save us we need preachers, but he's but a lad – just twenty-one, so they say. How can a lad of twenty-one hope to steer us, when our situation is so wretched?'

Hannah left soon after that, but Helen pondered what she had said about this James Renwick. Could the young man possibly provide the leadership, the instruction, the care that they so desperately need? Pray God it would be so, and the Lord might anoint him and make him a deliverer to Scotland. It would matter little to her though, for she would soon be on the other side, with the saints. She would never meet James Renwick in this life.

Yet still the days slipped by. Each time the door opened and a summons came, Helen wondered if this might be her time. Today the guard who stood at the top of the steps with light behind him was the tall, skinny one – the one who thought he was a bit of a comic. He wasn't as bad as some. 'Cooncil met the day.'

There was a shuffling and murmuring among the prisoners, as everyone waited to see which of them would be the recipients of judgement. Ann Stewart let out a thin wail, and someone kicked her.

He held up a paper and made a bit of a show of clearing his throat, and gobbed. At last he was ready to read out the words. 'First. Captain George Lockhart has been granted a warrant to transport prisoners to the Plantations. Any prisoners wishing to be considered for transportation should make their names known. Lord Livingstone and the Bishop of Edinburgh will be comin here the morn to select such prisoners as they see fit.' He looked up from his piece of paper. 'Ye should be goin, I tell ye. The Plantations. Got to be better than this dump.'

Something quivered within Helen, and she clasped her bony fingers tight. Could that be the answer? Not death – but transportation? Either way, she would never see her children again, but at least they would inhabit the same earth, breathe the same air, sleep under the same sky. Should she ask to be considered?

'Second,' the guard continued. 'Alexander Black, you

53

are to be released since you have taken the Test.'

Helen turned aside in disgust at the grateful babbling that came from Alex Black. At least thirty of their people had taken the Test during her time in prison. What a grief of heart it was to see and hear them so far left by God. Alex Black might live many years at liberty on this earth, but he had sold his eternal freedom. A poor exchange.

'Third,' the guard said. 'Robert Andrew, you are to be freed on account of your age and infirmity.'

Robert Andrew! He was lying beside her, and Helen touched him gently on the shoulder. 'Rab! Och, Rab! They're letting you go. Oh, praise be to God, praise be to God.'

He was dazed, stupefied, looking at her. They had all thought auld Rab would die here. And Helen was so busy trying to convince him that he was to be set free, that she almost missed the next part.

'Widow Alexander,' the guard said, 'your petition has been granted and you are to be freed.'

She was bending over Rab. The joy which bubbled up in her heart was all for him, dear Rab. But his pale, milky eyes were searching hers, and his withered hand reached up to touch her face. They looked at each other and understood together that in this pit they were on holy ground, for the Lord was surely working a miracle. Slowly, Helen raised her head. 'Me?'

'Rather stay, would you?'

She ignored his sarcasm. 'But – I presented no petition.'

'Well, I canna help that.' He tossed another paper across at her. 'It's all there. A Mr Robert Umpherstone is coming to tak you awa this evening.' He turned. 'That's it.' The door slammed behind him, and Ann Stewart let out a stream of foul-mouthed curses directed at Helen. She picked up the paper he had thrown and took it beneath the window for enough light to read.

The Lords having considered a petition by Helen

Alexander, widow, prisoner in the tolbooth of Canongate for harbouring Andrew Guillon, one of the murderers of the late Archbishop of St Andrews, which she acknowledges was out of ignorance and that, if she had known him guilty of that crime, she would not have in the least harboured him, craving that she being a poor widow with several fatherless children to maintain, and having remained a long time in prison, might be set at liberty, they hereby ordain the bailies of the Canongate and the keeper of their tolbooth to set her at liberty, as she has found caution in the books of the Council in 3000 merks to compear when called.

It made no sense. She had submitted no petition. Someone had surely done this on her behalf and put up the money too. But – she read it again, and again. There was nothing here to which she could not own. It was true that she had not known what Andrew Guillon had done when she had sheltered him. It might even be true that she wouldn't have taken him in, had she known – although who could tell? But there was not a word here about taking the Test, about acknowledging the king's authority or renouncing the Covenants. She was being released without taking the Test. It was unheard of. It was a miracle.

Aye, four long years had now passed since her time in prison, but she wouldna want to forget. Darkness and light.

Helen eased herself up from the bench where she had sat for a moment, overcome by her memories, and lifted a pot over to the hearth. She had been so weak when her good-brother Robert came and led her from the prison that her first mouthful of fresh air in many months made her dizzy. She remembered the interminable ride back to Pentland, with Robert's arms around her holding her upright on his horse. Strange, how she had resigned herself to never seeing her children again – yet, when she knew she was travelling back to take them in her arms once more, she near went mad from desperation on that final journey. Then there were long weeks of illness back at home, when she did not know where she was and her friends cared for her. Those same friends, when she was better, told her just how afraid they had been during her imprisonment, and pleaded with her never to harbour fugitives again.

But gradually her strength returned, and with it her conviction. The Lord had spared her. She never learned where that petition had come from – some believed it was submitted by her good-brother, some by Sir Alexander Gibson himself. But in her own mind she knew she was spared by the sovereign intervention of the Lord Almighty. And if that was true, then, like Joseph with his coat of many colours, she was spared for a reason.

When, shortly after, she heard the 'young lad' James Renwick for herself, she began to catch a glimmer of what that reason might be.

Chapter Four

Sunday 27ᵗʰ November 1687

This is the third Sabbath of Jonet Gothskirk her appearance in Sackcloth in the place of public repentance.

Jonet Gothskirk rebuked for her absence three days from the place of public repentance, and admonished to wait more punctually in time coming, or if at any time she happen to be absent, to signify by herself or some other in her name the reason thereof.

Rebuked?

Aye, she would be rebuked right enough if Mr Mackenzie kent the places she had been, the people she had met. It gave her secret pleasure, sitting there on the stool, to picture the minister's apoplexy if he caught hold of even a grain of it.

For she had had to return during the course of the past week. Pleading sickness for those absent Sabbaths – well, that much was true! She felt it now, the queasiness of the bairn, though it was getting easier. And strangely, enduring her sentence felt easier, too. Maybe Mam was right, and she'd just needed to get away for a while. Though in the name of heaven she had had no notion at all of what she was going to! Fragments from her weeks with Kirstie flitted through her head; her sister's unexpected certainty, Helen with her sorrow over the prisoners from Bothwell Brig, the quiet man in the background.

She was glad to be away from them and their madness. She couldn't quite rest easy, knowing as she did the danger that lurked close to her sister and her family, but what to do? She was better away from them. Her life here in Calder might be under a shadow, but at least it wasna the shadow of the noose.

The last part of her weekly ordeal was the walk from kirk to home, still dressed in the hated gown. She held the material off the ground, and held her head high too, for no longer would she shuffle along behind them. The people spilled out from the darkness of the kirk and spread out across their land, and Jonet breathed the clean, cold, sparkling air. The frost had not lifted, though it was midday. There was Mamie looking the other way as usual, but the youngest of her lassies gave Jonet a shy half-smile, which she returned. Aye, and there ahead was Davy, walking briskly, with that man she'd seen the last time she'd stood here – the one with the unsavoury gleam in his eye. Davy was the only person from her family to witness Jonet's penance, as Mam still stayed away. One of the elders had come to the house remonstrating with her, but Mam blankly refused to attend the kirk, or to bring wee Mary, while Jonet was in sackcloth. 'That's no way for the bairn to see her sister.'

'Perhaps it would keep her from going the same way.'

That was when Mam showed him the door. But they won't take Mam on. They need her too much – need her remedies when they're sick and her help when their bairns are pushing into the world. So Mam and Mary stayed home, and Davy came but looked the other way. Davy – proud and dark and thinking himself man of the house since their father had gone. Which he was, of course. He did well at the hairst, bringing in the crops and getting them stocked up for winter. As a strong and fit young man, he could have found plenty work on the larger landholdings too, once their own community's yield was brought in. But a couple of years back, Davy began working for their father's friend, Highland Angus, who kept the smithy. Angus had been good to the family since their father died. He spared Davy whenever he was needed to help on the land but gave him work in the smithy when there was less to do, like now, in the winter. It meant there was still a wage coming in, although Jonet had lost hers.

And now Davy was to marry Highland Angus's lass, Elspet.

Jonet turned along the track towards home. That had been the news awaiting her when she returned from Pentland. Wee Mary had come running and told her, all excited. Jonet was pleased for her brother. She'd only met Elspet once or twice, but knew her for a bonny thing, with thick brown hair and a strong, capable figure. She was Angus's only child, so it was a good marriage for Davy too. But oh, for all she was glad for him, it stirred the grief within her heart once more. Grief that lay quieter now, hushed like a wee bairn, aye, but still there. Slumbering. All that she hoped for, and all that she'd lost.

As she approached their home, she could see Davy in the doorway, speaking to their mother. She couldn't hear what they were saying, but Davy was gesticulating. Then he left the house and came hurrying towards her. Barely a nod and he was past, not meeting her eye. Ach, Davy had aye been like that. Even when she hugged him and wished him well in his marriage, he shrugged her off, awkward as a gawky lad. But never mind him, she was home at last. Behind the house to rip off the foul garment and scrub off the stench with icy water from the barrel. There would be some food and then, because it was the Sabbath, they would do no work.

Aye, but Mam was restless, that much was clear. When Jonet rose to clear the plates, she caught her wrist. 'Sit you down, lass, there's something you must hear.'

Some moments slow down and pull you into them. The winter sun, streaking through the open doorway and falling between them across the table, opaque with swirling smoke. Mary watching, anxious, for she would have heard them talk before now. And Mam, her face a mask.

'You may as well ken now, and Jonet, try to see it as a

guid thing for it's an answer to your trials. You are to wed.'

Slow down, and even stop.

Wed.

Will?

She must have said it aloud, although she knew it couldn't be true, for Mam made an impatient gesture, brushing the escaped name beneath the table and out of sight for all time. 'You are to wed a friend of Highland Angus. He is a widower in need of a wife. And he must be a kind man, Jonet, for he has said he will take your bairn as his own, and because he lives far frae here, naebody will ken different. Your shame will be no more, and in time you'll have more bairns and you will be a family like any other.'

There was a skelf on the edge of the table. She must work it free or it would catch on their clothing, or maybe in wee Mary's soft hand.

'I ken it's unexpected like, but I have thought and thought on this, and I can see no better way for you and for the life of the bairn that's to be born. It's no that I want to lose you, my lass, but if you're sensible about this, you have the chance to make a new life. The minister will surely allow you to make your repentance afore the kirk and be restored in order to be wed.'

But carefully, or she would leave a jagged edge when she broke it off. That would be worse.

'What say you, lass?'

And there was something jagged within her too, rising from the deepest part of her and ripping through her with a pain that, for all she'd already gone through, she had never dreamed she could experience.

'Jonet?'

'Where?'

Strange, that that was what she asked, for it was not the question which was uppermost. But she was far, far too frightened to ask *who?*

'Inverness.'

Inverness! She had barely a notion where that was, except that it was somewhere in the godless wild Highlands where they all spoke the Irish and dressed like savages. So far away that she would never see her family again. Aye, and that would suit her brother. She lifted her head then and looked right at her mother, the first flames of anger stirring.

'This is Davy's doing, is it no?'

And now that the first telling was done Mam's mask had slipped a little, and Jonet could see the wearied pain on her lined face. 'Aye, pet, that it is. But he wants the best for you, my lass. You canna bide here, and better, far better, to be somewhere you can start afresh. Your ain hame, your ain family. And although I dinna ken this man I have met him once, and you will be well enough provided for.'

'You have met him?'

'Briefly. He is staying with Highland Angus and Elspet.'

And then Jonet felt the gorge rise within her, for she knew without the slightest doubt that the man she was to wed was the man who had accompanied her brother to the kirk. The man with the curly grey hair, the belly hanging over his breeks, the man who had undressed her greedily with his eyes. He must be forty if he was a day, maybe even fifty. Dear God. Dear God. She struggled to her feet, hand clasped to her mouth, and was barely through the door and among the startled hens before she vomited.

And then Mam was behind her, a hand resting on her shoulder. 'It's a shock, and no what you wanted, I ken that. But Jonet, it's the only way, and God willing it will turn out to be a guid way.'

She wiped her mouth and stayed kneeling on the wet ground. 'I want to bide with you.' Like a child.

There was a weariness in Mam's reply. 'All things must change, Jonet. You ken Davy and Elspet are to wed. This will be their hame. I will help them keep house, of course, as

61

Davy's mother. And Mary must stay here for a year or two until she's old enough to get a place somewhere. But–'

'Go on.'

'Ach Jonet, I dinna like it. But the fact is Elspet's no willing to start her wedded life with Davy's unmarried sister and bairn in the house. They could have turned you out, lass, and neither the one of us able to do a thing about it. But they havena. Davy has found a guid man who will take both you and your bairn, and you can make a clean start of it.'

Mam's voice, so gentle, offering hope where there seemed to be none, as she had been doing all Jonet's life. And yet ... She shook off her mother's hand. 'And if I will not?'

'Then I canna help you further.' Her mother stepped back. 'You're a grown woman now, Jonet. You ken what life your bairn can expect, born a bastard. This chance willna come twice. Now, Davy will bring the man to meet you this evening. Tak some time to yoursel and then make yoursel tidy and be ready. You ken there's no other way.'

And she did. For all the protest in her heart, for all the revulsion at being handed over to a man the age of her father, for all the panic that rose within her at being separated forever from her home and her family, she knew from the outset that there was no other way. This was an old tale, after all. She knew the bleak prospects for a woman alone in their land, especially a woman alone through her own wantonness. She knew too, the shame which would dog her child through all its days, through no fault of its own. She had glimpsed these things that first night in the kirk, yet she had pushed them aside, caught up in the immediacy of her troubles and foolishly believing that her boxbed with Mary would aye be there for her. She had given no real thought to the future, but it seemed that others had, and here they had a solution that was watertight.

But oh – to have to submit to his touch. To belong to him. To lie under him, his weight pressing down, his body invading hers. How could she ever endure it?

She would run, run, run. She would go to Kirstie. She would go anywhere. She wouldn't do this. She wouldn't. They couldn't make her. She would kill herself and her bairn. She wouldn't be the first to do so.

Yet when he came calling with Davy that evening, she was seated by the fireside, her napkin tight over her hair and her hands demure on her lap. His voice and his turn of phrase were strange to her, but at least he spoke her language, though his accent was thick and hard to understand. He spoke to her only the once, to tell her that his married daughter lived a mile away so she would not be without friends. She nodded her head, unable to trust herself to speak as she listened to them deciding her fate between them. He had business to attend to in the south which would take some time, but then he would return to Calder and they would be wed quietly here. He could not say when – perhaps six weeks, certainly no longer than two months. And then he would take her north to Inverness as his wife, and because he had been away so long there should be no questions from folk there about the bairn. And perhaps Mam was right and he was kind, for this was the only reference he made to her shame with his words – and yet what he did not say with his lips he spoke with his eyes. She barely looked at him, but she could feel his gaze aye on her, and there was something there which made her flesh crawl. What kind of a man was he really, this Highlander who had decided to take her away as his own? She sat motionless until they rose to leave, he and Davy both. They reached the doorway, and she called her brother back. Surprised, he turned towards her. She beckoned and he bent low, so only he could hear what she had to say.

'Dinna think I will ever forgive you for this. Your betrayal will haunt you to your grave.'

He looked startled, then flushed and turned away. She watched him go, a tiny glimmer of satisfaction among her grief.

'Aye, lass,' said Mam when they were gone, her voice low. 'That's it done then.'

Jonet nodded her head.

'I will go to bed.'

Her boxbed. Mary was not yet there. She curled into herself and pulled the blanket over her head, buried her face in the straw mattress, and finally, fully, she wept. Tears enough to flow all the way from Calder to Inverness – aye, and back again too. But that would never be.

With all that had happened, the trouble in Pentland had flown far from Jonet's mind. It was disconcerting, therefore, when Beatrix appeared from the pasture late the following afternoon. The frost had broken to be replaced by a raw dampness, and the girl had walked over the hills through the grey smirr, told where to come by Kirstie. Jonet was outside, returning from delivering a tonic of her mother's making to a neighbour, her shawl round her head and shoulders to keep off the rain. She saw the lass approaching and tightened her fingers on the empty flagon, seized by an awful panic. She hurried towards Beatrix. 'What's become of Kirstie?' she demanded, catching Beatrix by the shoulders. 'Tell me. Is it the soldiers?'

But the lass was smiling, though weary. 'Dinna fear,' she said at once. 'Your sister is well. I've come with a message, though. My mother would like you to come through as she is joined in marriage with James Currie on Wednesday.'

Slowly, she released the girl, took a step back, trying to catch up. 'Marriage?'

'Aye.'

The full meaning came in on her then, and abruptly she came awake. Turned, looked round furtively – no one was near. 'But surely that will be dangerous?'

'We dinna believe so,' said Beatrix, her calm and

composed voice echoing her mother's tones. 'Naebody kens he is in these parts. And my mother would dearly like you to come. Your sister too, she urges you to join them. She would have written you a note but it wouldna be wise.'

It wouldna be possible either, reflected Jonet, as neither sister had ever learned to write and could read only a little. But were Helen and Kirstie unhinged, to think she would come to such a gathering? As if she had not enough to worry about! 'Lass, I dinna–' She broke off. Someone was coming. Mam, wondering what was keeping her. She had pulled her cloak around her against the steadily increasing rain, and her head was bowed. Jonet stood, unsure what to do. Guilty.

But Beatrix surprised her. 'Good day, mistress,' she said in her soft voice, stepping forward.

Mam pushed back her cloak, fear quickly following recognition. This time Beatrix was ready for the reaction. 'Your daughter is well,' she said quickly. 'I come with a message for Jonet.'

Mam looked between the two of them. 'Well, come out this weather, lass, afore you catch your death.' She turned and walked briskly back down towards the house. Beatrix and Jonet followed, stepping carefully over the slippery ground. Mam was soon busy, removing their wet things and ushering Beatrix near to the fire in the centre of the room. The girl had been well wrapped up, but was still damp and shivering. 'You get warm, lass. Mary, build up the fire some more. Jonet, fetch the bairn some soup.'

Silent and wondering now, Jonet did as she was told. Soon Beatrix was seated at the wooden table, a bowl of soup and some bread before her. Jonet sat down on a low stool and waited. She was not surprised by Mam's immediate concern for the cold and weary child – she would have done the same for any traveller, be they friend or stranger. No, what surprised her was the familiarity with which Mam was treating Helen's daughter. Right enough, Mam had visited

Kirstie in Pentland several times, and had stayed with her for a few weeks after the loss of the wee lad. Maybe Jonet was foolish never to have considered that she too would have come to know Kirstie's dangerous neighbours. But then, why had Kirstie never given the slightest hint of their mother's feelings on the matter?

What *were* their mother's feelings on the matter?

Mam would not let Beatrix speak until she was warmed and fed. Only then did she ask, 'So, lass, what's this message you bring?'

Beatrix repeated her invitation. 'My mother is to be wed to Mr Currie on Wednesday. She would like Jonet to join them.'

Mam said nothing for a moment, just looked at the quiet child, who looked back, unwavering. Then she turned her head sharply. 'Mary, awa see if the hens have been laying.'

Disappointed, Mary knew better than to argue. With a last quick glance at the visitor who was only a few years older than herself, she was gone. Mam eased her body slowly down into the one carved armchair in the room. That in itself was something of a wonder. She rarely sat in daytime – especially in winter, when the light for working was so short.

'So, your mother is to be wed.'

'Aye.'

'And she would have our Jonet join her?'

'Aye.'

Mam sighed, shifted her body a little, looked across at Jonet with a look which said she knew all there was to know about Kirstie's new friends. 'Ach well, I kent this might happen when you went visiting, lass. You never said, when you returned, that you'd spent time with Helen Alexander.'

No more did you! Jonet said nothing.

'And Kirstie will be there too?'

'She will.'

'Will he marry them in your house?'

He. The name no one spoke. The man in the shadows. So Mam knew that too.

'We'll go to a place we know in the hills. It's safer there. The preaching will take place at dawn.'

Her mother shifted her sharp glance from Beatrix to herself. 'Do you want to go?'

Jonet opened her lips to refuse. 'Aye,' she said.

Aye?

Of course. If ever she needed to see Kirstie, it was now. If ever she needed to escape from Calder, it was now. Perhaps she could even – but no. Capture that thought, lest Mam sees it drift by on the smoky air.

Mam looked between them then with a sombre softness in her eyes. 'Then you should go. But tak tent, girls. And Jonet, you must be hame for the Sabbath. I'll no be able to divert the minister a second time, and it matters even more now.'

It was too late and Beatrix too weary to set out that day. Instead the girl joined Jonet and Mary in the boxbed and rose early next morning, rested and ready for the return journey to Pentland. It would be a long, cold trail through the wintry hills, but Mam helped them prepare, putting together a bundle of food for them, along with some wee sweetmeats for Helen and her man, and ensuring they were both well-wrapped in the thickest woollen cloaks. Then she hugged them both. To Beatrix she said, 'Your mother is a brave woman. Be proud of her.' Then she placed her hands on Jonet's shoulders. 'Look to your sister, Jonet,' she said. 'I aye thought you were the risk taker, till Kirstie got hersel mixed up in this. She's thrawn, for all she's quiet. My prayers go with you.'

'We'll be fine, Mam.'

Her mother nodded. 'Aye, and it will do you no harm to look to your ain eternal soul,' she said surprisingly, before

67

turning back into the darkness of the house.

At first, they spoke little. The rain fell in a steady, fine mist which spread a silvery blanket over the moorland, but thank God there was no snow, not even as they wound their way along the pass between the hills. Now that the sickness had lessened, Jonet felt little effect of the bairn within, which was not yet big enough to make walking uncomfortable. The rain began to ease. As she set off, Jonet felt herself still bowed under the weight of the events of the last couple of days, but gradually a sense of freedom fluttered within her. She was leaving Calder, and all that it held for her, behind.

She glanced down at the young girl beside her. Beatrix, though small, was clearly strong and seemed to make nothing of her second journey in two days.

'It was kind of you to come for me.'

Beatrix gave a shy smile. 'My mother will be glad.'

Jonet remembered the walk with Helen to Roslin Castle, how she'd spoken of her own harsh stepmother and then of her first marriage to a man she had barely known. Aye, an old tale right enough. Stepping from tuft to tuft over the boggy ground, Jonet began to wonder if it might be Helen, rather than Kirstie, who could give her counsel on this visit? Jonet had paid little attention to Helen's story at the time, being more concerned about the unexpected appearance of James Renwick, but now she realised that the older woman had walked a path not so very different from her own. Perhaps she could ask Helen for advice. But of course, that was unlikely to happen, for Helen would be taken up with her new man – a man of her own choosing. And what of Beatrix? How might she be feeling now, on the eve of acquiring a new father? 'And you, Beatrix?' she asked. 'Are you pleased that your mother is to be wed?'

'I am,' Beatrix said at once. 'My faither's death was a sair trial to her, though I was just a bairn at the time, of course.

And since then she's had many burdens to bear alone. Now the Lord has provided a godly man for her, and a faither for Jamie, Charlie and me.'

Jonet glanced a little curiously at the young lass walking at her side. Beatrix could only be four or five years younger than she was herself. Her slight build made you think she was no more than a bairn, yet there was an unsettling intensity about her for someone so young. Jonet thought of Helen's story of taking her three small children to witness the wretched line of Bothwell Brig captives stumbling towards their doom. Beatrix would perhaps have been old enough to remember the occasion.

'I mind that,' Beatrix said in response to Jonet's question. 'I was maybe five or six years old. I mind the poor wretched prisoners, and the folk crying out such foul things as I had never afore heard. And I mind my mother greeting most of the way hame to Pentland – and the lads and I were greeting too, though we didna ken why. That was when my faither was still living,' she added.

At that point they stopped talking, for the way required them either to walk through the fast-flowing waters of an icy burn or to scramble a little way uphill where they could cross from one boulder to another. They chose the second option and Jonet crossed first, then reached back to help the smaller girl over the water. Once they were on an even pathway again, however, Jonet returned to the conversation.

'How old were you when he died?'

'I was eight,' she said. 'Jamie was five and Charlie just three.'

'That must have been hard,' said Jonet. 'My faither died too, three year syne. I still miss him.' She breathed coldness into her lungs as she thought of him; the darkness of his looks, the strength of his arms, the hands, lined and calloused with work in the fields, but so gentle as they gathered her to him. He would not have allowed this dreadful thing to happen to her, surely he would not. She caught her breath as, just for a moment, the horror of her future loomed before her once more. But Beatrix was speaking again, her voice low.

'That wasna the hardest time for us. The hardest time was when they took my mother.'

'Took her – I dinna understand you,' said Jonet, hurrying to catch up. Beatrix's voice was so soft that she could only hear properly when she walked directly alongside. 'Who took her? Where?'

'It was Sir Alexander Gibson, and his son with him, and some of his men. They kent my mother wouldna attend their kirk, nor pay their fines. And then she gave shelter to … to some folk she believed were godly. So they came and they took her away to Edinburgh, to prison, and she didna come hame again for weeks and weeks.'

Right enough, had Kirstie not said something about Helen being imprisoned? Jonet had assumed she meant for a day or two at most. Now she looked at the young lass at her side, and the spectre of Marion loomed once more. 'So your faither was deid and your mother was in prison? How could you live?'

'The Lord provided. And it was at that time I signed the Covenant.'

The Covenant? That document binding the people of Scotland to God and against the rituals imposed by the Stuart kings? Jonet began to wonder if everything Beatrix was telling her could be strictly true. 'A bairn like you couldna sign the Covenant.'

'Aye, but we have our ain children's Covenant.' They were, at last, descending the hillside and drawing close to Pentland. Perhaps because they were leaving the shelter of the hills, Beatrix's tones had dropped lower than ever. 'My mother had gathered about her some bairns from nearby, some of my friends, you ken, and had explained the evils of our time. When she was imprisoned, we kept meeting and

70

we drew up our ain children's Covenant with a wee bit help from one or two godly women. We pledged oursels to the Lord. My name was the first to be added to that paper,' she said with some pride. 'I was ten years of age. And we prayed faithfully for my mother to be released unharmed. And she was. The Lord heard our prayers and honoured our pledge of our lives to Him. *Cast thy burden on the Lord and He shall sustain thee.'*

Her mother's daughter, right enough. Jonet didn't doubt her story for a moment, but she wished she had never heard it. Almost, she wished she had never come. But only almost – for there was Kirstie's house, and right now her need for Kirstie was far greater than any sense of danger. She stopped. 'Thank you for coming for me.'

'Grand.' It was the shy smile again – the intensity disappeared, and she was just an ordinary wee girl. 'I'll see you the morn.' The lass held up her hand in a strange little salute and was gone. Jonet watched her go then took a breath and pushed open her sister's door. What would Kirstie make of her proposed marriage to a Highlander?

Next morning, they stepped out into a darkness which wrapped itself comfortingly around them. Sandy walked ahead holding a lantern, with wee Bel on his shoulders. The two sisters followed behind, arm in arm, and Kirstie carried a second flickering light. Sandy led them not by the path she and Beatrix had taken the day before, but along to the end of the little cluster of houses and up a sheep track which led towards the hills. 'Is it far?' Jonet asked, her voice low.

'I havena been to this place, but Sandy kens these hills as well as he kens how to thread his boots. He chose the place for the preaching.'

Jonet said no more. It was the last day of November, and it was cold and damp as they made their way silently along the track, but at least the steady rain of the day before had passed. No moon or stars lit their way, and there was as yet no glimmer of dawn to the east. She kept her eyes on her feet, nervous of stumbling over a protruding root or boulder, for the light from the lantern dipped and danced unsteadily. Ahead, on the hillside, a few other tiny pinpricks of light told her that others too were making this same journey. Perhaps one of those lights was Helen. Perhaps one was James Renwick himself. She shivered as she thought of all that she'd heard about him. Madman. Traitor. Murderer. Leader of those wild people who disowned the king.

The way here was too narrow to travel side by side, so Kirstie released her arm and dropped behind. Now her voice sounded, low. 'We havena had a preaching in the fields here for some time. Mr Renwick is so anxiously sought by the faithful all across Scotland, it's rare we see him here. I am so pleased you are to hear him, Jonet, more so than ever now that you are to leave us.'

For she had told her sister last night, and Kirstie had been bereft at the thought of the distance that would be between them. Yet for all her grief, and for all her schemes of visiting which they both knew were but a comforting dream, she sorrowfully accepted Jonet's fate. 'You will have your own hame and bairns, and you will be able to make something of that, Jonet, I ken you will.'

Six weeks. Six weeks in which to see as much of her dear sister as she possibly could. Even in the company of Mr Renwick. Jonet pictured again the man she had seen sitting on the floor in the shadows in Helen's house, and then later leading the little gathering in prayer. The man who, even now, was being hunted with all the power and might that the king's forces could raise against him. And yet, Kirstie assured her, time and again he was miraculously preserved to continue his work. 'In his company I believe we are in no danger, for the Lord protects him,' Kirstie had said as they left the house. But now, in the darkness, with only those little moving lights to betray that anyone else was out on this hillside, Jonet was not so sure.

At length, Sandy led them off the main path and down a steep bank. They turned a corner, and there, sheltered by sloping hillside on one side and by the spreading branches of an overhanging tree on the other, they came upon a company of people. The slope of the hillside was sparsely occupied by men, women and children, some sitting and some standing in groups of three or four. Beside the tree, however, the people were crowded more thickly together. This was clearly where most of the listeners wanted to be, and it was to this area that Sandy led them. All around, people shuffled and changed position, but barely a word was spoken. They waited in silence, a silence which hung heavy with anticipation and was disturbed only by the sound of the burn rushing over the stones on its journey down the hillside, and the song of a single blackbird summoning the dawn. Sandy found them a position on the banks of the burn. He handed Bel over to her mother, and Jonet watched as he turned away and climbed up to stand some way above them. The darkness was lifting a little, and she could see quite clearly now. Standing with his back to them, her sister's man set his legs a little apart and raised his musket, clearly outlined against the grey dawn. She took a quick breath and looked around. Three other men were positioned at different points on the hillside. Each, like Sandy, stood with his back to the gathered congregation, his firearm held ready.

Jonet pulled her cloak closer and turned her attention to the people grouped together on the bank. There was Helen, with her three children, and James Currie stood a little to the left of her, waiting for the moment, after sermon, when the preacher would pronounce his blessing on their union. She wondered how James Currie had fared climbing up the track, with his lame leg. Beside him was a younger man with untidy black hair who had a sleeping infant cooried against

73

his shoulder. She let her gaze move past them both, looking for the field preacher. Kirstie had told her that Mr Renwick sometimes spoke from a wooden preaching tent, but today it had been considered too cumbersome to carry all this way. 'He doesna aye use it, anyway,' Kirstie had said. 'Last month, I heard that at one preaching the rain was thundering down, and Mr Renwick chose to leave his tent and stand with the people, to share in their discomforts.'

And there he was. James Renwick. He stood a little distance away, his eyes fixed on the path from which they had come. Jonet took advantage of the shadowy light and the people around her to look at him more closely than she had dared in Helen's home. He wore a dark cloak which hung open, and she could see that he too had a pistol thrust into his belt. So it was true that these rebels came to worship fully armed. In his hands, he held the Scriptures and a small pocketbook. The sight of him was alarming, true enough, and yet she was struck at the same time by how young he looked. He could only be a few years older than she was herself. He was not small in height, but so thin and slight in build that it added to his apparent youthfulness. He was clean shaven today, with sandy coloured hair reaching to his shoulders. How could this unremarkable-looking lad possibly have caused such uproar throughout all Scotland?

And then, quite unexpectedly, he turned his head and looked directly at her. She had no time to look away. The brown eyes in that pale face held hers, clear, quizzical, perhaps working out where he had seen her before. Then he smiled, a quick, warm smile, and turned away. But not before his gaze had unmistakably dropped from her face to her belly, and back again. He knew.

And all at once Jonet felt a hot rush of rage – rage at the man for that so-familiar swift, appraising glance, at her sister for bringing her here, and above all at herself. *What, in the name of heaven, hell and all that's in between, possessed you to come here? You have the wrath of Mr Mackenzie, the lust of your new husband – do you need the scorn of this fanatical field preacher also? And risking your life for the pleasure, you damn fool? What is Helen Alexander and her marriage to you? Nothing, nothing, nothing. You should never have come.*

On her right-hand side stood her sister, her head bowed, no doubt in prayer as befitted her new holiness. Jonet laid a hand on her arm. 'Kirstie, this is a mistake. I shouldna be here.'

Kirstie didn't even raise her head. 'Ach, Jonet. Hush. It's all right.'

'No.' Jonet was sure now. 'No Kirstie, I mean it. I'm going to go now. You stay here, I can find my way.'

Kirstie looked up this time. 'Dinna be such a fool, Jonet,' she hissed, her voice low.

'The folly was to come in the first place. I'll be gone.' She had dropped her hand, but her sister gripped her elbow in turn, and her fingers dug through layers of cloth into Jonet's flesh.

'You canna leave now. They'll shoot you for a spy.'

Jonet looked towards the hillside and the armed sentries posted there. No way she could slip away unnoticed. 'But Sandy–'

'Jonet, you come here, you see who's here, you discover our meeting place, and you leave afore a word's been spoken? Of course they'll think you're awa to betray us.' Her sister stopped, took a half-step back. 'Are you?'

'Of course not!' Her voice had risen a little, breaking through the reverent silence. A few people nearby turned to look, some frowning, some curious. Kirstie dropped her hand and looked down. Jonet glanced across at Mr Renwick. He was watching them too. And though her heart beat in fear and her cheeks were flushed with humiliation, she knew her sister was right. It was far too late. She had no option but to stay. Angrily, she took a step away from her sister, happed her cloak protectively around herself, and waited for their meeting to begin.

The untidy man she had noticed before handed his infant to an older woman, stepped forward, and climbed onto a boulder. He raised a hand and gave out the psalm, then began to lead the praise in a voice which carried the depth and power of an older man. The words of the psalm, which Jonet had known since childhood, were picked up by men, women and children, and rose into the open air utterly unlike anything she had heard or felt within the kirk walls. But surely such a voluble swell of praise was unwise? She glanced up towards Sandy and was relieved to see that he stood as steady as ever, unheeding of the worship below, his eyes fixed on the vast sloping moorland.

God is our refuge and our strength,
in straits a present aid;
Therefore, although the earth remove,
we will not be afraid.

Kirstie's eyes were closed as her lips took on the words of the psalm. Jonet looked across at Helen. She too sang the familiar words, her hands pressed together and her gaze fixed on Mr Renwick – aye, and her eyes burned once more with the strange mix of hunger and tenderness which had so perplexed Jonet that first evening.

The heathen rag'd tumultuously,
the kingdoms moved were:
The Lord God uttered his voice,
the earth did melt for fear.

The resonant voice rang out, leading them just as the precentor in the kirk would do, but there was no mumbling, coughing or faltering here. And gradually, as she listened, she could not but recognise the sharp truth of the ancient words that this little group of hard-pressed worshippers embraced and made their own. Until now she had thought these people foolhardy – earnest, no doubt, but misguided and blind when it came to the risks they were taking. But as they sang there among the hills, she understood all at once that Renwick's flock knew exactly what they were risking. With eyes wide open they were prepared to take the hard path for themselves and their children, trusting all to God.

But why? In God's name, *why*?

> *Our God, who is the Lord of hosts,*
> *is still upon our side;*
> *The God of Jacob our refuge*
> *for ever will abide.*

Aye, that's what they believed, as clear as the daylight that was spreading over the hillside.

The notes of praise died away, and Jonet became aware of one young woman sobbing openly now. Those around her sought to comfort her, but not, as you might have expected, to silence or reprove her. They were so tender with her that Jonet guessed they knew and understood the cause of her grief. What horrors had this woman already faced? What sacrifices had she perhaps been called on to make?

After a pause to allow the woman to compose herself, the man with the untidy black hair turned and took the Bible from Mr Renwick, leafing through the pages, then read from Isaiah. The people stood in a silence which was only broken by occasional pitiful gasps from the woman. When the reading was done, he stepped down from the rock. He placed a hand on Mr Renwick's shoulder, bent his head and murmured something, then stepped aside. The slight, fair preacher mounted the rock and, raising his face to the vast skies, prayed to God to open their minds and their hearts to the Word.

What had she been expecting? Fire, perhaps. Wrath, certainly. A stream of treason against king, country and government. Yet Mr Renwick seemed not to be over

77

concerned with these things. True, he refused to give the king his title, referring to him only by his former rank, the Duke of York. That in itself was treason. And he spoke passionately against the Toleration, that recent royal proclamation which many ministers had accepted in return for limited freedoms to preach. He scorned the very idea of the life-giving, liberating, true Scottish kirk being *tolerated*. When something is good, he declared, we dinna merely tolerate it as we tolerate, say, a sore throat or an uncomfortable bed – no, we rejoice in it, we embrace it.

He was convincing enough, but she could almost hear her father's voice in her ear pointing out that for all his talk of freedom, Mr Renwick wouldna be extending those same freedoms to those who thought differently to himself. But in reality, it was only a very short part of his sermon which was given over to such matters. Mostly, his concern was for the people – for their strengthening during present and future sufferings, and ultimately for their salvation. *Close with Christ*, that was his phrase, as he urged them to make sure they were right with the Lord. His voice was not strong – at times she had to strain to hear him, and more than once he broke off into a fit of deep and painful coughing. But still he continued – *close with Christ* – do not miss out on the beautiful riches of a life lived with Him, which will far outweigh present hardships.

Close with Christ. Jonet felt the warmth as Kirstie clasped her hand, interlocking their fingers. Quite deliberately she moved the hand Kirstie had slipped into hers and placed it against the swelling of her pregnancy. *These words are not for me.*

'Never think these words are not for you.' She raised her head quickly, startled. His eyes were roaming over his flock as he spoke but did not stop to rest with her. 'The greater your sin, the greater you have need of Him.' Now he faced in her direction. 'Though you have all the sins of the world, He welcomes you. Only He can help you. Seek a heart to repent, and grace to believe in His name, that He may justify you.'

And her heart was beating swiftly now, and her limbs were tingling, and perhaps she had been standing for too long, so she leaned a little against her sister. Kirstie seemed to understand and swiftly slipped an arm around her waist. For there was more grace, and a glimpse of a different sort of God, in this lad's words than in all the dry preachings she had ever sat through.

But look around you! Look at Sandy with his musket, the preacher with his pistol. That's the cost.

Yet his brown eyes, his outstretched arms and his pleading words inspired a strange sort of confidence in her, so much so that she almost thought he could be right, and it was worth the risk. Worth everything, to have what he had, to have what he was offering. The Spirit of God was in his every breath, and if she would only give way as he entreated, that breath could be hers too. His, hers, the Lord's. In unison.

But the cost.

Many people were seated on the sodden ground by the time Mr Renwick had finished, among them Kirstie and Jonet, for he spoke a long time. But even the bairns sat quietly, though Bel was sleeping in her mother's lap. Jonet watched, quiet and thoughtful for all the turmoil within her, as he finished the preaching and pronounced his blessing upon them all, charging them in God's strength to go and be faithful. The woman who had wept before was white-faced and silent now, but there were sighs and sobs from elsewhere among the gathered people. As for the preacher, he seemed weak and spent now that his work was done, and sat for a while on the rock with his head in his hands. His dark-haired friend handed him a leather flask and he took a long drink. But his work, of course, was not done. Here and there people were detaching themselves from the crowd and moving towards him, many with small children in their arms

79

or by their sides. Jonet watched as Helen Alexander and James Currie spoke softly to one another and then joined the flow of people. Others fell back to make space. Mr Renwick got to his feet, helped by his friend, and smiled as he faced them.

The baptisms were carried out first, Mr Renwick scooping icy water from the burn onto the heads of the wee ones as their parents made their vows with all solemnity. At the head of the line was the young man who had led the singing. He had taken his tiny child back in his own arms. It had a thatch of hair which was even blacker and untidier than its father's. Jonet wondered if the mother was perhaps at home with other children. Once again, she let her hand rest on her stomach. Her own bairn would be birthed and baptised far away in Inverness, among strangers. She could not bring it to Mr Renwick, even if she wanted to. And strange though it might seem, there was a voice stirring within her which whispered that that was exactly what she did want.

*

Helen walked towards Mr Renwick, and he met her with a smile. She breathed slowly as he reached out and lifted her hand with his cold, slender fingers, and gently passed it into the firm grasp of James Currie. She glanced quickly at her soon-to-be husband standing at her side. He was beaming, his pink face shining with pride and joy as he listened to the minister's words. Helen listened too. Mr Renwick was seeking God's blessing for their union. *Yes, Lord, I will be faithful.* Heads around her might bow in reverence, but she stood erect. Her eyes remained open, fixed on the young preacher, taking in his every word, his every gesture, in the solemnity of this moment under the breadth of the pewter sky. Only when Mr Renwick finished did she turn, giving a little sigh, and allow her new husband to pull her into his arms.

And then there was a clamour of excitement and

conversation. The meeting was done, and some people began to slip away in twos and threes, but her children rushed up to them and others came too, hugging and laughing and greeting them. Her new husband had an arm around Jamie's shoulder – how the lad was growing, he was nearly as tall as his stepfather. Helen clasped Beatrix to her and glanced round for Charlie. There he was, he had scrambled up onto the great boulder and was chatting away eagerly to Mr Renwick, who was seated beside him. And amid the merriment Helen felt the touch of an icy breeze, for although James Renwick answered the boy with a smile, it was clear the exertions of the morning had drained much of his strength, and he coughed as often as he spoke. She turned to her husband. 'It's time he was away from this place.'

James followed her gaze. 'Aye,' he said at once, and looked toward the sentries. Most people had now left, and Sandy and the other two were coming down from their positions. Sandy walked across to join the little group who remained. It transpired Mr Renwick intended to head for Lanarkshire.

'You must wait, sir,' said Sandy at once. 'You are fatigued after such a morning. Have a day's rest afore you set off.'

'You must come to us,' said Helen at once.

Mr Renwick laughed as he turned to her. 'I think not, Helen! It will scarce do for you to have a guest on your first day and night as man and wife together!'

'The bairns are coming to us,' Kirstie said shyly. 'Will you not join us, Mr Renwick? You are welcome to bide for as long as you need.'

Helen pulled her cloak tight around her shoulders and tried not to mind. It was right, of course. For the next hours she belonged to her husband alone. And yet it was hard to watch the preacher making his way down the slope, leaning for strength on his friend. By the next day he would surely

81

be gone.

Without the cover of darkness, the route would be easier than on the way up, but they would be far more exposed. They must travel separately. Kirstie and Jonet would set off first with wee Bel, who was full of energy after her long nap, and with Beatrix. The boys would take a different route with Sandy. But as they turned to go, Helen sensed Jonet hesitating, and then the younger woman caught hold of her arm. 'I need to talk to you,' she said, the words coming out in a rush. 'Can I?'

Helen was startled but before she had a chance to respond, Kirstie called to her sister. 'Jonet! We really must go.'

Jonet snatched her hand away again and hurried off after her sister. Helen stood, looking after her. What on earth had the girl meant? Was she perhaps moved by the sermon, and in need of some spiritual counsel? Or was something else troubling her? Maybe she was perturbed by the thought of Mr Renwick going back to Kirstie's house. Aye, that would likely be it. Helen had been slightly surprised, though pleased, when Beatrix had returned last night with the news that Jonet had accepted the invitation to join them. Helen couldn't really say why she had sent for Jonet, other than by the prompting of the Lord. There had been something about the younger girl, the way she was at once so wounded and yet so defiant, that had stayed in her mind these past weeks. But this morning, Helen thought, as she continued down the slope arm in arm with her new man, this morning there had been a different look about Jonet. She had stood there, hunched into herself, and she had looked every bit as desolate as the barest hut left abandoned on the hillside. A light had died in the girl's eyes.

James was slowing. The old pain in his leg, the result of an illness several years ago from which the Lord had mercifully rescued him, was bothering him. He needed to rest, but she knew that they must keep going. If word reached the authorities that a preaching had taken place, they would scour the countryside for likely travellers, and force them to reveal their principles at gunpoint. Failure to do so would mean a bullet through the head and a grave among the heather, at the decree of the tyrant king who pretended to be offering freedom. 'Can you walk no further?'

His face was tinged grey with pain, but he breathed in deeply, just as aware as she was of the need to press on. 'Aye. In just a minute. I'm sorry, my love.'

She leaned in and kissed him. 'We'll be hame soon,' she said.

'Aye.' James shifted his stick to his other hand and slipped an arm round her waist, pulling her close. 'Hame with my wife. Hame to the hearth and to the bed that at last will be ours to share. I can scarce believe my guid fortune, but aye, I can walk on to *that* hame right enough.'

She felt his desire hard against her as he held her close to him, and something stirred within her too, though whether it was desire or fear she was hardly sure. 'Come then,' she said quickly, pulling away to resume their journey, and he eased himself into a steadier rhythm. They did not waste their breath in further speech, and eventually were back down in Pentland. Helen glanced across at Kirstie and Sandy's home, wondering if everyone had made it back safely, but her husband was holding her hand tightly and leading her towards her own front door. They stopped on the threshold.

All at once she remembered coming here as an eighteen-year-old bride when the wedding festivities were over. Charles Umpherstone had lifted her in his arms and kicked the door open, then carried her into his home. 'Welcome hame, wee wife,' he had said, lowering her onto the bed and bending over her. He had smelled of beer, and she had been frightened.

But now this was *her* house, and it was her own choice to invite James Currie to share it with her – indeed, to share her life with her. There had been no dancing this time, but there had been a sacred moment of binding up there on the hillside, and now another union awaited. He was standing back, expecting her to open the door. 'You do it,' she said. 'You live here too.'

And so he pushed the door and walked inside, and she followed him into the cool, dim room. She removed her cloak and bent to get the fire going. 'I'll heat some soup,' she said. 'You must be hungry. It was an early start.'

He had lowered himself onto the bench with a groan, glad to take the weight off his leg. As she turned back from the hearth towards the table, he reached out and caught hold of her, turning her to face him. 'The soup can wait,' he said, one hand on either side of her waist. She stood there above him and felt her heart begin to race. It was six years since the death of her husband – a long time since last she lay with a man. She had not expected this moment quite so soon, but if he was ready now then so was she. But then he pulled her down onto the bench beside him with one hand and slipped the other into his pocket, drawing something out. He held it towards her. 'I wanted you to have a gift to mark this day, but didna ken what you would like.'

She took it from him. It was a small bag made of dark red cloth with something hard inside. Gently she shook it out onto her lap. A brooch lay there, gleaming silver, its simple heart shape topped with a crown. Unexpected tears pricked her eyes. 'James, it's beautiful,' she said.

'Do you like it?' His voice was eager. 'I got it in one of the luckenbooths when I was last in Edinburgh. You can use it to pin your shawl.'

'So I can.' She lifted her trembling hands to unpin the simple clasp she used and replaced it with the new brooch. 'Grand.'

'Grand,' he repeated. He raised a hand and brushed away the single tear that had run down her cheek, then lowered his fingers to undo the brooch once more. He laid it carefully on the table, and slipped her shawl from her shoulders. 'Helen.'

She took his hand and eased him gently to his feet. 'Dear James,' she said, and helped him to remove his jacket before wrapping her arms tight around his neck and drawing him down into an embrace. As on the hillside she felt him respond, but now there was no need to pull away. She no longer wanted to. His hands caressed her tenderly and they kissed ever more deeply, all the while working at each other's clothes, removing the warm layers until their skin tingled in the cold air. The bed with its thick curtain stood at one end of the room, and Helen led James towards it. 'Come, my love,' she said.

Chapter Five

Sunday 4th December 1687

This is the fourth Sabbath of Jonet Gothskirk her appearance in Sackcloth in the place of public repentance.

On the following Sabbath, as Jonet perched in her place of humiliation, the congregation in Calder Kirk sang the very same psalm that the rebels had sung in the open air. An irony no doubt sent by Heaven. She looked around them all, gathered through fear and duty with one eye to a little-known deity and one eye to the authorities, and thought how little they understood. How could words which had brought such courage and strength and reassurance out there on the hillside sound so dry and meaningless here? As for Mr Mackenzie, he paid her no attention that morning. Perhaps he had at last sated his excitement over the thought of her lustful doings with Will. Oh, but how his little black eyes would sparkle with relish once more, if he knew, if he knew.

But he must never know.

It had been many hours before Mr Renwick and his companion made it down from the hill after the preaching. They had been obliged to take cover from some passing soldiers, and then to come by a different route for fear of bringing the authorities straight to the door. Jonet had intended to return to Calder immediately, but her sister pressed her to stay one more night. She was easily persuaded, for, whatever the danger, it was good to push the thoughts of her terrifying fate aside for just a little longer. The light was short in winter and was already beginning to fade when at last Mr Renwick and his friend arrived. The preacher was in a bad way, wet through, shivering and coughing, his hair bedraggled and plastered to his head. They gave him some spirits, though he protested that he could not tolerate strong drink, and saw him off to bed to sleep for as long as he could.

Glancing through the narrow window, Jonet saw Helen and her new husband making their way home. She had been foolish, of course, to hope to catch a moment alone with Helen earlier, but the idea lingered.

Kirstie joined her at the window and Jonet stepped back to make way for her. 'I wonder if they've gone hame for some religious discourse in their bed,' she murmured. Kirstie giggled, then glanced across to the bench where the dark man, whose name they had learned was Nathaniel, had turned one of his boots upside down and was attempting to mend it. He made no sign of having heard, but Jonet thought she detected a twitch in his shoulders. She watched him. That morning his infant daughter had been baptised with the name Sarah, and he had gazed on her with a look ablaze with love before handing her back to the older woman. He had said little since he and Mr Renwick had arrived at the house, other than begging materials to mend their boots, and apologising to Sandy for not accompanying him out to see to the beasts on this wild evening. 'I must get this done, or we will struggle to walk the morn,' he said. Who was he, this man? Was this his life, accompanying the hunted preacher from gathering to gathering, leaving his wife and children at home somewhere?

Meantime, Jonet and Kirstie embarked upon the regular household chores, which had not been carried out earlier as they'd been out on the hills. But after some time, Kirstie turned to her sister. 'I'm ready to get off my feet, after all we've done today, and you must be weary. You had the walk from Calder yesterday and all. Come Jonet, let's sit.'

The light through the small windows was dim, and Kirstie had lit the cruisie lamp. Jonet watched her sister in its yellow glow. The unreality of their situation was pressing in on her more and more. 'Does it no seem strange to you,' she asked with a sideways glance at the man with his needle, 'that we carry on here same as ever, and there's a wanted fugitive asleep in your bed?'

Kirstie pulled up a stool and sat down by the fire. 'Aye it's strange, right enough,' she said. 'Strange that a man should be hunted down for preaching the plain gospel you heard this forenoon.'

Jonet was not willing to accept this. 'He's a bonny preacher,' she agreed. 'But they say he believes he is the only godly preacher in all of Scotland. How can that possibly be anything other than wicked arrogance?'

The man paused in his stitching and laid his boot on the bench beside him but said nothing. Kirstie gave him a nervous glance. 'I dinna think–' she began. Jonet interrupted her. There had been questions dancing around her mind all through that day, and she needed to find some answers.

'There are ministers aplenty in the kirk. I have no love for them, as well you ken. But I have heard Mr Mackenzie of Calder say that James Renwick tells people no to pay their taxes and calls for violence against all who oppose him. Surely those are the words of a proud man, no a prophet.' She swung round to face the man. 'Am I right, sir?'

'My name is Nathaniel,' he said mildly. 'Or Nat, if you prefer. And I have never met a man more humble, more full of kindness and grace, than James Renwick, despite all the lies that are spoken about him.'

Really? She frowned at him. 'What's your part in all this anyway?'

'God has given me the gift of leading praise, as my faither did afore me. Where possible I use that to help the persecuted remnant in their gatherings.'

'Do you travel much with him?' Kirstie asked. The man shook his head.

'I live not so very far from here. I am needed to tend my land and to care for my daughter.'

'The bairn who was baptised. Sarah.'

'Sarah.' The word hung in the room. After a pause he looked up, though his face was still in shadow. 'My wife is deid.'

And with a child so young, that was surely a fresh grief. The two women exchanged a glance and allowed the conversation to die away. Kirstie picked up some more of her beautiful embroidery, while Jonet returned to mending a tear in her gown. Soon Sandy and the boys would be back and looking for their meal. Still James Renwick slept on, still there was that sense of unreality about the presence of the weakened wanderer in their midst, separated from them by no more than a curtain. But as she began to scoop Kirstie's steaming thick stew into the wooden bowls, the curtain which hung across the boxbed was pushed back. James Renwick sat there, dressed in the crumpled nightgown of Sandy's which had been given to him, his fair hair untidy and a rueful smile on his face.

'Kirstie, the scent of your delicious stew has roused me! How long have I slept?'

'For some hours, sir,' Kirstie said shyly. 'But I hope it has done you good. Your clothes are dried and waiting for you.'

He took his garments and retreated behind the curtain to dress in privacy, then came to join them at the wooden table, climbing onto the bench beside Nathaniel and the two boys. Kirstie brought him his food, and they ate in near silence, listening to the wind as it howled round the house, tearing at the thatch and rattling the shutters. But once the meal had been cleared away and the children had been sent to bed, the five adults sat together around the hearth. 'I'm grateful to you, dear friends, for your hospitality, but we must now be on our way.'

89

'Now?' exclaimed Kirstie. 'But it's a wild night out. Please, stay with us until morning.'

'You are very kind, but it's generally best that we travel under cover of darkness.'

Sandy joined in. 'There's a great storm about this evening, sir, but it should pass afore morning. If you will but wait another few hours you may be gone by daybreak.'

'Well ...' James Renwick hesitated. 'I do feel much stronger for the warmth and rest and food you've given me. Perhaps it would be wiser to wait a while. What do you say, Nat? Nat is to accompany me to this next preaching, you know, afore he returns hame to his dear wee lass. But we will be gone in a few hours. You're very kind – I ken the risks you take. May the Lord reward your faithfulness.'

Jonet had barely spoken since Mr Renwick rose from his bed. Instead she watched him, watched both men. Mr Renwick had turned to Sandy with a query about the farm work, and there was a warmth in his glance, in his smile, a winsomeness in his very way of speaking, a sense of genuine interest in his manner. There was something about him, right enough. She had to remind herself that he was a very dangerous man to know. Never mind to shelter. A man with a price on his head.

It was easy to believe that on the hillside, with Sandy standing guard and Renwick himself preaching with a pistol thrust in his belt, while the words of the psalm drifted on the damp winter air. But now, in the familiar surroundings of Kirstie's cottage, as he took his supper and spoke softly with adults and bairns alike, she could scarce comprehend that this gentle lad was one and the same with the notorious Mr Renwick whose pride threatened kirk and kingdom.

And what of his friend, he of the dark untidy hair, the tiny baby and the deep voice? He said little and smiled less, dour and watchful as the conversation went on around him. She wondered whether he knew anything of her story, her

90

sentence. And thinking that brought her back to her other sentence, her sentence of exile and of marriage to a man she had scarcely met. All at once the stew was hard to swallow. With a huge effort she pushed thoughts of her own perilous situation aside and tried to focus on the conversation going on around her, which had reverted to the issues of the day.

Until now, the controversies raging in their land had meant little to her. She knew her parents had sworn the Covenant in days gone by, and family worship had been part of the rhythm of her childhood. But then each year seemed to bring a new division – an oath to be sworn on this side, an imposition to be resisted on the other. The voices of the passionate grew more strident, while the ordinary folk just grew weary. The preaching in the kirk and the ways of the government were not to her family's taste, but they would never dream of losing their land or their lives for such things. Like many others, they were driven not towards the field preachers, but away from things of the spirit altogether. Attendance at kirk was an obligation, and worship by the fireside a distant memory. Then her father died, and the slippery path of their daily existence became even more treacherous. Her mother still sat apart for a short time some evenings with her Bible open on her knee, but she would not have wanted her children to join her.

Jonet had escaped the confines of Calder soon after, finding her place in the dairy loft and sending wages home to ease any guilt. For more than two years she'd toiled and laughed and argued and sung with the other girls. And then had come Will, his eyes laughing, and his arms held out with promises of future happiness if she would only give way to him. And she'd walked right into that dream and found only the anguish of betrayal, the bitter taste of the kirk, and now the desperate prospect awaiting her in Inverness. If Mr Mackenzie was right, then she was despised not only by all good people on earth, but by God himself.

But now here was Mr Renwick, and a glimpse of something at once more dangerous and more enticing than she had ever encountered before. But who was he really, this man? Was he a deluded criminal with a persuasive way of speaking, who had deceived her sister and her husband? Kirstie and Helen would have her believe that he was a prophet speaking with the voice of God. But surely a true prophet would not bring down such wrath upon his head from government and kirk alike.

Or was that really so unlikely?

Was it not in fact always this way?

Whoever this man was, he was seated by her sister's fireside, so close that she could reach out and place a hand on his knee if she wanted to. In maybe an hour or two he would be gone, probably forever. There was so much she needed to know. She had seen his presence as a danger, but maybe it was an opportunity. Jonet was not often scared to speak her mind. 'Sir, may I ask you something?'

James Renwick raised his head, and his brown eyes looked directly at her. His face was still gaunt, but sleep had done him good. 'Of course,' he replied. Beside him, Nat turned his head. She could feel his darker gaze on her.

'We have a minister in our kirk in Calder, who likes to proclaim against the ways of the Society and against yoursel, sir. I have no reason to respect him, but he makes some powerful accusations.'

'Jonet–' Kirstie interrupted at once, her forehead creased with worry. Mr Renwick raised a hand.

'No, Kirstie. Your sister should say what's on her heart. It grieves me that so many lies are spread about us by people who once would have stood by our side, particularly since this wicked Toleration. I welcome the chance to bring clarity. Go on.'

Jonet held his gaze. 'Is it true for instance that you have called for the murder of the king?'

Kirstie gave a tiny gasp, but Mr Renwick did not even flinch. 'The Duke of York might be the late king's brother, but by the Word of God and the ancient laws of this kingdom, he has no right to rule. The king's authority isna absolute whatever he may wish. It comes frae God and is held on behalf of the people. If any ruler thinks himsel above the law and uses his power to abuse the people of Scotland, I canna own him king.'

'And murder?' she pressed, watching him carefully.

He frowned. 'Our followers must carry arms, to defend themsels against this terrible persecution we face. How can we do other? We are commanded by Almighty God to gather for worship – we must resist those who would prevent us. But I dinna call for violence.'

'So what of the murder of Archbishop Sharp, or that curate who was killed?'

James Renwick was silent for a moment, looking into the fire. His friend was now completely still. Outside, the wind was gathering strength, and the timber cruck frame creaked. Jonet waited. Had she gone too far? Unexpectedly, she did not want them to think badly of her. But when Mr Renwick looked up and faced her, it was not anger or irritation that she saw in his brown eyes, but a great weariness.

'Our land and our kirk are in a wretched state. Soaked in blood. Riven with division.'

Jonet couldn't help herself. 'But surely that canna excuse–' she began. He made to continue, but whatever he would have said was lost in another bout of that deep coughing which had overtaken him repeatedly on the hillside. His friend passed a flask across the table to him and he took a quick sip, then spoke quietly.

'The murder of the curate was wrong. I said so at once. And I acknowledge that many things have been done and written and said which might have been done and written and said mair wisely. But we are broken, and we are bleeding.'

No one dared speak. Jonet glanced at Kirstie and saw her face pale in the darkness, her frightened eyes fixed on the preacher. After a pause he continued.

'These are no thieves and vagabonds; they are ordinary men and women whose only wish is to continue in the stated principles of our reformed and covenanted kirk. They have seen their hames and their fields ravaged and stolen from them, their loved ones shot dead without trial or dragged awa to be tortured in their foul prisons. For what crime? For continuing in the faithful footsteps of their ancestors. Aye, for nothing more than that they are hounded. Little wonder that some among them are driven to actions which are mistaken. I'll no be the one to condemn them.'

'But you condemn others,' persisted Jonet. 'This morning you had harsh words for those who accept the king's Toleration. Yet it is surely a guid thing that the king has granted new freedom to preach?'

There was a spark in his eyes then. 'Freedom, aye, but to preach what exactly? Only what the authorities permit. The gospel is in chains. What the Lord Himsel gives me, *that* will I speak, and nothing else. This Toleration hands Christ's authority over to civil powers, and that I will never do.'

'But where will that lead?' asked Sandy. Young James Renwick stared into the fire, and its glow flickered across his face.

'I sometimes wonder if it will take something more than mere words to help the people of Scotland realise the truth of what we say.'

There was silence for a moment. His meaning was not so hard to understand. 'But there has been so much blood shed already, and it changes naught,' Kirstie said.

'It will bring change, Kirstie, mark you that. Our River Jordan is very deep but it isna very wide. At the moment we canna see where all this might end, and I fear God has a great reckoning for Scotland yet, but the blood of His martyrs is never shed in vain.'

His words had a chill about them, a frosty winter air stealing into the cottage, and Jonet shivered. He was convincing, aye – but was he right? Or was his own vainglory leading him towards the scaffold, not through sacrifice but through pride? After all, he wanted freedom to worship, but he wouldn't afford that same freedom to others. Those words he'd spoken seemed to hang there among them. *Our River Jordan is very deep but it isna very wide.* To brush them away, she asked, 'But surely there are other godly men who want what you want, yet they dinna cut themsels off from all others as your people do. Men like Sandy Peden, for instance, long admired by my mother. They say even he wasna guid enough for you.'

Sandy Peden. For all Mam kept her distance from the struggles of the day, she had a wholesale respect and admiration for Prophet Peden. She'd heard him once, in her youth, when she was a farm girl in Lanarkshire. She'd followed all his struggles, never ceasing to pray for him during those years when he was imprisoned on the stinking island they called the Bass. She had rejoiced at his freedom and mourned at his passing. If anyone had authority among the disparate, leaderless, confused remnant, it was surely Sandy Peden – and he reputedly had harsh words for James Renwick's ministry.

But Mr Renwick was not dismayed – far from it! He stretched out his legs before him, and the warmth slipped back into the room with his smile. 'Ah, Sandy Peden! The old bear himsel. I have the greatest regard for Sandy Peden. Did you ever hear the tale of my meeting with him, shortly afore he died?'

Jonet shook her head. 'I heard he wanted naught to do with you.'

'Well, that may be true, or it may no. Words again. So many words in this Scotland of ours. All I ken is that Mr

Peden sent for me in his last illness. If truth were telt, I was more than a wee bit feart when I received his summons.'

'But you went?' Kirstie asked.

'Of course I went. This was about two year syne. It was winter, January I think, and the day I received his message was foul with driving rain. I rode to the farm in Ayrshire where he lay, but when I came there was nane but a young lass there to see to his needs. She showed me into his room. I pushed the door, and it was a room smaller than this, and lit just by the one small window – which on a dreich January afternoon was near no light at all. At first, coming in from outside, I couldna see a thing. But I could hear him. I could hear the harsh, heavy breathing of one who's no lang for this world. Then I heard the groan as he raised himsel up, and I saw him.'

'What did he look like?'

'Like Samson,' said James Renwick and laughed – a laugh that ended in a cough. Then he shook his head. 'I mean no disrespect, but he was lying on his bed, leaning on his elbow, and I could scarce see his face for the fullness of his beard and his long, tangled grey hair. Even his eyebrows were wild! He'd lain sick for many months, you see, and he would allow nane to care for his person, so his hair was uncut. The air in the room was near putrid too.'

'Did he ken you?' Sandy asked.

'Och aye. He'd sent for me, remember? His body might have been failing but there was naught amiss with either his spirit or his mind. I walked towards him, and he asked me, "Sir, are you the James Renwick that there's so much noise about?"

"Faither, my name is James Renwick," said I, "but I've given the world no ground to make any noise about me." I told him, as I have told countless afore and since, that I follow no *new* principle or practice, but what our Reformers and Covenanters maintained. So he reached out his hand –

96

withered and brown and bony – and he summoned me close. Think how surprised I was at what he said next. "Turn about your back," said he. Well, I wondered, of course, but I did as he said, facing away from him and towards the door, which was a wee bit ajar. I was as feart as a lad that's to be beaten! And then I heard his voice once more. "I think your legs are too small," said he, "and your shoulders too narrow, to tak the whole Kirk of Scotland on your back." And then he took my hand in his and pulled me down to sit on his bed beside him, and he asked for a complete account of my conversion, and my call to the ministry, and what I believed, and why it was I withdrew from the other ministers.' Renwick paused. 'Such a man,' he said softly. 'Such a godly man.'

'And was he satisfied?' Jonet persisted.

'He was. He had the grace to admit his error in believing ill reports, though of course his only motive had aye been the glory of God. We prayed together. He kent his time was near.' Renwick shook his head, then smiled at Jonet. 'Your mother is a wise woman if she trusted in the guidance of Sandy Peden. Shall I tell you his last words to me?'

Jonet nodded, feeling her cheeks warm under the directness of that soft gaze.

'"Go on in a single dependence on the Lord," he said to me, "and you will win honestly through when many others that hold their head high will fall and lie in the mire." I dinna mind admitting that the path I must follow is oft times lonesome, and loneliness can lead to dark thoughts. I have my demons, and aye, my shoulders are far too narrow. But Sandy Peden's words remain a great comfort and strength to me. *Go on in a single dependence on the Lord.* I can do no other, and if that leads me to separate from those who choose to place their dependence elsewhere, so be it.' He shifted his position and turned his head, looking towards the darkened window. The rain seemed to have eased for the meantime. 'But friends, Nat and I must awa.' He turned to face her once more, and his smile was kind. 'I hope that helps you, Jonet?'

Jonet had almost forgotten that the conversation had begun because of the doubts she'd expressed, but he had not. He used her first name as if he knew her, but he didn't. He couldn't. Yet there was a question in his voice. Perhaps he already knew that the issues she had raised were not the ones she really needed to understand. Jonet dropped her eyes, looked at her own hands lying on her lap. Her fingers were twisted together so tightly that the knuckles were white. Her heart was beating forcibly with the inevitability of what was about to happen, as she heard her own voice say, 'Sir, my bairn–'

An arm slipped through hers, and Kirstie's warm hand was laid on her clenched fingers. Mr Renwick said nothing. Jonet took a quick breath and continued, her eyes fixed on the earthen floor.

'My bairn is a bastard, Mr Renwick. What's more, because the man is married to another, though I swear I didna ken it, they say I am guilty no just of fornication, but of adultery. Week after week I must put on their sackcloth and sit afore the congregation in the kirk of Calder while the minister abuses and scorns me. I dinna ken how many mair weeks I must endure, to satisfy the kirk session. And after that …' She broke off. There were not words enough to tell her horror at what must follow after that. Breathe deeply. She kept her eyes down and spoke more evenly. 'This forenoon, sir, you spoke of closing with Christ. You speak of the principles of the Covenant. But none of this is for the likes of me, is it?'

There. She'd said it. *None of this is for the likes of me.* She felt Kirstie's hand tighten on hers, but for herself, the sensation was of tension easing out of her. Relief. She'd said it. It didn't matter any more.

When at last he spoke, she wondered at first if she'd misheard him. 'Church discipline,' was all he said, very slowly.

Jonet looked up quickly, uncertain. She had no idea what she would see in his brown eyes. Perhaps the harsh glare of Mr Mackenzie; perhaps the warmth she'd seen earlier, the warmth that had finally prompted her to speak. But when she raised her eyes, she found he wasn't even looking at her. Instead he seemed to gaze beyond them all, thoughtful. Then he shook his head.

'Strange, that you should raise this matter,' he said, and his tone was unruffled, dreamy even. 'I've been thinking on this for some time.'

'Well so have I, sir,' she said dryly, before she could stop herself. He looked up then and smiled.

'Of course you have.' He was grave for a moment. 'The gospel of grace, the gospel you heard this morning, is the reason for everything. The desire on my heart – as should be the desire of every preacher of the Word – is to bring each person to know Christ through repentance, faith and obedience. But the kirk in Scotland is so broken that procedures which are designed to help lead people to Christ are instead abused. The result is chaos and despair.'

Jonet didn't understand a word, but it didn't sound as if he was condemning her completely.

'What do you mean, sir?' Sandy asked.

'In our small remnant of the true kirk it's my prayer that we can bring healing and order once more. Just a few weeks ago, as you Sandy and Nat ken, we introduced ruling elders to the Society at Tinto and at Darmead. Church discipline is necessary,' – here he glanced across at Jonet, – 'to help us all grasp our wretchedness afore a pure and holy God, and our desperate need of the forgiveness for which Christ died. But we canna *earn* salvation. All spiritual discipline should be applied with tenderness and compassion, and where genuine repentance is evident, there should be forgiveness.' He looked directly at Jonet, and there might have been no one

99

else in the room. 'Is your repentance genuine?' he asked her.

She thought of Will and caught her breath. The laughter dancing in his eyes as he came towards her, arms outstretched. The closeness of his mouth as he whispered into her ear. But what pleasure was there now in such memories? How empty her treasures had turned out to be. And in the shifting sands of those turbulent weeks the only refuge she'd found had been among these hunted people, whose eyes were fixed not on the world or the flesh, but far beyond. She nodded.

'Then Christ has forgiven you.' He paused, and it seemed to her that the steadfastness of his brown eyes was wide enough and full enough to swallow up every little crumbling fear she had within her. 'Go in a single dependence on the Lord, Jonet,' he said quietly.

She was suddenly unmade by the kindness in his voice. She lifted her head to answer but could not speak. He seemed to understand, getting to his feet, asking Kirstie for his cloak. Gradually she was winning the battle against tears. She looked up as the two men said their farewells. Mr Renwick was no longer looking her way, but Nat glanced across, and she thought there was a certain curiosity in his expression. And then the door closed and they were gone, leaving an empty silence in the room they had so recently occupied. For a moment or two, Sandy, Kirstie and Jonet stood looking at one another. 'I'm awa to bed,' Kirstie said at length.

Jonet agreed but she knew sleep was very far away. Her mind replayed firstly the conversations of the evening and then the events earlier in the day. There was much she didn't understand but she sensed that the comfort of these hours would stay with her. But it wasn't long until, inevitably, her thoughts drifted to the coming day, her return to Calder, and all that awaited her there.

She turned on her side and closed her eyes. Fine words were bonny enough, but they wouldn't do her much good in Inverness.

*

Helen stepped outside in the cool morning air. She had left James arranging his goods in the byre while she meant to walk to the burn to fetch fresh water. Beatrix usually did this, but the bairns hadn't yet returned from Kirstie's. She would leave them for now and call for them later if they didn't turn up of their own accord.

She hummed quietly to herself as she walked. She and James had had a day and a night together and had shared breakfast this morning, smiling at each other across the table as they gave thanks to God. Now, with the coming of the day, the work must begin again – his work as a travelling merchant, hers to tend her land and care for her family, and the work of the true gospel which they both shared. She wondered about Mr Renwick. Was he safe? Where would he be now?

As she stooped to lower the bucket into the burn, a movement caught her eye and she turned. A figure was walking away from her along the track, pace slow and head bowed. It was Jonet, surely, leaving her sister's home to return to Calder. She would have the latest news of Mr Renwick. Helen set her bucket to one side and hurried after her. 'Jonet!'

She had to call twice before the younger woman stopped and turned. She did not move towards Helen, but stood still, waiting, arms folded. Helen was breathless by the time she caught up with her. 'Are you leaving?'

'Aye.'

Helen allowed her breathing to steady before she spoke again. 'Did Mr Renwick get away safely?'

'I think so. He stayed with us until well into the night and left when the wind had died down a wee bit.' The girl was looking down at the path and avoiding her eye. It was only then that Helen remembered the brief, strange exchange they had had yesterday on the hillside – the urgent hand on her sleeve, the look of desperation in the girl's eyes, as the words almost fell out of her. Helen spoke gently.

'Yesterday you said you would like to speak to me, Jonet. How can I help you?'

'You canna.'

Helen hesitated. 'Shall I walk with you a short way?'

The girl shrugged. 'If you like.' There was little welcome in her tone, but she began walking slowly along the path once more, and Helen accompanied her. The girl was surly, but yesterday Helen had glimpsed real need. Returning home with her new husband and all that followed had pushed Jonet's behaviour from her mind, but now she was determined to get to the bottom of it.

'It must be hard to go back to Calder with what awaits you on the Sabbath,' she began.

'Aye.'

'It willna last much longer, though, surely? And your mam will help you with the bairn when it comes.'

Jonet's face was turned away, but her words were clear enough. 'My mam will be far away when my child is born.'

'What do you mean? Where is she going?'

'Mam will be at hame in Calder. I'm the one who will be gone. They're sending me to Inverness to marry an auld man. I've just met him the one time, and that was enough.'

The girl's voice trembled, and below the defiance Helen could hear fear. Dear God. No wonder she had seemed so haunted yesterday. Helen reached out and took Jonet gently by the shoulders, turning her so that they were facing each other. She looked into the girl's tormented eyes and saw just how much speaking out her pain had cost her.

'Is this what you wanted to talk to me about?'

Jonet nodded. 'That time we were walking to Roslin, you said you were young when you first wed. You said you didna ken much. I thought you might … but it's no matter. There's nothing you or Kirstie or anyone can do to make this any

102

better.'

'Can you tell your mother how you feel?'

'What good would that do?' Jonet demanded. 'My brother willna let me bide in his house. My mam has agreed to this, and even Kirstie thinks it's the only way. Soon he will come for me, and what choice do I have then? None at all.'

Choice. Aye, there was little choice right enough for an unwed, pregnant lass. Helen saw the tears in Jonet's eyes, but the younger woman brushed them away angrily as soon as they appeared. 'I must get back,' she said.

Helen breathed a swift prayer for help. 'Aye, you must go, but I'm glad you've told me,' she said. 'I will think and pray on the matter. There might be another way.'

Jonet stared at her. 'It's mair than prayers I'm needing,' she said abruptly, and pulled her hand free of Helen's grasp before setting off along the path once more. Helen stood still for a long time and watched her go. The joy and the comfort she had known this morning had slipped away, and her heart was troubled over the fate that awaited Kirstie's sister. Slowly, she turned towards home. She wanted to help Jonet, but what could she do? As she made her way back, she wondered what James would think when she told him. How *good* it was to be able to tell him. How good, when troubles came, to have another adult to talk them over with. A smile came to her lips once more. Her heart was grieved for Jonet, aye, but it sang for herself and her man.

Chapter Six

Sunday 11th December 1687

This is the fifth Sabbath of Jonet Gothskirk's public appearance in Sackcloth

The weeks were slipping by far too quickly.

Chapter Seven

Sunday 18ᵗʰ December 1687

This is the sixth Sabbath of Jonet Gothskirk's public appearance in Sackcloth for her Adultery.

Soon the man she had to marry would return.

Mam knew it too. There was a tightness in her words, an abruptness in her movements. She would barely look at Davy and refused to discuss plans for his marriage to Elspet. 'Time enough,' she said, and Jonet knew just what she meant. Time enough when it was all over, when Jonet was gone and never coming back.

Yet still the relentless humiliation at the front of the kirk continued, and somewhere in the midst of it all Jonet found time to run over and over in her mind that strange evening in Kirstie's home with the hunted James Renwick. An evening at once so ordinary and yet so startling. The kindness of his tone and the warmth of his eyes contrasting with the uncompromising certainty of his words. And then there was the quizzical curiosity she had glimpsed in the eyes of his companion. But no use to think on any of it, for she would likely never see any of them again.

She would see Kirstie, though. She and her sister had talked about that, and one or other of them would try to travel through each week, to make the most of their time before Jonet was gone. It was December, so there was always a fear that snow might prevent them, but thus far it had been a wet rather than a frozen winter. She hoped Kirstie and Sandy would make their way through tomorrow.

When she had returned from Pentland, Jonet had told her mother much of what had happened. She repeated the story of Sandy Peden, knowing how her mother had revered the old preacher.

Mam was deeply moved by the description of the squalor of the old man's last days. 'Well is that not a sin. What an ending, what a sad ending for the Prophet. That's what we cried him, you ken.'

Jonet knew that but found she didn't know much else. 'Tell me, Mam,' she said.

Her mother took her time. 'I was young,' she said eventually. 'It was afore I wed your faither. Maybe the year afore – aye, that's right. Peden the Prophet, he'd been hounded out his kirk down Wigtown way like so many of them. Those were the early years of the reign of the second Charles, and the return of the bishops who were puppets of the crown. But no for Mr Peden an easy escape to the Low Countries, like so many others. He took to the fields, and he continued to minister to his flock.'

'And you went to hear him?' Jonet asked. She could feel her skin tingling. *He took to the fields.*

'I did. I was a farm lass then, working in Lanarkshire, and he was preaching nearby. My friend bade me come. We were covenanted folks, but it seemed to us that the days of the Covenant were done. Still, we walked many miles through the dawn, and we spent the whole day at worship among the hills. It was right fine. He was a preacher like none I ever heard – truly he was a prophet. And there on the hills they spread out the cloths, and we celebrated the sacrament of the Lord's Supper. Och Jonet, when I think on that day, I canna believe we have to thole what we do in our kirk these days, and cry it worship. I made my personal covenant that day, lass. So did my friend. But ach …' She stopped, turned her head suddenly aside.

Jonet said nothing. She knew the rest of the story. Mam had married Faither, a man with a good heart who would whistle a psalm tune but had little time for fanatics of any persuasion. And shortly after they were married and settled back in Calder there came the so-called Pentland Rising, when the government forces defeated the Covenanting army just over the hills. Sensible folks kept their heads down at that time.

Oh Scotland, bloody Scotland, how can it be that a generation has passed, and nothing has changed?

So she sat by her mother's side and told her the rest, the parts she'd planned to keep to herself. All about Mr Renwick, and the power of his preaching, and his words to her in the house that night. And Mam said little, just rested her hand on her daughter's hair and smoothed it now and then. But ever since that day she'd caught Mam looking at her, when she thought she wasn't seen, looking at her with a kind of wary expression.

But now it was Monday, she was free of the sackcloth for another week and wee Mary was at her side, jumping up and down with excitement. Kirstie and Sandy were at last riding over, but it seemed they were not alone.

Mam looked at her. 'Did you ken this?'

'How could I?'

'Hmph.' Mam stalked ahead. Jonet waited at the door of the cottage, leaning against the wall. Truth to tell, she was more wearied by her weekly ordeal than she would ever suggest to Mam. She was coming on for six months into her pregnancy now, and she was starting to tire more easily. So she waited – and when the riders dismounted, she saw Helen Alexander and James Currie follow on behind her sister and her husband. Her cheeks burned as she remembered her last brief conversation with Helen on the track leading from Pentland. As for Kirstie, what good did she think it would do to bring that woman with her fervent fanaticism *here?*

Mam shrugged off her irritation as she opened her arms to Kirstie and wee Bel. Jonet moved forward and greeted Helen. 'Mam, you ken Helen?'

107

Mam had swung her wee granddaughter up in her arms. She nodded her head. 'I do. We met when the bairns were poorly. Though I dinna believe you were hame last time I was in Pentland with Kirstie.'

'It's possible. I've been obliged to spend a guid deal of time on the road.' Helen and Mam stood some distance apart, eyeing one another warily, as Kirstie and Jonet embraced. Then Kirstie turned to her mother.

'I asked Helen and James to join us, Mam, because I think they can explain many of the things you were wanting to understand.'

Jonet watched Kirstie carefully. She really was very pretty, with her brown curls peeping out from below the scarf that framed her small heart-shaped face, but there was a waver in her voice as she spoke. She risked wrongfooting Mam with this step, and Mam would not take kindly to that. Yet for all her timidity, there was a determination about Kirstie now, which Mam could not possibly miss.

Soon they were inside, out of that biting December air. Jonet built up the fire. Delighted not to be the wee one for once, Mary took her niece aside to play. Jonet busied herself pouring ale for their guests and looked round the crowded room as she did so. James was aglow with pride and happiness. A big man, he leaned back on the bench by the table, watching his wife and largely content to let her do the talking. Mam had ushered Helen into the chair in the centre of the room by the fire. She had removed her travelling cloak, but still sat with a brown shawl wrapped around her, pinned at the neck by a pretty silver brooch. Her black hair, sprinkled with grey, was held back from a face which was too worn to be youthful and too angular to be beautiful, but in which deep lines suggested a character more compelling than either youth or beauty. Kirstie and Sandy sat on stools; Jonet preferred for comfort to sit on the bench and lean back against the rough wall. They spoke about the bairns – about

Bel, about Mary, and about Helen's three. Then Mam said, 'Jonet telt me of your marriage.'

Helen glanced over at Jonet, then back to Mam. 'Aye,' she said. 'We give thanks to God that we were able to be wed by a godly minister.'

'Are you no feart?' Mam asked bluntly. 'They'll catch up with him eventually, and then where will you be?'

'It's in God's hands,' Helen said simply.

Mam stared at her for a moment then swung round to face Kirstie. 'And you?' she demanded. 'Are you willing to risk everything for this man?'

Kirstie couldn't help but flush at her mother's accusatory tone, but she held her ground. 'It's no for Mr Renwick, Mam. You ken that. It's for what's right and guid. It's for a kirk in Scotland which has Christ, no the king, as its head.'

'Bonny words,' said Mam.

Jonet looked across at her mother. Her hands were twisted together on her lap; hands that had done nothing but work and care for her family all these hard years. Yet once Mam too had stood in the fields, with the fresh breeze whipping across the moor, and had been moved by the words of a great preacher. When Mam had spoken about that day, the young lass who covenanted her life with the Lord had not been so terribly far away, for all she might sound dismissive now. 'Aye, Mam,' she said quietly. 'Are they no words you once held with yoursel?'

Her mother turned towards her. For a moment she glared at Jonet, then she shook her head. 'You ken that's true,' she said. 'And maybe that's why I was glad to let you go, for all the man is dangerous. You will be needing an inner strength from somewhere. But I never *dreamed* ...' this to Kirstie, 'I never dreamed for a moment that you would harbour that rebel in your ain hame.'

'It wasna like that, Mam,' said Kirstie uncomfortably. Mam sucked in her breath, and the air whistled where a tooth had long been missing.

'Tell that to the judge, or to the trooper who aims his musket at you, mair like.' She shook her head. 'Since the days when I listened to Peden the Prophet, not a thing has changed, for all the blood that has been spilt across our land. Must I watch my ain bairns mount that scaffold?' She turned to face Helen. 'For I'm right, am I no? That's where all this is headed. They imprisoned you once. They willna set you free a second time.'

Helen didn't answer straight away, and a shadow of something tortured seemed to pass over her face. After a pause she said quietly, 'The Lord may choose to preserve me – but even if he doesna, I willna serve their gods. Though they drag me back to their foul prison once more, aye, and even to the scaffold.'

Jonet shivered. Mam looked across at her. 'You'll be well out of all this, Jonet, you and your bairn. A new life far from these fools is just what you're needing.'

Jonet opened her mouth to protest, but before she could form the words, Helen was speaking. 'Jonet told me that she is to marry some man she doesna ken frae the Highlands. I wonder if it's really necessary?'

'*Necessary?*' Mam spat. 'Of course it's necessary. What would you have, the lass discarded and her guid name in the ditch? What chance survival for her bairn then?'

'There might be another way.'

Another way? Jonet looked at Kirstie, who was pale and frightened, and then at Helen, who was calm.

'Jonet could come to live with me. With us. For now. James and I would be pleased to have her.'

Mam laughed then, a harsh laugh without a drop of humour. 'And that's your *other way?* I might as well deliver her to the Tolbooth with my own hands.'

Jonet's head was swimming. Helen. She found it hard to know what to make of the woman. At first, she had blamed her for dragging Kirstie into danger, and even now she found her intensity and religious certainty disturbing. But Helen was offering to help her. To free her.

Why?

Then Helen spoke in a low voice. 'I ken what it means, mistress, to be a young lass at the mercy of an older man. I dinna want it for Jonet.'

'And you think I do?' Mam's blue eyes flashed with fury. 'You think I want her to go to those heathen mountains, and never see us again? You think I wouldna like her to have a nice young lad from these pairts as her man? Dear God, if there was another way do you no think I would find it? You are doing her no favours at all with your false promises and foolish ideas. You'd take her in for now, perhaps, but her name would still be tainted – aye, and tainted twice over in your company. This man is offering a hame and a future to her and her bairn both for the rest of their days.'

'At what cost?'

At what cost? As the argument raged around her, Jonet got unsteadily to her feet. She couldn't bear to hear any more. She left the cottage and followed the sound of children's voices to the edge of the burn, where her little sister was teaching Bel how to twist together a light twig with a dried leaf and make a wee sailboat. It was something her father had done with each of them. Bel's fingers hadn't quite mastered the knack, and Jonet gently helped her. 'There you are. Now, in the water with them – here's best, where the water's rushing down the side of that rock. One, two, three – go!'

Both girls laughed in excitement as their makeshift boats were carried downstream. Mary's soon caught in the brown weeds at the edge of the burn, but Bel's bobbed on before twig and leaf separated and drifted onwards sadly. 'A shipwreck and a grounding,' Jonet laughed, as the girls began to look for materials to try again. She watched them, thinking how good it was to laugh, and how rare too, these

111

days. Such a short time it seemed since she and Kirstie had tried floating their boats downstream, and now look at them.

Just look at them. She put her hand to her stomach, feeling the child move. Of all the things she would teach this bairn, how to make a sailboat from a leaf and a twig might not be the most important, but she would make sure it happened for all that. She was resolved to do what was best for her bairn – but for the life of her, she really didn't know what that was.

*

Helen thought she had a fair idea what was best for Jonet and her child, and it certainly wasn't marriage to a stranger at the other end of the country. She and James said their farewells soon afterwards, leaving Kirstie and her family to stay on in Calder. Jonet's mother was not for changing her mind. Fear of association with the Society people somehow outweighed any fear of what might happen to her daughter in the north.

'How can the woman think that way?' Helen was still vexed when they arrived home. 'I can understand that she wants Jonet married, but the lass is scared near to death. A fool could see it.'

'Ach, maybe it willna be so bad,' said James, bending to loosen his boots.

'And maybe it will!' She turned towards the hearth, where Beatrix was busy preparing some broth. Her tone softened. 'Thank you, my love.' She shook out her damp cloak. 'It wouldna be for aye, just until the lass was through the birth and could see her way ahead. She would have her sister nearby for company too. I really canna see why the woman is set against it.'

James had sat down by the fire and now stretched his legs out in front of him. 'I think you can, Helen. She kens we keep company with Mr Renwick and she's feart. Maybe it's best that we dinna keep reminding her of his association with us – for his sake.'

Helen looked across at him. 'She wouldna betray us,

James.'

'No, I dinna think so,' he replied, 'no when that would bring such trouble on her Kirstie. But for all that, we must be canny. It doesna do, Helen, to become so involved in another family's troubles. No at a time like this.'

Helen pressed her lips together. Of course, she agreed that Mr Renwick's safety mattered above all else. She, of all people, was hardly likely to forget that. But as for not getting involved, that was not her nature, and it wasn't her calling either.

She knew there were people – Jonet's mam just one among many – who found her commitment to the cause unsettling, but she simply knew no other way. That commitment might bring her into danger, but it also helped her to live life to the full in a world that was all too ready to tell people like her what they could and couldn't do. She had learned her earliest faith at her mother's knee, but it was her mother's death and all the troubles that followed which really opened her heart to the words of the persecuted ministers. She had been in such need, struggling under an unbearable burden of fear and doubt, when those godly men had drawn her into the presence of the Lord. From that time onwards she dedicated her life to Him, whatever hazard or discomfort might come her way. She and James had talked about this and she knew he had a similar story of awakening. His commitment was not in doubt, but she suspected he had a hankering for a quieter life for all that.

A quiet life was not an option for Helen, not while the powers of the land were arrayed against them.

She looked across at him, dozing now in front of the fireplace, comfortably leaning back in that same spot where Mr Renwick had so often sat. For a moment her steadiness faltered as memories pushed to the fore and she seemed to see the young preacher lean forward, listening to her intently, or moving his delicate hands in the shadows to illustrate his story. But she was married now, she had made her choice. Aye, and for Jonet there was no choice. Helen might not be able to change Jonet's fate but perhaps she could still make a difference, encourage the girl to see there was usually another way.

'Soup's ready. Will I call the lads?' asked Beatrix.

James awoke with a little grunt at his stepdaughter's voice. 'I'll do it,' Helen said, gladly sliding back into this place and this time. She stepped towards the door as James got to his feet and moved awkwardly towards the table. 'Thank you, Beatrix love,' she said.

Chapter Eight

Sunday 25th December 1687

This is the seventh Sabbath of Jonet Gothskirk's public appearance in Sackcloth for her Adultery.

Aye, even though it was Yuletide, still they made her stand here.

When Mam was a bairn there were no Christmas services in the kirk, and the elders were on the watch for any sign of the old feasting and revelry, calling it Popish. But over these years since the second Charles came to the throne, the feasting and dancing had grown more popular again, and the curates held services on Christmas Eve and on Christmas morn. Now it had even been made an Act of Parliament, with King James VII – the Duke of York, as Mr Renwick cried him – decreeing that the people of Scotland should celebrate Yuletide once more.

And so there was a service, and for Jonet there was sackcloth.

*

Helen Alexander, of course, paid no attention to such a decree. She was no more likely to attend kirk or to celebrate Yuletide this day as any other. There was no preaching nearby that she and her family would contemplate attending, so the Sabbath would be spent quietly in worship and prayer at home. Next day James was heading east, and she helped him load up Moss, the packhorse, in the darkness of a December morning. He would take with him the spices, soap, utensils and oddments he had purchased in Leith and Edinburgh, seeking to sell or trade these along the country lanes. Tucked away among the bundles, strapped securely to Moss, were some tracts and small books which could be slipped into a sympathetic hand. As James travelled from one faithful house to another, he traded not only in goods but also in news, hoping to pick up word of Mr Renwick as he went. Today, for the first time, Jamie would accompany him, and the boy was brimful of suppressed pride and excitement. Helen, however, was hesitant. 'He's but a lad yet,' she had argued the night before. 'He should still be at his books. If he goes along with you, he'll think the merchant's life is for him, and then where will we be?'

James had laughed. 'Would that be so bad? There's aye trade to be done, Helen, and I'd like fine to train the lad up and have him alongside.'

Helen was silent. She had hopes stored up in her heart for her boys which had little to do with trade – yet they would remain just that, empty hopes, if she could not find someone to help with their studies. She'd had no difficulty teaching all three bairns their reading, writing and calculations, but she was aware that Jamie, at least, needed to begin Latin if, as she longed, he was to progress in his education. The boy was eleven now and would soon either need to be apprenticed to a trade or find a sponsor to enable him to continue his studies. She feared she knew which he would prefer. It was good that the boys now had a father once more, but for all her new husband was good with them, he was first to admit he had never been much of a scholar. Now she watched as Jamie carefully checked the strapping on each bundle and nodded to his stepfather. 'All fine, sir.'

James clapped him on the shoulder. 'Then we'll be off. Kiss your mother, lad.'

Jamie ducked his head away and grinned. 'Och, we'll be back in a few days.'

She smiled despite herself. The boy was nearly beside himself with pride to be working like a man, and what harm would it do? 'Tak tent, then, and James, mind he's but a lad.

He needs more sleep than you do.' She kissed her husband and watched as they set off at a steady pace into the gloom on either side of the packhorse, then turned back into the house.

All was silent. Beatrix had already gone out to collect the eggs, and Charlie was still sleeping. Helen allowed herself a moment's seat by the fire. It was now almost a month since that sacred early morning in the hills when she and James had been joined together before God. A month of remoulding the shape of their family to make a space for her new man. The rhythms of his voice in prayer, the warmth of his body in bed, the size of his appetite at mealtimes. Aye, she was becoming used to having him around – but there was something merciful nevertheless in this little snatched moment of time when her house was her own again.

For she had been many years without a man about the place, and it had been during those years that she had come to know James Renwick. Although he was but one among many taking shelter in her house, there was a loneliness at the core of him which whispered to her. The trust between them grew gradually, until one particular evening when they sat here, by this fireplace, and he wearily told of yet another trusted friend who had crumbled in the face of persecution. He was unable to hold back his tears that night, and rather than attempt to comfort him she let him weep, for the same grief was tearing apart her spirit too. But then they came together, to pray and seek God's forgiveness and strength, and from that place of humility they began to talk as never before. He asked her about herself, drawing out the story of her father's wife, and then the difficulties of the years of her marriage to an older man who did not share her convictions. He listened, and in return he told her about the Lord's call on his own life and the many struggles he had gone through as he attempted to respond. There had been periods when his own faith had been stretched so thin that he could look

117

right through its translucence into the dark void of a life without God. 'It's hard for a leader to speak of his own doubts,' he said, his chin resting on his hands. 'No because I want to pretend to a stronger faith than I really have, but because God has called me to build others up, no to shake their foundations.' The glow of the fire began to dim as the evening drew into night, and their words eventually died away too, but she knew that a bond had been forged that evening which was surely stronger than most.

Eventually he yawned and stretched. 'I am keeping you from your bed. I should continue on my way while it's dark.'

'Please, not yet.'

'I must.'

They both stood up at the same time and moved towards one another. The cords of their earlier conversation had slipped around them and were drawing them together. The light was almost gone, and when their lips met it was natural, it was inevitable, it was complete. She closed her eyes, and felt her arms encircle him, pulling him closer, engulfing him in a love and a hunger which was a world away from any embrace she had known when her husband was alive. Desire rose within her as his thin body responded to hers, as long months and years of desperately clinging to what was good and true amid persecution and fear came together in a tremor of fierce comfort. They held on and on and on, sinking deeper into one another. But then he pulled away. 'Helen …'

She did not stop him.

'We canna …'

'No,' she said.

She did not stop him. She reassured him and she turned away. She picked up his cloak, helped him into it, handed him some food as she would always do. She opened the door, standing aside to let him pass. He pulled his hat down on his head, but as he turned to go, she saw that his face was wet with tears. She squeezed his long thin fingers hard, and he was gone.

She did not stop him.

But that was more than a year ago. Now she was married to James Currie, and it was good and right, and she was adjusting. And thinking of the change that marriage had brought to her own life, she could not but think of Jonet once more. She had seen the fear in Jonet's eyes, and had seen reflected there all the panic of the early months of her own first marriage, and her heart was troubled for Jonet – and for Kirstie too, who was whitefaced and sorrowful at the loss of her sister to the distant north. James was right, there was little she could do to help without endangering Mr Renwick, but she would speak with Jonet next time she came through to Pentland and try to prepare her a little for what surely lay ahead.

She got to her feet and walked over to the boxbed, pulling the thick curtain aside and rousing Charlie. It was time he was awake, for with her husband and older son both away there would be additional work for him to do. She thought of them on their travels. There should be no danger – except, of course, there was always danger. The danger of being associated with the Society, known supporters of Mr Renwick. The danger of falling in with the wrong person, offering a tract up where money had already changed hands in the hunt for the persecuted. Helen built up the fire and put on some water to boil. It was a danger they had all lived with for many, many years, but there was no doubt the heat was increasing as the authorities grew frustrated in their efforts to find Mr Renwick. And where was he now? That was aye the hardest part – week upon week could go by with little news, when she could do nothing but imagine him out there on the hillside, skulking in the dark, or leading worship in constant danger of discovery, arrest, torture and death. All she could do was pray, and comfort herself with the knowledge that word of his capture would travel faster across Scotland than an eagle in full flight.

Almighty God, keep him safe. Keep them all safe.

Chapter Nine

Sunday 8ᵗʰ January 1688

The eighth Sabbath of Jonet Gothskirk's public appearance in Sackcloth.

Her Sabbath humiliation over for another week, this time it was Jonet who walked through to be with Kirstie in Pentland. For already nearly six weeks had passed, and the Highlander would soon be returning to claim her. Mam nodded when she announced she was going through to Pentland, but there was little to be said.

'Three days, no more, mind.'

'Aye. And Mam, if he should come–'

'If he does, he can wait three days.'

And so she was gone, and after a cold and weary journey she was with her sister once more. 'I must be back for the Sabbath, though,' she warned, as Kirstie folded her into the warmth of her arms and the safety of her home.

'Are they no done with you yet? When will you be free?'

Jonet shrugged off her damp cloak. 'There's no word. Maybe Mr Mackenzie means me to drop the bairn at his feet.' She sat down close to the fire and held out her hands, reaching for the heat to penetrate her chilled and aching bones. 'All that's been said is I will be released to be wed.' She glanced up at her sister. 'Is that what you call free?'

Kirstie brought her a steaming mug of spiced wine. 'You'll be free of the judgement of the kirk, at any rate.'

'Aye, maybe.' She sipped from the mug and let the warmth and the spices spread though her. The ice began to thaw; the heat of the fire was doing its work. She looked across at her sister, the person who knew her best. 'You think the shame of the kirk is the worst that could happen to a body, Kirstie. You're wrong. I would wear that gown every Sabbath that remains in my life rather than marry him, if I had the choice.'

'Ach Jonet, ye dinna mean that.'

'But I do.'

Kirstie shook her head. 'Soon you will have your bairn. That will change everything,' she said with certainty.

Jonet had thought she had no tears left, but she felt her eyes prickling in frustration at her inability to make Kirstie hear what she was saying. She turned her face to the fire and struggled for control. Even her sister believed they had found the best possible solution, and the knowledge filled Jonet with an intense and weary loneliness. A home, a man, a bairn. Everything Kirstie had herself, and all any woman could want. Never mind that the home was in the distant Highlands, the man a stranger near as old as their father, and the bairn not even his. No one seemed to think any of that mattered.

No one but Helen Alexander.

'He may be waiting when I return,' Jonet said, when she was sure her voice would be steady. 'This could be the last time.'

'I will come—'

'Aye.'

Somehow, Helen had understood. Helen had looked at her with warmth and concern and compassion. Helen had offered to find another way. She must speak to Helen. 'Is your friend Helen at home?'

'I havena seen much of Helen and James this last week or two,' said Kirstie at once, grasping gladly for a new topic of conversation. 'They were awa at a meeting of the Society, I believe, for I had an eye out for the bairns. They've no been in this way since they returned. We'll call on her the morn, tell her you're with us.'

There was no need to call on Helen, however, for she was there to see them early next morning. She welcomed Jonet, but absently, and made sure the door was closed before saying, 'I have our friend with us once more. He's for Edinburgh but will bide here this evening. Will you join us?'

Our friend – Mr Renwick. If the fugitive preacher was present, there would be no opportunity to speak to Helen about her own situation. Yet for all that, Jonet felt a quiver of excitement at the thought of him. A month or so must have passed since she had sat in this room alongside him and listened as he spoke so frankly of his mission. She had taken the goodness of that evening into herself over the following weeks, wrapping it around her heart to protect it from the barbs of Mr Mackenzie, and of her own brother. She had been afraid that day, but this time she cared nothing for the troops. Soon she would be gone, and she would never see Mr Renwick and his associates again. 'Aye, we'll come,' she said, before Kirstie had framed her answer.

Helen nodded slowly. 'There will be no preaching, for the times are too dangerous, and besides, he's gey weary.' Concern flitted across her face. 'The business in Peebles has taken a fair bittie out of him, though of course he'd never say so.'

'What business in Peebles?'

'Did you no hear?' Helen shook her head. 'The saving power of Almighty God – though four of our number are in prison this night as a result. But I've no time now. There are others I must ask to join us for a house meeting. You'll hear about it later.'

*

Helen stepped out into the sharp January air, took a deep breath, and exhaled a stream of mist as she looked up at the Pentland Hills stretching away to her right. For all she was glad to see poor Jonet again, she would rather, just this once, that Mr Renwick was not so welcoming. It was far

123

too dangerous for him to be present at a gathering. But he was so conscious of their plight, sheep without a shepherd, that he let no opportunity pass to strengthen his friends. He had given up the notion of a field preaching reluctantly, as she persuaded him to get some rest during the day. He had entrusted her to alert their friends to his presence in her home and invite them to a meeting late in the evening.

She did as he asked, of course, but her heart was in rebellion. Perhaps it was the nearness of the terror she had known at Peebles, though the Lord knew they had lived through many close escapes before this one. What was so different this time?

Fear. This last day in looking at him, in watching him eat, in catching his easy smile, she had been near paralysed by a terrible fear that never, in all these turbulent years, had she felt before.

And aye, some of it was caused by what he told her last night, but it began before that. Though she didn't realise it at first, it perhaps began the last week of December, when Mr Renwick sent word that he was holding a meeting near to Peebles in the night-time. It was just within travelling distance, so she and James resolved to go. They journeyed on foot, for James was not long back and Moss needed to rest. The days were so short at this time of year that most of their way passed under cover of darkness and without incident. 'Along here,' James said as they drew near to the town, leading her away from the road by a track which passed through dense trees. Helen took his arm, weary but expectant. But just a few paces later they both stopped abruptly. Her husband's grip tightened on her arm, and he pulled her from the track into the thickness of the undergrowth. A shot, and another. Shouts, and running feet. Friend or foe? The sounds were coming closer.

James hauled her down and held her close. She felt cold moisture soaking into her skirts from the long grasses and

124

withered nettles. She clung to him. 'James—'

'Ssh.'

They crouched there in the dampness, completely still, unable to see a thing. Around them they could hear the continued sounds of disturbance. Then a horse galloping by on the path directly above them, its hooves shockingly loud, the rasp of its breathing in their ears. Soldiers. Oh God. Mr Renwick. Oh Lord God.

The horseman was past, and the other sounds had died away completely. Still they remained in their hiding place, motionless. Helen's legs were already aching after the long journey and were now cramped in an uncomfortable position. She shifted. 'Is it safe, do you think?'

James moved cautiously. 'Let me go first.' He clambered out of the ditch. She followed him and, hand in freezing hand, they edged back to the track. Both knew that there would be no mercy if they encountered soldiers in these circumstances. They would be challenged to swear allegiance to the king on the spot, and when they refused to do so they could expect nothing other than a bullet to the brain. They waited on the fringe of the trees, where the faint moonlight at least offered more vision than the complete blackness of the ditch.

'We canna go back the way we came,' James murmured. 'The meeting has surely been betrayed, and they will have watchmen on the road. Let us continue up the hill and see if we can find our way hame ower the moor.'

Helen found she was crying. 'We have walked five hours to get here. How can we return without rest? And oh, James, what of Mr Renwick? What have they done to him?'

The second part of Helen's question could not be answered. The first was a problem. They had counted on receiving shelter and sustenance from Society members who lived nearby. 'Well, we canna stay here. Do as I say, and we may come on somewhere we can rest.'

In the end, that was indeed what happened. They walked

for perhaps a mile, silent for the most part, both afraid to put their thoughts into words. Helen's whole being was filled with dread for the fate of Mr Renwick, while she knew her husband was fretting over the identity of the traitor in their midst. They did not see another soul. And then, a light flickering in the window of a cottage. 'Let us try the byre,' Helen said quietly. 'This may well be the Lord's provision. Even if we can sleep a few hours, and rise to carry on afore dawn, it will strengthen us.'

There were obvious dangers, but James did not argue. They slipped into the darkness of the byre and took shelter among the diminished supply of winter feed. Cold, wet and exhausted, they lay together, cloaks over them, each trying to gain some warmth from the other's chilled body. And slept.

When Helen woke, it was to the sound of voices. She started up in alarm, but James hobbled to her side. The exertions of the day before had aggravated his leg. 'Dinna fear,' he said quickly. 'This is Hughie, and he has news of the events of last night.'

Hughie turned out to be a lad in his late teens. How he had known they were there she never learned. He warned they must be gone as soon as possible, as the farmer was no friend to the remnant, but he had brought them some bread and some ale, and the story of the events of the night before. It seemed they were not betrayed – a point of huge relief – but their discovery was rather a strange chance. There had been a robbery in Peebles earlier that day, and the authorities were watching the town exits for the thieves. Instead of thieves, they found small groups of people slipping out of town at a time when honest folk had no reason to be abroad. The Society people were stopped and questioned, and four were captured. As for Mr Renwick, he had been staying in the town and had been on his way along an alleyway when the man accompanying him sensed the danger. Had he taken a few more steps and reached out a hand, he could perhaps have touched the officers. As it was, he slipped away, but the alarm was raised, and chase was given – hence the sounds James and Helen had heard the night before. Where he was now no one quite knew, but he was believed to be safe. All glory be to God.

Helen and James listened to this tale, and then did as they were bid and hurried away before the light began to dawn, making their long journey back home to Pentland. But the whole episode had shaken her more than she might have expected. She had scarce slept since the encounter at Peebles, and she was weary and fraught as a result.

For some days they heard nothing more, beyond the names of the four who had been taken, and the whisper that Mr Renwick was safe. She found herself thinking of him constantly, not quite able to name what it was that had changed, but sure that something had. And then, late last night, when she and James were in bed, there had come the soft knock on the door.

She was awake when it came, and slipped from the bed, not disturbing her husband, who, as she'd quickly discovered, was the soundest sleeper she'd ever met. She picked up her shawl and pulled it around her, before walking softly to the door with a flickering candle held before her. Listened. Not a sound – so not the troopers then. Quietly, 'Who's there?'

'James Bruce.'

She knew both the alias and the voice, opened the door. He had his hat pulled down low over his forehead and his dark cloak covering the lower part of his face, but she recognised him at once, ushered him in from the bitter cold of the January night. 'Come,' she said, thrilling to clasp his slim, icy hands in her own. 'I'll build up the fire. Come, get warm. Och, it's right guid to see you. James is sleeping but I'll waken him.'

'No – dinna disturb him. Please. Go to your bed again.

I'm right glad to find you hame but dinna want to keep you from your sleep. I can rest on the settle here by the fire.'

'Ach, sit yoursel down and dinna be daft.' Helen busied around him, all the while aware of the quick beating of her heart within her. It was him; he was here. He was safe. 'You need some food and a drink. I'll bring you some wine and we've bread and cheese. For I warrant you'll no have eaten for many hours, am I right?'

James Renwick did not answer her. He had loosened his cloak, though not yet removing it, and had added a log to the fire before sitting himself down on the settle. Now, he looked into the slowly rising flames. 'I am on my way to Edinburgh, Helen,' he said.

She was pouring some wine from the tappit hen into a pewter mug as he spoke. Her fingers tightened on the handle, and she placed it carefully on the table. Her hands, when she released her grip, were shaking. 'Edinburgh?'

'Aye.'

For a moment, she said nothing more. She lifted the mug, carried it over to him, and then lowered herself onto a low stool on the other side of the hearth. 'James – *why*?' Her voice would have betrayed her if he had not already known all there was to know.

He took a long drink and then smiled at her – that calm, gentle smile she loved so well. 'Dinna fret, Helen. It's where the Lord would have me go. What use is it for us to prepare so careful a paper exposing the dangers of this Toleration, if it's never read by those who most need to understand it? I will take our paper direct to those ministers in Edinburgh who, for the sake of a roof over their heads and food in their bellies, would lead our kirk into destruction.'

She shook her head. 'It's too dangerous, James. Let someone else take it. They will hang you – or worse.' Her voice was little more than a whisper, and her gaze was on the floor, so it came as a surprise to her when he reached out and

128

took her hand. She raised her head and looked into his eyes. Even in the dim, flickering light of the fireglow and the one little candle, she could see his fervent conviction. He was not smiling now. Instead, he held her gaze and she sensed he needed her to understand what he was trying to say.

'Aye, Helen, I'm well aware of the danger. But what price my head against the destiny of Christ's kirk in Scotland – His Bride? I'm no fool – I ken they will only listen if the Lord melts their hearts. But they can never say I didna warn them. I must do all that lies in my power. Do you see?'

And it was why she loved him, the passion in his tone, the sense of purpose that encompassed him. He was still holding her hand. It was the first time they had been alone together since her marriage. Gently, she freed herself from his grasp. 'Go then, and God go with you. But you will rest and eat and keep warm with us for a day or two first, I hope?'

And then the fervour was gone, and it was the easy, twinkling smile again. 'And why else do you think I came here?'

She gave him his soup and brought him a blanket, all without her husband stirring, and then she returned to bed. But if her sleep had been restless before, it had flown completely now. She lay in bed, facing away from her husband but pressing her body and her icy feet against him to gain some warmth.

Such a turmoil of emotions. Warmth and gladness – he was safe, and he came to *her* for shelter and friendship. Her mind ran over the few precious moments of conversation again and again. *Why else do you think I came here?* Her dear friend. But for all she savoured his presence, his intentions pressed down on her like some great boulder crushing the breath from her body. She knew all about the paper which had been a matter of discussion among the Society people for many months now. It had been carefully prepared by Mr Renwick alongside Mr Shields, who had returned to them in repentance after a period of backsliding. She knew it was to be printed and distributed, and she and her husband had agreed to be responsible for a proportion of the copies. But she had never thought that Mr Renwick himself, the most wanted man in the kingdom, would carry it to the city and hand it over to the very ministers who had welcomed the Toleration with open arms. It was more than foolhardy. He could not possibly come back alive.

And yet, there was no prospect of dissuading him, not if he believed the Lord was calling him in this direction.

And so, in that case, he must not go alone.

But first, there was the coming of morning, and they laughed openly at her husband's bemusement as he emerged from his bed to encounter their house guest. A bit sheepish, James Currie welcomed the preacher and shook his head. 'Sleep is aye my master. I've been thinking we should maybe get oursels a guard dog.'

'Oh please!' This was Beatrix. 'I've always wanted a dog, please may we?'

Helen laughed. 'We dinna need a guard dog, for you may sleep like the deid, but the slightest sound wakens me.'

'And I'm glad of it,' said Mr Renwick, smiling merrily at her. *Last night he took my hand.* They were seated at the table, sharing porridge. The children were used to Mr Renwick appearing unexpectedly and knew to say nothing of his presence to their playmates.

Charlie had manoeuvred his way to the young man's side and was now pressed up against him. 'Will you play jacks with me?' he asked.

'You have work to do, my lad,' his stepfather said at once.

'Later then?'

Mr Renwick laughed. 'Aye, we can play, Charlie. I have a new game to show you, one I learned from some bairns in a house where I stayed down in Galloway. But you eat your porridge and see to your chores first of all.'

'And your lessons,' said Beatrix quickly. Charlie scowled at her.

'What's it got to do with you?'

'Charlie, watch your tongue!' Helen said at once. 'Beatrix is right. But perhaps Mr Renwick would help you lads with your lessons, too. He's a very clever man.' She turned to their guest. 'The boys canna go to the school, for I willna have them taught by that curate-loving schoolmaster, so I've been teaching them mysel, as I did with Beatrix.'

'Well lads, I'd be very interested to see your schoolwork. If you want to be useful to the Lord and His kingdom, it's important you get a guid education first. So do your chores, and then we'll have a wee school of our ain here this forenoon.'

This seemed to take Charlie's fancy. Jamie said nothing. Mr Renwick turned to him. 'You'll join us, Jamie?' he asked lightly.

'Aye.' Helen shot him a look, and he reddened. 'I'm very grateful, sir, thank you,' he said.

She gathered the dishes together. It was good of him to offer to teach the boys, but of course it just reminded her how much she needed to find someone to help with their studies. Since Jamie was a tiny thing, she had prayed that the Lord might call him into ministry, but it was looking less and less likely. The boy was determined now to become a merchant like his stepfather. Her thoughts turned to her younger lad, lively, mischievous Charlie. Perhaps the Lord had plans for him? But oh, if they were to lose Mr Renwick, how hard it would be, how hard. As she left the house later that morning, heading out to alert their friends to his arrival, she glanced back. The two boys had brought out their workbooks and had spread them before the preacher. Her throat was so dry she could barely swallow. Would this be the last time they were all together?

Oh Lord God, if he is not to come back to us, may his conversation with Jamie and Charlie this morning shape their lives for all time to come.

*

As Jonet entered Helen's house, she could taste significance mingling with the woodsmoke in the air. A far cry from that first time she had visited here, oblivious to the atmosphere around her. She recognised one or two faces from that time, or maybe from the field preaching. But there was a sombre mood among them. Everyone knew Mr Renwick was near taken at Peebles last week. Everyone knew the persecution was growing hotter. Everyone knew what a privilege and what a danger it was to be nourished by him this evening.

There were perhaps eleven or twelve of them crowded together in the house. Mr Renwick himself was seated by the fire. He smiled and greeted her by name as she came in, asked how she was keeping. 'Very well, sir,' she replied, blushing a little. She desperately wanted to say more, to tell him of the dreadful fate that awaited her, but he asked no more and she dared not continue the conversation. She looked round for somewhere to sit and caught the eye of a tall, dark-haired man sitting on the ground, his bairn asleep in his arms. Nathaniel. He was watching her. She looked away and sat on the bench by the table, and Bel cooried in against her legs. She gloried in the warmth of the child's presence.

Helen had been standing by the door, and now she closed it. 'That should be everyone,' she said. Jonet moved up and indicated space on the bench, but Helen shook her head, and leaned back against the wall in the shadows. 'I'll stay here. Keep watch.'

Jonet had not yet given up her hopes of speaking to Helen about her own fate but, looking at her now, she seemed so strained and distant. This morning, Kirstie had remarked on

132

the change in Helen, how exhausted she appeared. Could it be that married life was not turning out to be all that Helen hoped for? Or was it the constant strain of expecting soldiers at the door?

Mr Renwick opened the meeting. 'We'll sing the 23rd psalm together,' he said in that voice which, though soft, could reach inside each one of them. He held his psalter in front of him, but no one needed to strain to read in the dim light. These words had been woven into the fabric of their earliest days.

The Lord's my shepherd, I'll not want.
He makes me down to lie
in pastures green; he leadeth me
the quiet waters by.

Yea, though I walk in death's dark vale,
yet will I fear none ill,
for thou art with me and thy rod
and staff me comfort still.

The shadow of Peebles prowled near. After the singing, Mr Renwick turned to prayer and then read from Scripture. Only then did he tell them that tomorrow he would make his way to the festering sore that was Edinburgh and confront the leading ministers who had accepted the Toleration.

'Heaven preserve us, no!'

'It's too dangerous, surely!'

Amid the exclamations, Jonet noticed that Nathaniel, sitting directly opposite her, did not stir. She guessed he had known of the plan already. His long fingers were gently stroking his little daughter's soft dark hair. Jonet found the gesture unexpectedly moving and placed her hand over her own growing child. He looked up and met her eyes, but she could not read his expression in the dim light.

Mr Renwick stilled their protests. 'Pray for boldness for me, friends, and for grace and wisdom in all I say.'

'And for protection, surely?' Sandy asked.

'As to that, it's in God's hands.'

Jonet remembered the uneasy sense she had had last time she sat in the same room as Mr Renwick, the sense that he was being drawn towards the scaffold. Or was it just that, walking so close to God, he could discern the first steps on the road that had been prepared for him? She listened, as he returned to his purpose.

'These ministers teach that the Toleration gives freedom to the kirk, yet they agree to say naught which might lead the people to question the authorities. That is no freedom at all. I watched Donald Cargill suffer and die with the truth that Jesus is Lord on his lips. And what of us? Will *we* now be found wanting, in the face of this new lie? No. I must proclaim that Jesus Christ alone is head of His church, whatever the cost.'

Whatever the cost. Jonet looked round at Helen and saw her eyes were brimful with tears. Her voice was steady enough, however, when she spoke.

'We support you in what you do, Mr Renwick, but you mustna go alone. Some of us will accompany you to Edinburgh.'

'How can we do that?' a woman asked abruptly. 'We'll only draw mair attention to him and to oursels. They're sure to seek out his companions when they take him.'

'As for oursels,' Helen returned swiftly, 'I would hope each of us ready to shed our blood for the kingdom, as so many saints have done afore us. But dinna fear, Jean,' – and there was sarcasm in her tones, – 'no one would dream to send you. No, my husband James is a merchant and often has cause to visit the toun. This week I shall accompany him, for I find I need some cloth and would prefer no to leave it to a man's choice!'

There was a murmur of approval. Jonet was watching Mr Renwick. 'I willna be deflected,' he warned.

'And nor should you be, sir,' said Helen, her voice taut.

He let out a long breath and his shoulders relaxed. He smiled. 'Then I'll be glad of the company, my dear friends. I hope to meet with those ministers who have come together in Edinburgh since accepting the Toleration, under the leadership of Mr Hew Kennedy. It will be a comfort to have your prayers and your support.'

Hew Kennedy. Jonet frowned. She whispered quickly to Kirstie. Helen, still standing nearby, intercepted the exchange. 'You ken this Kennedy?'

'No,' Jonet said slowly. 'At least, no directly. But we ken him by repute – all who come frae Calder ken him by repute. Mr Kennedy was minister in our kirk for many years. When our mother was a lass.'

She noticed Nathaniel lift his head quickly at this.

'And what can you tell us, then?' asked Helen.

It was Kirstie who answered. 'Little more than stories. He was a man of God, so I believe, and gave up his kirk when King Charles returned rather than submit to the bishops.'

'That's true,' said Mr Renwick quietly. 'In fact, I understand that when Mr Kennedy was a student his mentor was Samuel Rutherford himsel. What sorrow has come to Scotland, what darkness, that a man such as he should give way to temptation.'

'Samuel Rutherford was minister of Calder too, for a very short time,' said Jonet. 'At least – he was going to be and then he changed his plans. I dinna mind the whole story. But in that short time in between, our mother was born, and Samuel Rutherford baptised her. In the famine years.'

Renwick looked directly at her. 'Then she is blessed indeed,' he said. 'I carry with me a copy of Samuel Rutherford's writings, and their grace and wisdom have sustained me through these weary years. And if our rulers had taken *Lex Rex* to heart rather than burning it, we would live in a Scotland which is better for all.' He smiled. 'But I begin to understand the heritage of faith that may be yours, my dear friends, if your mother was prayed ower as a bairn by one such as he.'

Jonet felt herself blush and was glad of the dim light. Could it really make a difference, that Mam was baptised by one who was, right enough, a giant of the kirk? True, Mam was aye proud of it, told the story often, but was there not a hint of magic and superstition, in some strange way, that it would make any difference *which* particular minister sprinkled the water on the head of the bairn?

But then she glanced across at Nathaniel and thought how he and others had risked everything to bring their children to be baptised by Mr Renwick in the hills nearby. And oh, how she wished she too could do the same. Perhaps it did matter.

Perhaps Samuel Rutherford's prayers laid the course for Mam to come under the preaching of Sandy Peden.

And now here they were, a generation on, and Mam's two daughters and even her grandchild were seated in the shadows, in the company of Mr Renwick.

There was a thread there right enough, linking it all together, but a thread as fine as one spun by a spider, unable to be grasped. So much was only partly seen. Jonet shook her head and brought the conversation back to Hew Kennedy. 'Mr Kennedy was a hard man, though. When he first came as a young man it's said he burned so fierce against witchcraft that several wise women in Calder were put to death within his first year among us. Others were accused and locked up for days and months, with no cause and no trial.'

'Thou shalt not suffer a witch to live,' came a voice from further into the room. Kirstie and Jonet exchanged a glance.

'Meg Thomson was no witch,' Kirstie said. 'They found naught against her in the end. But no afore he'd kept her locked up day and night, naked but for sackcloth.'

Jonet shifted slightly, feeling the roughness of the material on her skin. 'Poor woman.'

'Aye, and you would say so.'

It was the same voice. Jonet felt the heat rise in her face, and distress churned in her gut. Surely not *here,* in her one place of safety? Or had she been a fool to believe these godly people would ever accept her among them? She looked helplessly towards Kirstie, but before she could respond, Helen spoke.

'Jean, I think it's time for you to leave. Jonet here is a friend of mine and–'

'–and a redeemed child of God,' finished Mr Renwick. 'But there's no purpose in us now remaining here; our time together is at an end. Idle chat willna serve the kingdom. Let me pray with you, my dear friends, and then let us part.'

The grace of the Lord Jesus Christ, and the love of God, and the communion of the Holy Ghost, be with you all. Amen.

With the words which had strengthened believers for centuries laid over them like a royal robe, they slipped away one or two at a time. Nathaniel lifted his sleeping daughter from the little nest of blankets he had made. He turned to Mr Renwick, his expression serious. 'You must be gone from here,' he said with urgency.

James Renwick nodded slowly. 'Aye, I think you may be right.'

Helen sat down then and put her head in her hands. 'I shouldna have spoken sharply, but och, she riled me.'

'She wouldna betray us, surely?' Kirstie asked, fearful. It was the preacher who answered.

'I dinna believe she will, she is a guid woman, but we live in troubled times, when a cross word between friends can cause a cataclysm. We didna mention, I think, where I will be lodging – though James and Nat, you ken it well. I will go.'

They were all on their feet now. Hands were clasped, hugs exchanged. Helen took Mr Renwick's hands, her eyes glowing. 'We will join in you in a few days. May God go

137

afore you,' she said, her voice low. James Renwick bowed his fair head in receipt of the blessing. As Jonet watched, the snide remark cast her way disappeared from her mind. It felt almost intrusive to be here watching them take their leave of each other – and yet so compelling was the intensity between them that she did not think to move.

But then Kirstie touched her arm. 'It's time for us to go,' she said, swinging a sleeping Bel up into her arms and following Sandy into the darkness outside.

Jonet glanced back. She had almost forgotten Inverness for those moments, but now the memory rushed over her with the cold air from the open door. She had begun to feel as if she belonged to these people, as they sheltered together against the night and against those who hunted them down, but now she would be unlikely ever to see them again. She turned back to the door and found herself trying to exit at the same time as Nathaniel. The doorway was not wide enough for them both. He stepped back. 'After you.' She nodded, but as she moved forward, she felt his hand take hold of her arm. She looked back. The light was dim, but her eyes met his and she felt an unexpected and unlooked for connection. An immediate swell of both intimacy and fear rose up within her. His dark eyes held hers. He felt it too, she had no doubt in that breath of time that he felt it too, though afterwards she would wonder.

'Go safely, Jonet,' he said, his long fingers still clasping the material of her cloak.

She couldn't speak. She pulled away gently and hurried after Kirstie, her heart pounding, her hands shaking. It was just the intense atmosphere in the cottage, surely, and the sense she would most likely never see him again.

Aye, but it was more than that. It was more than that.

But no matter. For the night was dark and the times were dark too. James Renwick would walk to Edinburgh to meet his fate, and she must return to Calder to meet hers.

For even now the impatient Highlander could be seated

138

in her mother's home, awaiting her return.

Chapter Ten

Sunday 15th January 1688

The ninth Sabbath of Jonet Gothskirk's public appearance in Sackcloth.

The ninth and the last?

She returned to Calder on the Saturday to find he had been there two days already. Mam was brittle but he was expansive, his legs pushed out in front of him as he leaned back in the only armchair. 'The prodigal daughter has returned!'

She froze in the doorway, leaning on the doorpost for support. For all she had expected this, the reality of his presence brought the chill of the north right into their home once more. He grinned across at her and waved his tankard, clearly in high spirits.

'It's glad I am to see you, Jonet,' he said in that strange, sing-song voice of his. 'Your Mammy here says you were away through the hills with your sister. I'm surprised that she lets a lass like you be travelling alone – *especially* a lass like you, understand me? That's not how we do things in Inverness, no, not at all. No need to go a-wandering there. But you'll be learning that soon enough.'

Her limbs, though weary, had seized up and were rigid. She couldn't move. Mam stepped forward quickly and pulled her by the hand. 'Ach, look at you, stood there like a pillar of salt. Come awa in, lass.'

She stared at her mother, mute, and allowed herself to be drawn into the room. He heaved himself to his feet. 'I'll be off then. Staying with Aonghas. Tomorrow, girl, you'll get your business done with the kirk and then we'll be seeing that minister mannie. Soon as he can marry us, we'll be on the high road for Inverness, the beautiful town that it is. I'll show you the river, the hills, and our own bonny home. Eh, Jonet?' He walked past her towards the door, and, as he did, he came so close that his body brushed against hers. He slipped his hand round her waist and gave her backside a quick squeeze. She made a sound – half gasp, half whimper – but if he heard he made no sign. 'Oidhche mhath, ladies!' he cried merrily, and was gone.

And so she was standing here before the kirk next morning, surely for the last time. He would see the minister tomorrow, release her from her sentence, and take her as his wife. And there was nothing she could do about it, not a single thing. Any hope that had lingered of seeking help from Helen was gone now. Helen. She thought again of that precious night in the cottage, and the light shining in Helen's dark eyes as she promised to accompany Mr Renwick to Edinburgh. Helen could well be in prison, even now. She was no longer in any position to offer help to Jonet. And as for Mr Renwick, it was just a question of time until word came of his arrest.

In distant Inverness, would she even get to hear?

*

James and Helen had arranged to meet Mr Renwick in Edinburgh on Monday. Jamie helped his stepfather ready the horses in the bitter darkness of the morning. Helen pulled her cloak around her shoulders and paused in the doorway. Beatrix was sorting through a pile of clothes to be washed, her head bent so that her mother could not see her expression. Helen moved forward and gently tipped her chin. Beatrix looked up, cat-like, her dark eyes solemn. 'Go on, Mam. We'll be fine.'

'Aye, that you will.' Helen kissed her daughter. 'But if we dinna return–'

'You will.' Beatrix spoke with quiet certainty, and Helen

141

smiled.

'Of course we will. We'll be back in a few days. Look to the boys. See Charlie minds you.' Then she stepped over the threshold into the raw cold of the January morning. A faint silvery light brushed the horizon, whispering a promise of daylight to the silent darkness. She kissed Jamie and mounted the borrowed horse, drawing her cloak close around herself.

Helen and James were constantly amazed that he managed to continue trading as a merchant, despite the disfavour of the authorities. He regularly loaded up the packhorse and sometimes the sledge with fresh produce from the countryside and carried it into the city, where he sold it to the traders whose booths and stalls lined the High Street. From those same booths, and from the bustling docks at Leith, he purchased all sorts of imported goods – cloth stuffs, pottery jugs from France, clay pipes for the increasingly popular tobacco, sundries like hair ribbons, bits of lace, and sweet smelling pomanders – and carried them back to men and women at the fairs and markets in the little communities on the road out to Pentland and beyond. He visited Edinburgh every few weeks, sometimes staying for several days at a time, but until today Helen had never accompanied him. The great walled burgh, with its dark, hidden closes and crowded thoroughfares, held no attraction for her. She knew it for a cruel, godless sort of place, where the blood of the faithful seeped out into the gutters and stained the feet of the inhabitants. She rode along beside James, watching quietly as grey light gradually stretched across the breadth of the sky and opened up their way for them.

Last time she had travelled this road her wrists had been knotted painfully with thick rope and her mind filled with fear for her children. At least Beatrix was old enough now to look after the boys, and Kirstie and Sandy would give an eye to them too, should anything go wrong.

No, four years later the icy fear within was not on

account of herself or her wee ones. She and James, they might be travelling into danger right enough, but there was every likelihood they would yet walk free. Mr Renwick, on the other hand, only a miracle could save him now. And we have such need of him, she said fiercely under her breath. Surely we canna be left leaderless once more. We have such need of him.

They passed over the pasture belonging to the burgesses of the town as they drew closer to the forbidding walls. The skyline was spread out before them, a great long warren of streets stretching from the castle high on its rock at one end down to the sinful palace of Holyrood, tucked in the shelter of the crags. A grey pall of smoke hung over it all. James reigned his horse in and stopped. 'It's grand.'

But Helen felt no stirring of anticipation as they passed through the Society Port, skirted the edge of the Grassmarket and made their way to the High Street itself. People, there were people everywhere, most on foot, some on horseback, all in a rush to go somewhere or other. A young lad chased a pig between them; another wheeled his barrow at their side, crying out his wares. The shouts, the harsh laughter, and, even more, the foul stink which filled her nose and her mouth, each of these near overwhelmed her with memories of the grim Canongate prison. Filth streamed down the streets. Edinburgh, they said, was overflowing. Certainly, with every scrap of land within the city walls as far as the noxious Nor Loch already filled in, the houses were piled on top of one another, reaching ever higher. Tall buildings loomed on either side of them, their wooden fronts sometimes leaning perilously close together, almost meeting above them, casting dark shadows onto the street below. James had already told her that they would be staying in the home of his friend and fellow merchant, John Lockup, who lived in the shadow of Edinburgh Castle itself. Reaching the Lawnmarket, she glanced down towards the great High

143

Kirk with its crown steeple, where once good John Knox had preached. It was now given over to the wicked Bishop, like the other kirks in the city. Helen averted her eyes from the sinister Tolbooth and looked instead towards the luckenbooths busy with trade near the entrance to the kirk, reminding her of the temple courtyard in Scripture. But they were heading in the opposite direction, higher and higher, narrower and darker, towards the Castlehill.

'John's a guid man,' James told Helen as they rode slowly to the top of the hill. 'He's an Englishman, you ken, and much of his trade is with his cousins in the north of England. He and I have done guid business together ower mony a year.' He broke off and turned, signalling to a lad in the shadowy entrance to the close. The boy darted forward and, after a brief exchange of words and a coin, led the horses through the passageway to the stable in the courtyard behind.

'How came this John to Edinburgh then?' Helen asked, lifting her skirts clear of the filth on the ground.

'He's frae a family of Newcastle Puritans. John tells a fine tale of how, when he was a young man, he and all his family sailed for Boston. But then came a storm, and their ship put into Leith until it passed. Somehow young John was left behind. He saw it as God's will and made himsel a life here. But his sympathies have aye been with the Puritans and with us.'

Helen knew of the godly English Puritans who had sailed in such numbers for the New World during the troubled reign of Charles II. Aye, and shortly before her release from prison she had even thought she might cross that sea and join them.

But James was now leading her up a steep outside wooden stair and had come to a stop on a platform beside a stout door. He reached out his hand to take hold of the tirling pin, but the heavy wooden door opened just before he

144

could run the ring along the rod to announce their presence. Helen looked with interest at her husband's friend. John Lockup was a portly man with wiry grey hair, dressed in an embroidered waistcoat which struck her as a good deal more lavish than she might have expected from a Puritan. But he bowed his head at once in greeting to her. 'Mistress Currie!' he exclaimed – and it was strange to be addressed by her husband's name in the English way. 'I have heard much about you, it's my privilege to meet you at last! And of course, your dear husband is not our only mutual friend.'

Helen allowed herself to be drawn into the warmth of the chamber, where a fire was burning brightly in the hearth. She turned her head to look round the room. The walls were adorned with rich hangings and several portraits, and the wooden ceiling was beautifully painted. The window shutters were almost shut, but through a gap she grasped with a start that she was looking at the great walls of the castle itself. She had not realised they would be staying quite so close to the authorities. Could this be wise? Then, after that first glance round, she forgot her surroundings completely. There, sitting on a carved wooden chair by the fire, leaning back with an easy smile on his face, was Mr Renwick.

She stepped forward. 'You are here ahead of us,' was all she said.

He rose stiffly to his feet. It was just days since she had last seen him, yet he seemed thinner, his skin stretched tight as parchment. But he came forward, clasping first Helen then James by the hand. His grasp was warm, fervent – the gratitude of the fugitive, outnumbered and hard-pressed, but safe for the moment. 'My friends,' he said. 'I canna tell how much this means to me.'

And she looked at him again, his youthful face, his long fair hair, his gentle smile, and then it was worth it, every bit of it, all the danger and discomfort and fear, to know that they were where they should be, where God had willed them to be. John Lockup busied himself around them, taking outer garments, providing chairs, offering drinks. 'I have a girl who lives in, but sometimes I send her home,' he said in his unfamiliar Newcastle accent. 'It depends what company I wish to keep.'

'How go your plans?' her husband asked Mr Renwick when they were all seated. A shadow of impatience crossed the preacher's face.

'Not so well,' he admitted. 'I hoped to discover a meeting of the so-called Presbytery of these ministers who were once our faithful brothers. I have made enquiries, but no such meeting is planned in the near future.'

A crack of sunlight through the shutters. If there was no meeting, there was no reason for him to remain in Edinburgh. 'What will you do?' she asked.

He turned and looked at her then, and from the faint lift of his eyebrows she knew he could see right into that quick blink of hope. 'I shall find Mr Hew Kennedy, and give it direct into his hands,' he replied simply.

The shutter slammed shut. She said nothing. *Mr Kennedy was a hard man,* that's what Jonet had said. Yet she knew it was a grief beyond comprehension to James Renwick, that so many of those who should have been standing by his side at this time had sold the truth of generations for this fraudulent Toleration. And one such was Hew Kennedy, who had stood firm for Covenant and Parliament, who had even given up his kirk rather than submit to the rule of the bishops. And now Kennedy and those like him were ready to accept a church controlled by a king who could rule in all things as he pleased, without heed to parliament, people or kirk. This new tyranny could decree where and when a meeting of God's people could take place, and worse than that, what a preacher of the gospel was permitted to say. To argue now with James Renwick was futile. He recognised only the lordship of Jesus Christ, and if he believed his Lord had told him to confront Hew Kennedy, then nothing she could say would make the slightest difference.

There was nothing left to do but pray.

They discussed their plans at length. John Lockup had already made discreet enquiries and learned that Mr Kennedy's lodgings were in Hooper's Close in the Lawnmarket. James Renwick would take the paper to the door and place it directly into Kennedy's hands, with a brief indication of its content. As to what further events or conversation might then ensue, that must be left to the Lord.

Next morning, when the moment came, the young man's pale face showed some colour and his eyes were bright. There was a sense of purpose about his quick, careful movements. Helen knew he had long since accepted his probable destiny, and in coming to Edinburgh he had set his face towards it. Yet for all that, she knew too that the thought of torture was a horror to him. He had told her once that visions of Hugh McKail's mangled leg had haunted his dreams for years. If they took him, it would be blood and screams and splintering bone long before it was the final act of martyrdom. Dear God, sustain him, sustain us all.

James and Helen had agreed to accompany him down the High Street and keep watch from a distance. John Lockup would remain at home, ready to receive them back into the safety of his house. But first the English merchant placed his hand gently on young James Renwick's thin shoulder and prayed God's blessing upon him. Renwick's fair head was bowed. Helen watched, tears pricking her eyes, her fingers clasped tightly together. It was time.

'Who can say?' Mr Renwick said quietly as they picked up their cloaks and hats to step out into the winter's morning. 'The words in our paper may persuade Hew Kennedy to our cause. We ken him to be a man of godly reputation, and one who might once have offered guidance. But we are now in the hands of our Lord.'

'Aye,' said James Currie, though with far less conviction. He reached out his hand and opened the door, leading the way onto the top step. 'But now, we must speak of these things no more.'

They had kept the shutters closed as a precaution, so it was only when Helen stepped onto the wooden outdoor stairway that she discovered yesterday's cold, clear skies had been smothered by the haar; that damp, hanging Edinburgh mist which crept along close and thoroughfare, blurring the city's hard outlines in its murk. They walked with their heads bowed against it. Helen glanced quickly from left to right and left again at passers by, their faces similarly shielded against the penetrating dampness. On this day the haar was surely heaven sent. Still, she feared discovery at every step. The cries of the streetsellers and the metallic ring of horses' hooves sounded out eerily through the gloom, setting her nerves further on edge. But it wasn't far to Mr Kennedy's lodgings, and all of it downhill, so their footsteps carried them there all too quickly. They came to the mouth of the close, a narrow, black void between two tall lands. No less than the dark entrance to hell itself. James Renwick slipped his hand inside his cloak and withdrew the printed pamphlet which she knew so well. He looked at them and nodded.

'Wait,' said her husband. 'I'll take a look first, make sure it's safe.'

Safe? She almost laughed. How could anywhere be safe for James Renwick when he had chosen to enter the lion's den? Still, she was grateful to her husband for his consideration – and for this interlude alone with Mr Renwick. There should be words to say, but there were none. She could see that his mind was not on her but on the importance of the meeting to come. Then her husband emerged from the close. 'I can see no one, and the door you want is to the right as you enter the courtyard.'

'I thank you, my friends,' he said, and was gone. So swiftly. Forever. Helen could not help but gasp aloud at the passing of the moment, and felt her strength disappear down the close in his wake. She leaned back against her husband. His strong arm supported her at once.

'We mustna stay here and draw notice to the place.'

He was right. With a quick glance around, they started walking once more, continuing with no real purpose further down the hill. Neither spoke of the events of the morning. Helen found she was listening – listening for the telltale shouts and running feet and horses' hooves and even shots, which would mean he had been discovered. Her fingers were clenching the rough woollen material of her husband's cloak. And then, unexpectedly, they came to a stop, for out of the mist loomed a dark and ominous shape.

'The Netherbow Port,' said James. 'This is the Gatehouse which separates Edinburgh from the Canongate.'

The Canongate lay beyond, then. She shivered, half fancying she could hear a thin wail drifting through the haar. That was where they held her for all those long weeks, the foul Canongate Tolbooth. She never wanted to see it again. 'Let's turn,' she said.

'Aye.' But James hesitated. She looked up at him.

'What is it, James?'

He reached out, took her hand in his, held it firmly. 'Look up,' he said, with a heaviness in his voice. 'There's something you should see.'

She obeyed and drew a quick intake of breath. The gateway itself was large and imposing, with a series of towers and turrets. Spikes projected from the turrets, and on these, ghastly white in the swirling mist, perched a row of grinning skulls, long since picked clean by the corbies. She snatched her hand from his and covered her mouth. 'Almighty God, have mercy.'

'I dinna ken who they all are,' said James quietly, 'but

Donald Cargill is one, and Richard Cameron another. I believe Andrew Guillon may be there too.'

Donald Cargill, the thin, humble man with wispy grey hair and an extraordinary gift for preaching. She had heard him first when she was just eighteen and newly wed. Donald Cargill's words set her feet on the path which had surely led her to stand here this day. Aye, and she minded Mr Renwick telling her how as a young student he witnessed the murderous execution of the godly Mr Cargill and resolved from that day to give his life to God's kingdom in Scotland. She looked up at those skulls, wondering which belonged to one of Scotland's greatest saints.

James, it seemed, was thinking along similar lines. 'Did I ever tell you, I heard Richard Cameron at a field preaching one time, preaching alongside Mr John Welsh. A man of twenty-eight was baptised and gave his testimony. It's aye stayed with me. The Lord was among his people that day sure enough.'

The tears were blurring her vision now. 'And Andrew Guillon,' she whispered. Poor, simple, tormented Andrew Guillon who supped with her, who slept in her home, who screamed in agony as his hands were hacked from his arms.

But they had been standing gazing upwards for too long and had drawn attention to themselves. A guard stalked forward from the gatehouse. He was a rough looking man, almost as broad as he was tall. He planted his feet right in front of them and leaned into Helen's face, so that she drew back instinctively from the sour reek of his breath. 'Yer gawpin a long time at the traitors' gallery,' he remarked with an unpleasant grin. 'Friends o yours?'

Friends? Oh dear God, what was happening to their true friend, even now? And how many days until his beloved head joined those on the parapet? How would she ever bear *that*? But James placed his hand firmly on her arm and drew her away. Dipping his head, he spoke in a voice she recognised

150

as rougher than usual.

'We are but travellers in from the countryside, seeing the sights of the great toun, sir.'

The soldier coughed and spat, then spoke once more, seeming to accept James's explanation at face value. 'Aye well, if it's sights like these you want to see, you should go doon the Grassmarket. There's a hanging due the day. Tak tent to get there early, mind, there's aye a crowd.'

'A hanging?' Helen asked fearfully.

'Aye, some thief or other nae doubt. You dinna get entertainment like it in the *countryside*, I'll wager you.'

James led her away. 'Thank you, sir, we might just do that.'

Heads lowered, they began to retrace their steps up the hill. 'A hanging,' whispered Helen, naked fear in her voice.

'It's a regular occurance in the city, Helen,' James said gently. 'It's naught to do with us.' He glanced behind him. The soldier had strolled back to his comrades and showed no further interest in them. Beside him, Helen was struggling to hold herself together.

'I hate this place. It's cruel and it's godless. What's happening to him, James?'

'Hush. Not a word, not in the open.' The mist was thinning and one slightly brighter patch of sky indicated where the sun was trying to struggle through. They passed the mouth of Hooper's Close once more, neither of them so much as glancing towards the entrance. 'Shall we return to the house?' her husband asked.

Helen shook her head. 'No yet. I feel certain he's still here, for we've heard naught. I want to be nearby in case … Let's do as the soldier suggested and go to the Grassmarket.'

'Are you sure?'

'I need to be prepared.'

Prepared for the inevitable. She could tell he was doubtful, but he led her onwards, past the great High Kirk again, and down the steep, twisting descent of the West Bow, towering lands once more looming up on either side and filth below their feet. As they descended, James pointed out a house which had sackcloth nailed across its windows. 'That's where Major Weir and his sister lived,' he said. 'They say no one will take the house now.'

No wonder. Major Weir was supposedly a giant of the Covenanting movement, a man of prayer, yet when the true secrets of his life were exposed, they included crimes of such evil as incest with his own sister and unspeakable acts with animals. He was throttled and burned, the reek drifting up from the Gallow Lee along with ever-darker tales of his deeds, while his sister flung off her clothes in one last gesture of defiance as she mounted the scaffold. Helen remembered the scandal well. She'd been living with her father and his new wife at that unhappy time, and the local curate – whom she still went to hear in those days – preached on the iniquities of Major Weir and his sister. How her father's wife had salivated over the details! Aye, Major Weir did much harm to the Covenanting people, and whispers of his name still attached themselves to the remnant even to this day. Helen averted her eyes from the accursed house with its sackcloth shroud.

They had reached the foot of the West Bow now, where it led into the Grassmarket. The haar had lifted, leaving a grey and colourless day with a dampness lingering in the air. Helen looked around an open space, surrounded by the usual tall lands and narrow closes, and heaving with noisy, jostling people, animals and carriages. Nearby she could see the old Greyfriars Monastery and the new well head which brought clean water into the city, while Greyfriars Kirk – site of the signing of the National Covenant – stood high against the skyline. But her gaze slipped quickly over all these, for directly ahead of them, at the eastern end of the Grassmarket, loomed the great black shape of the gallows.

The shadow of death.

They stood still and silent, their fingers interlocked. Dark and forbidding, it was surrounded by a scaffold, with a ladder at one side. It drew their eyes, compelling them to look and look again, towering above them. And yet, other than themselves, no one seemed to pay the gallows the slightest attention. Streetsellers cried out, boys and girls moved livestock along the Cowgate and into the Grassmarket, the wheels of handcarts rattled by. James Currie reached out, caught the shoulder of a young lad rushing past. 'When's the hanging to be, lad?'

The boy twisted free. 'No till the afternoon, mister,' he replied, and was gone.

The ground beneath her feet was unsteady, insecure. Around her, the whirling babble of another ordinary morning in the beating heart of the city; in her whole being, an incessant pounding fear. And ahead of her the blackened instrument of death, on which so many of their beloved brothers and sisters had already had the breath choked from them.

I saw under the altar the souls of them that were slain for the Word of God, and for the testimony which they hold. And white robes were given unto every one of them.

She turned then and looked up at him. 'We must go back. We need to know what has happened.'

They retraced their steps up the West Bow. Up on the Lawnmarket there was still no sign of any disturbance; traders plied their trade while people gathered in small groups, laughing, blethering, shouting. They turned left and made their way up Castlehill, glancing behind themselves repeatedly. The tavern at street level, the close, the stair. No soldiers, no watchmen. They looked at each other. 'Wait here,' James said, 'and be ready to run. I'll enter the house and see if all is safe. Wait for my signal.'

They had already discussed this. If there was danger,

she should make every attempt to escape, for she would not be freed a second time. For the sake of the bairns she had agreed. So she stood at the mouth of the close, her hands clasped tight in prayer, as her husband climbed the stair and raised the tirling pin. The heavy door creaked open, but she couldn't see who stood in the shadows beyond. Then James leaned forward and beckoned to her. She resisted the desire to sprint up the steps and instead walked up as calmly and unobtrusively as possible. In the doorway her husband stood alone. As she entered, he closed the door behind her. He was smiling, thank God, he was smiling.

'James?'

He caught her hand and led her into the parlour, even as she wondered whose name she had just spoken. 'Safe,' said her husband. And there, smiling as though he had not just undertaken the most dangerous mission of his life, was James Renwick. Safe.

*

He had gone to see Mr Mackenzie to arrange their marriage for later in the week. Jonet knew she should wait inside for him to return but she could not. She could not. Begging an errand from her mother, she carried a pot of salve to a neighbour and then walked as slowly as possible back towards the house. As she walked along the lane she had known since childhood, she tried to take in the reality of not seeing these fields and dykes and homes ever again. It was not that Calder held much happiness for her – not since the death of her father – but it was home in a way the terrifying heights of the Highlands surely would never be.

And there he was, waiting outside her home. At first, he didn't see her. He was leaning against the byre her father had built, and she thought how large and ungainly and out of place he looked. He didn't belong here. Then he lifted his head, spied her walking home, and began to stride out towards her.

154

It took all her self-control not to turn and run the other way.

As he drew closer, she could make out his scarlet face, his scowl. Gone was the over-familiar merriness of the other evening. He reached out and caught hold of her wrist. His huge hand encircled it tightly and, for the quickest breath, she thought it might snap in two. 'Been out walking again, Jonet?'

She tried to pull away, but he held her tightly. She was aware of a neighbour watching across the way. How they would all be enjoying this. Her humiliation was complete.

'I had something to do for Mam. Would you let me go, you're hurting me.'

He stared at her, then dropped her hand abruptly. She covered her wrist with her other hand. He turned his head then and looked away from her. 'Damn fool of a minister.'

Something shifted. His barely-contained fury was not directed at her, but at Mr Mackenzie. But that could surely only mean … 'You went to see him?' she asked.

'Of course I bloody went to see him. And he claims he can't be releasing you without a formal rebuke at the front of the kirk, a meeting of his kirk session *and* a summons to you. Which means at least another week, probably two.'

A week, at most two. Not long, but still. She had thought he might take her tomorrow. She swallowed and said nothing.

'Trouble is, I have to leave for Inverness by the end of this week. Simply have to. There's a ship landing from Flanders with a grand load of furs, and if I'm not there to meet it, someone else will snatch them up.' He rubbed his large hands up and down his greasy coat. 'I'll just take you with me. We can be getting round this certificate business somehow.'

Jonet tried to breathe steadily, with the sense that much hung on her reply. She guessed from what she had seen of

155

him so far that he was not a man to be challenged but to be flattered. Steeling herself, she slipped her hand into his and pulled him gently so that they were out of sight behind the byre. He looked surprised but did not shake her off. 'It means a great deal to me that we are wed properly,' she said quietly. 'I have made one mistake, and for that I have repented sair. You have done me this great kindness of offering me the chance to be your wife. Surely our marriage will be the stronger if it is built on the approval of the kirk and of God?'

'Hmm.' She felt his gaze looking her up and down, undressing her as he had done that first Sabbath in the kirk. She cast her eyes downward. He needed to see her as a repentant, modest wife, not a whore to be taken at will. 'Perhaps. But you can see the difficulty, surely? By the time I return for you and carry you north, you will be so far gone no one will be believing the child is mine.'

That was when she saw the way forward. Glancing up at him as intimately as she dared, she said, 'Then tell them all about your new wife when you return to Inverness this week. You've been gone several months, have you no? Tell them we were wed some time ago, and I am expecting your bairn and staying with my mother until the birth. Then you can return for me once the child is born and bring me to Inverness, and no one will be surprised.'

He shook his head then. 'Oh no, not so long as that, not so long as that. But your thought is a good one, nevertheless. Yes. I will tell everyone I meet about my bonny young wife in the Lowlands. I will be back for you in weeks though, my lass, not in months. That bairn of yours will take in the northern air with its first breath.'

It was not much, but it was something. He would return to Inverness immediately, for there was nothing to keep him here and much to draw him back. He would come for her in a few weeks, once his business was transacted. Meantime

156

she would make her repentance and be restored to full communion of the kirk. She submitted to his wet, probing kiss and his hands slipping under her shawl and inside her gown, squeezing her breasts, but pulled back when he began to lift her skirts. At first, she feared he might force her, but then he laughed and gave up. 'You have little to be modest about, lass, but let's keep up the pretence. We can make up for it once that minister mannie of yours has seen sense. You'll be panting for it by then. A mare in foal is oft the most eager, I tend to find.'

I tend to find.

Repulsed, she forced a smile and watched him go. When he was gone, she crept into the darkness of the house and dropped to her knees beside her bed, shivering. *Almighty God, thank you that he is gone. Almighty God, let him fall and break his neck on the journey home. Let him never return. Let him marry someone else. Dear God, forgive me, but whatever it takes, let him never return.*

*

It turned out Mr Renwick had been back for some time. Hew Kennedy was leaving his house just as Renwick appeared, and took the paper thrust upon him with no more than a nod and no sign of recognition. 'I was sorry not to engage with him,' Mr Renwick told them frankly, as John Lockup passed round much needed goblets of wine. 'You ken what I had hoped. But then I reflected that perhaps this too is in God's Providence. This way Kennedy and his colleagues may read the paper for itsel and, God willing, be stirred by its clear arguments. If he had suspected my identity, if I had engaged him in lengthy discussion, then there was surely a danger he would toss the paper on the fire without reading it. This way, he may digest it, he may share it with other Tolerated ministers. The Lord must do the rest.'

Helen nodded, gripping her goblet in a hand which was shaking in reaction to the strain of the morning. Her husband had told the story of their wanderings through the streets.

157

'You have done what you came to do, and the Lord has protected you once more,' she said, scarcely able to believe it herself. 'And now we may leave Edinburgh.' A laugh escaped. Sheer relief.

He looked at her then and smiled the smile she loved so dearly, but there was a sadness in it. 'Helen, you are a dear friend. Dinna think that I shall ever forget your faithfulness in coming here with me. You are a true Barnabas, an Encourager. But our ways part here for now.'

'What are your plans?' This from James. Herself, she could not speak. Dear God, what now?

'I go to preach in the Braid Hills, and from there I will travel into Fife. We have so little support there. The folk of that locality have been prepared to sit back while their brothers and sisters suffer. But there are a faithful few, and I hope to encourage them and to challenge others. And you, my dear friends, you must return to Pentland.'

'We would come with you,' said Helen, her voice breaking.

'I ken you would, but I'm aye best to travel alone. And your place is back hame, with Beatrix and the lads. There is much of worth you can do from there.'

She knew he was right, even as everything within her screamed a protest. Did she really feel relief just moments ago? All that was gone, and bleak reality threatened to overwhelm her. James Renwick now faced greater danger than ever, for the people of Edinburgh would soon know he had been right in their midst. The Braid Hills were just outside the city walls. He would be gone, and she must return home, return to not knowing where he was, if he was free or captured, if he was alive or dead. Not knowing and having no right to know. She had spent these last days, for all their fear and danger, alive with the inestimable comfort of being in his presence and helping his purpose. All that, once more, would be gone.

She turned her face away so that he would not see her tears.

Chapter Eleven

Sunday 22nd January 1688

The tenth Sabbath of Jonet Gothskirk's public appearance in Sackcloth, on which she had a public rebuke by the Minister.

'Jonet Gothskirk is an example to each of you of sic godlessness. A woman without morals, whose sexual depravity and wickedness have brought her to this place. You see afore you the Whore of Babylon, who has brought shame on her family, and has condemned her unborn bairn to the life of a bastard. Be warned, each of you, where those moments of flattery or of desire may lead you. For Satan is aye in our midst, in the guise you are least expecting. Let the downfall and the shame of this fallen woman be a lesson to each of you. You maidens, hold your purity fast. You lads, keep watch on your desires. You married men and women, mind that adultery was gey recently punishable by daith in this land and be sure that heavenly justice will far outweigh aught you may encounter on this earth. And *you*, Jonet Gothskirk–' the finger quivered, and spittle sprayed from his mouth, '–may you aye be conscious of the depths of sin and wantonness into which your wicked and shameless desires have brought you, and may you repent for all eternity afore a holy and just God who isna fooled by the outward form but sees the black wickedness of your whorish heart.'

It was surely the beginning of the end.

*

Helen had not forgotten her resolve to prepare Jonet as best she could for what might lie ahead, but it was hard to know what to do. The snow had come at last, sweeping across the sheep tracks and making travel through the hills more

160

difficult. Even without the bad weather, there were barely enough hours of daylight to fit in the essential tasks of each day. There was no possibility of a visit all the way to Calder and back in one day.

When at last the weather had eased enough for her husband to set out on the road, she placed his porridge and ale before him and said, 'I'm anxious to speak to Jonet. Will you be travelling anywhere near? I could come with you.'

James took a mouthful and shook his head. 'There's no way. I'll be gone several days, and although I may pass fairly near to Calder I wouldna then be coming hame. I'll bide with Archie.'

'But you could get Jonet a message, perhaps?'

James considered. 'I suppose Jamie could take a message ower and then meet me at Archie's in the evening.'

'Then that's the thing to do!' Helen reached for paper and ink and then stopped. 'No need to write it. Jamie, lad, will you do this for me? Tell Jonet if it's fine on Friday she's to meet me by the shieling above the place where the burn divides. You ken where I mean, aye? That way neither one of us has to walk the whole distance.'

'And if she doesna come?' her husband asked.

'At least I will have tried.'

But Jonet did come. Friday dawned bright and cold, and though there was still snow in the heights of the hills, it had mostly disappeared from the lower slopes. Helen rose early and walked through vanishing gloom. She breathed in the sharp, clean, cold air and thought of Mr Renwick, wondering what had befallen him since they had parted in John Lockup's elegant Edinburgh home. Not a word since. She followed the track up towards the stone and turf hut she had mentioned, and there was Jonet, already here ahead of her. The girl didn't see her at first. She was leaning against the rough wall, her eyes closed, her face lifted towards the weak sunlight. A frozen branch snapped under Helen's foot and Jonet opened her eyes. They embraced.

The shieling was dark and smelled strongly of sheep shit. As their eyes gradually adjusted to the dim light, they could see a few oddments lying around, left by the shepherds and dairy girls at the end of the summer: a creepie stool, some wooden bowls, a couple of folded blankets. The winter months were taking their toll, and the roughly woven screen had fallen away from the open doorway, while the central hearth was just a circle of cold, blackened stones. Still, the hut was dry, more or less, and by sitting at one end they could avoid the draught from the door. Helen pointed Jonet to the stool, spread a blanket on the floor, and sat down. She had brought some oatcake and cheese in a bundle and shared these with the younger woman. 'I'm glad you got Jamie's message,' she said.

'He was frozen, poor lad. He was anxious to be on his way, but we gave him some broth afore he set off again.'

'He's a guid lad,' said Helen. 'At one time I thought he might go to the university, but he's far happier on the road. And he really is a help to James, for there are times his leg causes him real pain and Jamie can run to and fro and fetch and carry. He's not been into the city yet though. I'm no quite ready for that.'

'You were there yoursel,' Jonet said carefully. Helen nodded.

'Aye. And all went well, thanks be to God. I have heard nothing mair, but we'd ken soon enough if he'd been taken.' She couldn't help casting a quick glance outside, although there was no one to hear.

'I dinna ken how you can live this way,' Jonet said, brushing some crumbs from her lap. 'Ever watchful, ever feart. Is it worth it?'

'Aye,' said Helen at once. 'Aye, Jonet, it's worth it.' She slipped her hand into the folds of her shawl. 'But here, lass, I didna ask you to come all this way just for a blether. I

162

brought you something.' She held out a small, worn book. 'It was my mother's. Take it with you when you go north.'

She watched as Jonet took the Bible in her hands, caressing the leather before opening the pages and carefully turning them. For a moment the girl said nothing and then she looked up, and Helen couldn't read her expression in the gloom but she could hear the tremble in her voice when she spoke. 'That's kind.'

'It's the best help I could think of to give you,' Helen said soberly. 'What's more, I wanted to tell you that the offer of shelter with James and me remains any time you might need it. Jonet, I ken your mother is set on you going to Inverness. Is that what you will do?'

'I dinna want to,' said Jonet at once. 'You ken well enough I dinna want to. But what can I do? I've been praying and praying that he willna come back for me. Maybe there will be a miracle, maybe your God will save me. There's no one else that can.' She shifted on the stool. 'Ach, this is far from comfortable. I'll come and sit by you.' She moved across, hand on her stomach, and lowered herself down beside Helen, leaning against her slightly. 'What was it like for you, the first time?'

Helen hesitated. 'Giving birth, you mean? Or with my man?'

Jonet giggled, and Helen was reminded that she was still just a lass really, for all she'd been through a hard time. 'Both, now you ask!'

Helen smiled in the darkness and took Jonet's cold hand. 'Beatrix came slowly, right enough. The first bairn usually does. But there were people to help me, and there will be for you too. Women are the same the world ower at times like this. I'm right sure there will be women in Inverness who will help you through, and then you'll have a bonny wee one to care for.'

'All my life, Mam has been helping women in Calder

birth their bairns. It seems gey harsh that she willna be nearby to help me, her daughter.'

'It does,' Helen agreed. 'And I'm sure she'll find that hard, but she believes this is the right thing for you to do.'

Jonet moved in closer, and Helen could feel her breath on her own cheek. It was strangely intimate. 'To be truthful,' the younger woman said in a small voice, 'I canna think about the bairn or its birth at all, I'm that feart about being wed to *him*.'

Again, Helen thought how young she sounded. She must choose her words carefully. She didn't want to frighten Jonet more than she was already frightened, but she did want to prepare her. 'You ken that I was a lass like you when I married for the first time,' she said. 'I willna pretend it was easy. The man I married wasna cruel, exactly, but he had little patience and expected to get his own way. If things werena to his liking, he was hard on me. But the Lord was a great comfort. That's why I gave you my mother's Bible, Jonet. Hold fast to Him and He will see you through. That's been the testimony of my own life.'

Jonet said nothing for a while, then she raised her head and looked towards the door. 'Is it snowing?'

Helen pulled away, gathered her skirts and got quickly to her feet. 'Surely not.' She hurried over to the doorway. The light had changed, right enough, and was now tinged with yellow. 'Oh God save us, it is! I'm sorry, Jonet, I should have taken more notice of the sky, but seated over here I just didna think of it. What a fool I've been.'

Jonet had come to stand beside her. 'It's no that heavy,' she said, but her voice was uncertain. Already the brown earth was turning white, as snow lay on the frozen ground. And even as they watched, the smaller specks were overtaken by thicker, larger flakes which whirled into a mesmerising dance. Helen pulled Jonet back inside the shieling.

'We must just wait for a while and hope it goes off afore

the light fades. Otherwise we are here for the night and we've no fire and little food.' She lifted the second blanket. 'We can keep warm at any rate. Come, let's sit down again, and if we sit close we can wrap this round us both and wait it out. It will likely just be a passing shower.'

The blanket was rough and reeked of piss, but it was thick and warm. They sat together, leaning against the stone wall, one blanket under them and another wrapped around them. There was still a little oatcake left, but Helen put it aside. 'We might need it later. At least we willna want for water, for the burn runs just below the shieling out there.'

The strange, eerie silence of falling snow had crept inside the shieling, and for a while they said nothing. Helen tried to suppress the familiar sense of panic at being imprisoned. This was nothing like the Canongate Tolbooth, she told herself, nothing at all. Jonet leaned her head on Helen's shoulder. 'I should be afraid but I'm no,' the girl said, eventually. 'This feels safer than hame.'

Safer than hame. Helen took a deep breath, and her own fear subsided. Jonet was right, this place was a God-given refuge rather than a prison. She wondered about those out on the hills, as she always did when the weather was foul. Without meaning to, she spoke her thoughts aloud. 'I hope Mr Renwick has found a shelter like this.'

'Imagine if he came through the door right now! Imagine if he was out in these hills, and needed somewhere to shelter, and stumbled on this shieling, and came in here and found us. Him and that handsome friend of his, Nat. What a surprise they would get.'

Helen shook her head. 'I dinna ken where he is, but I hope he's far from here. I hope he's far from any place where they might be looking for him.'

Jonet shifted a little and blew on her hands. 'Tell me how you first got to know him,' she said.

Helen paused, gathering her thoughts. 'You ken I was

165

in prison,' she said. 'It was while I was locked up that Mr Renwick returned from Holland, where he had been ordained. I heard all sorts of stories about him, no all of them guid, and I didna hear him preach or meet him for some time. I had been told that he was proud and harsh and unfeeling, but when I finally met him for mysel he was none of those things. I could see he was a guid man. I gave him shelter in my home as I have done many others, and I – came to know him well.'

'You have been a guid friend to him,' Jonet said.

'I hope so. I have done what I can. But och, it's hard, Jonet. Day after day, week after week, I wonder where he is, I wonder if he's safe. I wonder if I'll ever see him again. And God forgive me, but if he's taken from us, I dinna ken how I will carry on.'

She hadn't meant to say so much, but somehow here in the chilly gloom, with the warmth of Jonet's pregnant body pressed against her, and the silence of the snow shrouding the hut, words could be spoken which could not be spoken elsewhere. And it seemed the girl understood, for her hand reached for Helen's under the blanket, and squeezed tightly. Helen found she was fighting tears as the pain and the despair threatened to wash over her. She was fast losing the battle. And then they held each other, these two women, one whose love had turned out to be a lie, and one whose love must remain unspoken. Together in the rank darkness their tears mingled, shared tears for what they had lost and for what they still had to fear.

Helen broke away first. 'I think it's getting lighter,' she said. She scrambled to her feet, and hurried back to the doorway. 'Oh thank God, thank God, the snow's nearly stopped.' She turned towards Jonet who was using the rough wall to ease herself to her feet. 'What do you think, Jonet? Can you walk hame? Or would you rather come back to Pentland with me?'

Jonet stepped outside, and Helen came with her. The world was white, and the sky was clearing to bright blue once again. Underfoot the snow was soft and powdery. 'I'll make for hame,' Jonet said. 'It might come on again and, for all I hate that minister, I must be back in the kirk by the Sabbath. You should have heard him last week! But if I go now I should make it afore nightfall.'

Helen stepped back into the darkness and picked up a blanket and the small bundle containing the oatcake. 'Take this then – you can eat it as you go. And wrap this round you for extra warmth.' She pulled the girl into a hug. 'Now I'll most likely see you when you next come to Kirstie, but just in case I'm no at home, God go with you.'

Jonet took the bundle and set off, while Helen stood outside the shieling watching. When the younger woman was a little way down the hill she looked back and waved. Helen waved back, then turned to gather her things and go.

She had done what she could for now.

Chapter Twelve

The eleventh Sabbath of Jonet Gothskirk's public appearance in Sackcloth.

She had thought last week's rebuke might be the beginning of the end, but still she was here, standing in the place of repentance and listening to the bell. The kirk bell at Calder had a strange note, uneven, almost like two notes in one. This morning it was ringing, ringing, ringing, sounding out vigorously across the parish.

Across the parish and across the land, from the grand bells of the great city churches to the smallest country kirk, they joined together that day in a chorus of triumph. *The queen - with child - thanks be - to God. The queen - with child - thanks be - to God. The queen - with child - thanks be - to God.*

Bonfires would be lit later, once darkness fell. Aye, and that would be about mid-afternoon in a northern January! Mr Mackenzie was puffed up with the pleasure of his position as he read the decree and announced the arrangements, then led the congregation in prayers of thanksgiving for the child promised now to King James VII and Queen Maria.

Had he any doubts at all, hidden beneath his complacency?

A Popish heir to the Scottish throne?

A continuation of the line which had brought nothing but tyranny to the people?

And as they bowed their heads in outward compliance, Jonet watched and wondered and thought of the way a seed grew in secret. Her own pregnancy, paraded in public, trampled in glaur. And the pregnancy of the Italian queen, announced to all corners of the land, greeted with celebration. Celebration by decree.

Two tiny, unknowing lives.

Of course, Helen and Mr Renwick would be dismayed at this news, would see it as a darkening of the skies over Scotland. The bells and the bonfires were just further tokens that their covenanted land had brazenly turned its face away from Almighty God. The screws were tightening upon those who held fast to Christ as head of his kirk, tearing flesh, splintering bone. For if this bairn should be a boy, he would replace Protestant Princess Mary as heir to the throne, and all their faintest hopes were surely at an end.

And no doubt they were right, but Jonet could think only of a bairn. A tiny bairn, not even born, and a woman treasuring that precious life within her. A woman who they said was given to brood over all the wee ones she had already lost. Jonet could not find it in her heart to hate.

No, she thought on the Italian queen, and there was a faint smile on her own lips, for no one was paying the slightest bit of attention to her this forenoon. Thank you, your majesty. They were all so stirred up by the celebrations for the royal pregnancy that she caught scarce a glance towards her own swollen belly. Auld news. And having cursed her for a whore last week, Mr Mackenzie seemed content to ignore her this week.

Let the bells ring out.

*

The bells rang out in Pentland too, but Helen paid them no heed. She was glaring at her husband across the table, hands flat on the wooden surface. 'Two months wed, and you think I canna bide here without you! Do you think I was helpless these past six years without a man?'

He shook his head slowly and, as was often his way, chose not to answer. Instead, he lifted a pamphlet from the table between them. The copy in his hands was just the top one in a pile. So many of their hopes rested in that little mound of papers, which would surely explain their position and counter the false allegations which were regularly made against them. Its tone was more measured than some earlier zealous publications, for all it still held to absolute truth. Mr Renwick had grown in wisdom during his years alone with the Lord on the desolate moors of Scotland. But whatever its truth and whatever its tone, it remained a highly treasonable document. James and Helen, like other faithful Society members across the country, had been entrusted with a quantity of the pamphlets to distribute and sell with discretion. But now James, who had intended to travel to Edinburgh tomorrow, was reluctant to leave her alone with the children when there were such dangerous goods in the house.

To Helen, who had harboured far more dangerous goods than a few pamphlets in her home over these past years, it would be laughable if she were not so concerned. But close on two weeks had passed since last they saw Mr Renwick. Word had come that he had returned from Fife, but since then, nothing. When James was in Edinburgh, he might hear some rumours exchanged over a market stall or muttered in a tavern, or perhaps John Lockup would have news.

Only now he was changing his mind.

She softened her tone. 'James, we'll hide the bundle, and gey few folk ken it's here. Besides, should the soldiers find it, none but the Lord could save us, whether you are here or no. Better by far that you should travel to Edinburgh and meet with our brothers there, see what news they have. I'm anxious, James.'

'We would have heard if he'd been taken.'

'Nevertheless, we know Edinburgh was much on his heart. You must go, James, or I may just go mysel!' She smiled to suggest she was joking, but across her mind flashed the vivid memory of that walk into the city in the wake of Bothwell

170

Brig, three young children clinging to her, her first husband oblivious. If James chose not to travel to Edinburgh … Her first obedience would aye be to her Lord. She reached out for the pile of pamphlets and the rough piece of sackcloth in which they had been tied. 'Here, let us bundle these up once more and agree on a safe place to store them. That may set your mind at ease. Then we will pray together.'

He did as she suggested, just as she knew he would. He was a good man, but he was never any match for her strength of will. They stored the bundle deep within the straw mattress, smoothing the covers over, and called for the children to come. Jamie appeared almost at once. They sat round the table, the cruisie lamp lit against the gathering gloom, and the Bible open at the 53rd chapter of Isaiah. They spoke quietly with the lad for a moment or two, but still Beatrix and Charlie did not appear. Helen's dark brows met in a frown. 'Have you seen them?' she asked.

Jamie shook his head. 'Charlie was with Adam earlier, but I dinna ken where they went.'

'And Beatrix.' Helen was vexed. It was the Sabbath, and the bairns were never far from home on the Sabbath. They had known too since they could walk and talk that each day when dusk began to fall, it was time to come in for family worship. She stood up, walked to the doorway. It was near dark out. Mingling with her irritation now came the first stirrings of a fresh anxiety. Had something perhaps happened to them? Charlie might forget the hour, but not Beatrix. Oh, dear sweet Jesus, not the soldiers. And then Jamie spoke reluctantly.

'I canna be sure, but they might have gone to the bonfire.'

She spun round. 'The bonfire?'

'You ken.' His face was flushed. 'The one *they* said we were to have. Up on the hill. Some of the lads were going.'

She could hardly speak. 'And you think – Beatrix – your brother–'

171

James heaved himself onto his feet and pulled his cloak around him. 'I'll go,' he said. But just as he reached the threshold there was a sound, and the two missing children were among them. Beatrix was flushed, holding her brother firmly by the arm, her long hair falling loose from its napkin. 'Mam, I'm sorry,' she said at once. 'I went to find him.'

Helen gave her a quick glance and nodded. Then she turned her attention to her younger son. 'Where have you been?'

Charlie lifted his chin, looked right up into her eyes. 'I wanted to see the flames.'

The slap across his face, with all the force in her arm, came from somewhere deep, instinctive and fearful. He staggered, and only his sister's firm grasp kept him from falling. With a cry he bent double, his hands to his face, but said no more. And nor did Helen. Rage and dread churned together within her with the terrifying abandon of the river in full spate. *Oh God, the wickedness of this world, and how are bairns to grow in the faith when they are surrounded by such evil?* Then her husband's arm was around her waist and he was leading her back to the bench. Charlie sat down too and buried his face in his arms. And somewhere, amid the festivities of this night across the land, she was sure that James Renwick held firm – but how long could they continue under such pressure?

How long?

James Currie left for Edinburgh with Moss next morning, intending to stay away for three or four nights. After the tensions of the previous day, Helen watched him go with a sense of calm. *He restoreth my soul.* Two days slipped by, and Wednesday brought in the month of February, with a cool sharpness which was welcome after such a dreich January. Helen and Kirstie stood together outside Kirstie's house while Bel played nearby. The sky was pale blue, with wisps of white cloud stretched across it, and the air was icy. Helen was reminded of her time in the shieling with Jonet and the snow swirling round outside. 'How's your sister?' she asked.

'The man she's to wed has returned north for now,' Kirstie replied. 'But he'll be back soon.'

'And Jonet?'

'Waiting to hear from the kirk session and praying he doesna find his way back down here. But he will.'

'And Jonet would never be willing to wed him if she werena desperate.'

'She's no willing. Even though she's desperate.'

'Ach, I wish–' She stopped, frowned. 'Hear that?'

Kirstie turned her head. They could both hear it now, a horse approaching at a fair pace. Helen stepped out into the middle of the track and tried to see, shielding her eyes from the sun. But although weak, the winter afternoon sun was low, and rays of light gleamed through the trees, throwing all else into darkness. She could just about make out a figure bent over the horse's neck. 'It's James,' she said, suddenly certain. 'But he wasna due back today, and that isna our horse. Preserve us.'

There was an icy edge to that February air, and the two women stood frozen in its grip. Aye, it was James, riding a hired horse. What had happened to Moss? He pulled up beside them. He had been riding fast and was short of breath. 'James – what –?' began Helen, but her husband cut her off.

'Where are the lads?'

'Here, sir.'

'See to her, boys.' He climbed down and faced the women. The gleaming sunlight both hid him and revealed him. She'd always thought him ordinary to look at, but there was that in the ordinariness of his face this day which would aye remain etched in her mind. And she found she didn't want him to speak, couldn't bear to hear the words that would change everything. She would cling to this last sweet second of ignorance – yet the agony of fear was surely more overwhelming than the horror of knowledge. 'James–'

That name again. Who did she mean, exactly?

'Inside,' was all he said, with a quick glance behind him. Then he turned to Kirstie. 'Bring Sandy. We need to talk, and we may not have long.'

Kirstie nodded and hurried away, the dread there in her blue eyes too. As soon as they were inside Helen turned to face him. 'Is he living?'

Her husband took her hand. 'Living, but imprisoned. They took him this morning.'

The sound which escaped was a strangled moan. She stepped backwards. *They took him.* James turned away from her, removed his outer layers, poured himself some ale. His hands were trembling and his breathing was still heavy. He sat down, and she sat opposite him. 'Tell me what happened.'

'I will, but we must wait for Kirstie and Sandy.' He reached out and his big hand covered hers. 'There's still hope, Helen.'

Hope? Hope, for the most wanted man in Scotland, now that he had finally fallen into the hands of the authorities who had been pursuing him for years? She shook her head and got to her feet, forcing herself to welcome Sandy and Kirstie as they arrived. *This, now, is where it has all been leading. Despite everything we've been through, even those months in prison, it has never been like this. What will they do to him? Even now, what are they doing to him? My terror, his pain. His terror, my pain.* 'Tell us, James,' she said.

Her husband took a deep breath. His eyes fixed somewhere beyond them all, he began to speak.

'I was staying with John Lockup. That young lad Nathaniel was there too – Nat, they cry him. He suffered in Dunnottar for the gospel, did you ken? Nat went to Bo'ness last Sabbath to hear Mr Renwick preach what he said was a

174

heart-stirring sermon.' He turned his head suddenly, looked directly at his wife. 'His text on the Sabbath past was from Isaiah 53, the very chapter we read together in our family worship that same day.'

There were murmurs, but his listeners didn't want him to be diverted from the main content of his story. James Currie, however, was picking at a ragged fingernail. It wasn't an easy story to tell.

'Nathaniel told us about the preaching at Bo'ness, where Mr Renwick spoke about the Toleration. For all his words were inspired, he seemed mair weary and burdened than usual.'

'But Mr Renwick wasna with you?' asked Sandy.

James shook his head. 'No at that point. Yet John feared he would come. He aye seems drawn to Edinburgh the now.' He stopped, his voice hoarse, and gulped a mouthful of ale. 'He arrived late yesterday afternoon, soon past dark. We shared a meal, spoke long into the evening.'

'You saw him. You ate with him. How was he?' asked Helen softly.

'He is as committed as aye he was, but there's no doubt he is weary. These past weeks he has travelled many miles, preaching widely against the Toleration – yet no matter how far he walks, how many words he speaks, he sees the spiritual condition of Scotland grow daily worse. He spake of the need to provide some sort of lasting testimony against the evil oppression – something which will have greater impact than any words he speaks or writes.' He hesitated. 'I mentioned young Nathaniel. Mr Renwick has a task for him. We were at prayer, though I confess I was having difficulty keeping mysel from drifting into sleep, to my shame. All at once, Mr Renwick directed himsel to Nathaniel, for in that moment of prayer he received a word from the Lord. He urged the young man to take heed of all that he has been witness to, and may yet be witness to in our cause, and to write it down for generations to come. It was a powerful moment.'

Helen was listening to all this, her hands clasped tightly together on the table in front of her. *Where is he? What are they doing to him? Oh, dear Jesus, keep him.*

James pulled the rough piece of nail free. 'We rose early this forenoon,' he said, his voice low. 'Mr Renwick had an appointment to keep, and I was bound for Leith docks. We had no warning, no word, else we might have managed to hide him. They were watching the house, there's no other explanation for it, for none but the four of us within kent he was present among us. We were readying to leave when we heard sounds beyond – and despite our urging caution, it was Mr Renwick himsel who opened the door.'

'Why in heaven's name did he do that?' cried Sandy. James shook his head.

'I dinna ken. He was nearest – it was just footsteps and voices – maybe he didna realise. And yet …' He was silent. The unspoken. The unspeakable. The question.

'Go on.'

'There was a man at the door, Captain Justice, one of the excise officers. I was a wee way into the house, but I heard his voice clear as could be, as he cried aloud, "My life for it, this is Renwick!" We caught hold of Mr Renwick then and pulled him back, and Nat slammed the door to, but we could hear footsteps and shouts and they were hammering on the door. We tried for the back stair down to the courtyard, but there were men there too – there was just nowhere to go. It seemed hopeless.' He buried his face in his hands. No one spoke.

The fire cracked. Eventually James looked up. 'He near got away. He pulled his pistol from under his cloak afore I'd even had time to think, and he fired it high above their heads. Well, they hadna been expecting that, and they scattered to the sides, and in that flash Mr Renwick, Nat and I pushed our way down the stair. They were after us, of course, as soon as they grasped what was happening, and one great chiel caught Mr Renwick such a blow with his staff that he staggered and would have fallen had I no caught him. Nat shouted, "Castle Wynd!", so we made for there and down that steep close to the Grassmarket. Nat was the fastest of us. I have never been much of a runner since the weakness to my leg, and Mr Renwick I believe was struggling with the effects of that blow.' He paused again. 'We shouldna have sought to run so far. We should have gone down the High Street, tried to lose oursels in some close or other.'

'You did what you could,' said Kirstie softly.

'Aye. Well, Nat was ahead. I was struggling to keep up, and I believe Mr Renwick was too. All the time the guard were running after us, shouting "Catch the dog Renwick!" But it was early morn, you ken, the light was still dim and there were few folks about. We made it through the Grassmarket, and I had my eyes on Nat ahead, and I saw him disappear into the Cowgate. If we could just reach him, that was all I was thinking, just reach him, and then there was another shout and I looked round.' He could barely speak. He closed his eyes, shaking his head. Helen reached out, laid a hand on his.

'Go on.'

A tear dropped onto her hand. Her own eyes were dry. Her man was greeting.

'I looked round. Some man from the crowd had him tight. Justice's men were almost upon him. It was hopeless. I stopped, I didna ken what to do. Then he lifted his head.' Another pause, another deep breath. 'He had lost his hat, and his hair was hanging half across his face, and he was struggling for breath, and they had twisted his arms behind him, but he looked right at me – right into my eyes – and he shouted, "Run". Just that – "Run". And I stood there, and I didna ken what to do, and I didna want to leave him, but there was no mistaking what he wanted. So I turned and I ran.' He lifted his hands, locked his fingers behind his head and looked up to the thatch above and to heaven beyond. 'Oh dear God, forgive me. I ran.'

Kirstie was crying. Sandy was shaking his head, staring at the table. Helen felt an unaccountable calm within her. She stood up and moved round behind her husband, placed her arms around his neck and kissed the top of his head. 'God gave you the honour of being with him in his moment of capture. Now isna the time for us to consider what might have been. We must pray, and we must plan.'

'I will return to Edinburgh,' James said, when they had spent time in discussion and in prayer. 'John Lockup brought me a hired horse, but couldna bring Moss for fear of drawing notice. But she's laden with goods we canna afford to lose.'

'I could go for you,' Sandy suggested. 'Surely it's dangerous for you to return to Edinburgh so soon.'

James shook his head. 'They willna expect me to return. I'll make for Edinburgh afore dawn. While I'm there I will hear what they have done with him.'

What have they done with him – done to *him.* 'I shall come with you,' said Helen.

'No. We'd be too noticeable travelling together, and you should stay with the bairns. Stay here and pray for us.'

She heard his words and she knew he was right – but how to bear it? How could she stay in Pentland, knowing he was in Edinburgh, knowing that even now he could be suffering the cruellest torture? The horror that had haunted his dreams, and hers.

'I'll come,' Sandy said. 'There must be something we can do. Men have escaped from the Tolbooth afore now, and I am a stranger to them. We willna travel together – we can arrange a meeting place. I will leave an hour or two behind you.'

And so it was agreed. Early on Thursday morning James set off for Edinburgh, Sandy following soon after. Kirstie and Helen tried to continue with the tasks of the day. Their men would be gone some days, and there would be no way of knowing if they had been arrested. Those who wait aye have it the hardest. The children were subdued and fearful, and no one slept much that night. Helen had not long since risen on Friday morning when she heard footsteps and hooves. The echo of her capture. The boys were already outside somewhere, but Beatrix was here beside her. *Dear Lord, help us.* She opened the door.

There were just two men and a lad there. The men had already dismounted, and the lad held their horses together with his own. Thank God they were not troopers, but nor were they friends. One was tall, with long brown hair and a dignified bearing, and wore the coat and hat of a man of wealth. The other was smaller and red-faced. The taller man spoke with a slight bow of his head. 'Mistress, I am James Clerk of Wrighthouses, and this here is Captain Justice, excise officer. We wish to speak to James Currie.'

She held herself straight and looked at each of them in turn. James Clerk of Wrighthouses – younger brother of Sir John Clerk of Penicuik, one of the wealthiest lairds in the area. His father was said to be a good man, but what of this generation? And Captain John Justice. The very man who had seized James Renwick, standing here, before her. A curse on him. Almighty God would have His revenge.

'I fear yours has been a wasted journey, sirs, for he isna hame.'

Captain Justice gave a rough laugh. 'You would say that.' Turned his head. 'Hold the horses, lad,' he said, then pushed past her. Clerk gave her a quick glance, then followed. There was nothing to do but accompany them back inside. Beatrix was standing by the table, her face pale and frightened. Helen motioned to her to sit down. *Keep quiet, and hope they move on.*

But Justice was making great play of looking in the hearth and under the table. 'Lost yer faither, have you?' he asked Beatrix, then reached out towards her. Helen took a quick breath as her daughter flinched. His stubby fingers touched her cheek, then tilted her chin. 'Fair bonny,' he said slowly, appraisingly. The girl's thin face was burning now, and her eyes burned too, but she said nothing.

'God's sakes, man, that's not what we're here for,' came the quick voice of his partner.

'Aye, well, what we're here for has clear flown,' said Justice sulkily.

Oh, please God, go then, go then.

'Currie is gone, but that's no surprise. Hold your peace, Justice, you'll get your reward for Renwick. But meantime, what else might we find? Stop your lechery and help me search.'

And Helen knew then that there was no hope at all. Silent, she joined Beatrix on the bench, and took hold of the girl's trembling fingers. There was some balm. Her husband must still be at liberty, and her sons were from home. *Please God, let them have the sense to stay away.* But for herself and perhaps for her daughter, there was nothing to do but pray, and she did that with all her heart, as she watched Justice toss linen from her kist. And her prayers seemed to have little effect, for Clerk had reached the bed now and was pulling the covers apart, and now the mattress too. Beatrix was crying quietly. Then a shout of triumph, and she knew he had found them.

'Just as I thought!' He held out the bundle of pamphlets to his partner. 'Here, take these, load them in the pack. They must go at once to Lord Perth, who will confront the prisoner Renwick with them. We'll see what he has to say about this treachery.'

Justice took the bundle, that precious bundle of truth and

wisdom and light, to be used to further blacken his beloved name.

'Come now.'

Justice stopped. 'The women?' he asked.

'I didna come here for women,' said Clerk, and he left the house without a backward glance.

Justice hesitated. 'I'll be back for you and your rebel-loving man, you fanatical bitches,' he spat, then followed the other through the open door. Helen and Beatrix sat, not daring to move, as they listened to the sounds of the men mounting their horses and setting off once more. Then Helen slipped her arms around her weeping daughter and pulled her close. 'No harm done, thanks be to God,' she whispered. 'No harm done.'

But of course, a great deal of harm had been done. They were looking for her husband. They had found treasonable documents and taken them to use in Renwick's trial. The link between the little family in Pentland and their friend in prison could not be stronger, and it would surely only be a matter of hours before they returned to arrest them all.

Kirstie's little heart-shaped face was white. She had seen the disturbance and intervened to prevent the two boys entering the house to rescue their mother and sister.

'For which I'm very grateful. What were you thinking, lads?'

'I was feart for you,' said Jamie defensively.

'Aye, and what good could you have done? As it was, they let us go simply because we were two women. Do you think your tender years would have saved you? Not in these wicked days, my lad, not now. These are the days of the great desolation, and you must be shrewd as a serpent. Hear me?'

'Aye, Mam.' He noticed she had conveniently forgotten the part about being gentle as a dove. Mam had never seemed particularly dove-like.

181

'Go to Jonet at Calder,' said Kirstie. 'You, and Beatrix too. The boys can bide here with me, at least until Sandy gets back.'

'But I must go to Edinburgh,' Helen protested. 'I must see my James, warn him, else he'll return here to look for me.'

There was sense in this, but Kirstie shook her head. 'For tonight, at least, go to Calder. They willna look for you there, but they will look for you here and in Edinburgh also. Please, Helen, at least for tonight.'

Helen was finding it hard to think. The strain of the last days, the panic of the last hour, and now new decisions to be made. All she wanted was to go to Edinburgh. 'I must see him,' she said, and she didn't mean her husband this time. 'What are they doing to him?'

'To walk into Edinburgh right in the shadow of those two men would be madness.'

Helen took a deep breath, tried to gather her thoughts. 'You are right,' she said more calmly. 'Very well. If you will look to the boys, Beatrix and I will go to Calder. I will ask your mother and Jonet if they would be so kind as to put us up for the night, and to keep Beatrix with them. But tomorrow I will carry on to Edinburgh.'

*

In Calder, it was Davy who brought news that the traitor Renwick had been taken. He had come to the house to tell his sister that her petition would be heard by the kirk session on the following Tuesday.

'What petition?'

'The one I've submitted on your behalf. You are to be wed, that's the only thing that matters. Mr Mackenzie will likely meet with you, hear your repentance and release you shortly.' He was sharpening his knife as he spoke and flourished it in her direction.

'And if I willna repent?'

'You're no sic a fool, surely.'

Jonet was ready to argue, but it was then he tossed his news into the conversation. 'Ken what I heard on my way here? That dog Renwick has been taken at last.' He laughed, careless. 'They'll be building a high scaffold in Edinburgh for that one.'

She looked at the knife he was holding and imagined plunging it into his heart. A noise from behind and she turned. Mam, normally so self-possessed, was leaning against the wall, her face grey and her eyes wide with fear. Davy seemed to notice nothing. He slipped his knife back into its pouch and turned towards the door. He spent little time here these days, and he and Jonet spoke no more than was necessary. Jonet knew that Davy and Elpset were just waiting for her sentence to be lifted before he could finally use that knife of his to slice through the ties that bound them together and, with his new wife, take over the house.

As Davy left, Mam sank into a chair. 'Dear God,' she said. 'It is the end for him. It must be. And what of Kirstie?'

Jonet said nothing. In her mind she could see the young preacher speaking from the rock with passion and fervour; tousle-haired and sheepish when he woke in Kirstie's house; thoughtful, tender and wise as he spoke with her amid the flickering evening shadows. And now, inevitably, his fate had caught up with him. A deep sadness draped itself over her shoulders like the cloak of mourning. She had never quite known what to think of him, but it was still dreadful to consider his fate. For of course, he would now be tortured and then would hang. There was no other possibility.

And what of those who supported him? What of Kirstie and Sandy? What of Helen and James, who had accompanied him to Edinburgh that last time? She could only begin to imagine how distraught they must be. She could not leave, not so close to her Sabbath penance, but how she longed to be free of the cruel, tangled thorns of Calder and hurry to be with her sister and friends in Pentland.

She did not realise that they would come to her.

It was late Friday afternoon when Helen and Beatrix arrived, tight with strain and weary from their journey. Davy, thank God, was still from home. The women ushered them in, full of fear. Reassurances first: Kirstie and the children were safe and well. But explanations had to follow, and Mam's lips were set thin as she heard that the authorities had already been to Pentland looking for James Currie, and that Sandy had travelled to Edinburgh. She interrogated Helen, her words serrated. For all Helen answered her questions, she seemed barely present.

'I would like to sleep, if you can spare me a corner. Then afore it's light I'll set off for Edinburgh and find them. But I'd like to leave Beatrix with you. Will you keep her?'

'Is that wise, lass?' asked Mam. 'Your bairn may already have lost her faither. Would you have her lose her mother too?'

Helen looked towards the bed where a worn-out Beatrix was already sleeping. 'Seek first the kingdom of God,' she said quietly. 'Beatrix is in agreement.'

'Of course, we'll keep her,' Jonet said with a glance to her mother. 'I only wish I could come with you.'

'It's kind, but I prefer to travel alone. But dinna fear, they willna be looking for me. It has all changed now, do you see? They have won their prize.'

And so Helen rose to leave early the next morning, and Jonet accompanied her to the door. The cold light of the moon sliced through the darkness which hovered over the waiting landscape. Helen tightened her boots and straightened up, smiling at Jonet. 'Thank you for caring for Beatrix. If you hear nothing, it will be safe for her to return to Pentland next week.' She paused. 'But what of you?'

'My case is to come afore the kirk session on Tuesday,' said Jonet. 'And he will return from Inverness soon enough.'

She knew Helen had plenty troubles of her own now and had resolved not to worry her further, but she couldn't hold back. She caught hold of the older woman's arm. 'What am I to do, Helen? I canna go with him. I canna.'

'Who says that you must?'

Jonet glanced quickly back into the darkened room. There was no sign of Mam. 'Everyone. But mainly my brother, I suppose.'

'Have you the strength to tell your brother you willna do as he says? And to take the consequences, whatever they may be?'

Jonet looked at Helen, her dark eyes set steady in her drawn and weary face. Aye, here was a woman who did not bend her beliefs or her will to others, no matter the consequences. It was a rare thing to see. 'I dinna ken. I might have.'

Helen pulled the younger girl into a hug. 'I will pray for guidance and courage for you. Now I must be away. Be strong, Jonet. Resist.'

There were tears in Jonet's eyes. 'We'll take care of Beatrix,' she said. 'Get word to us as soon as you can.'

Helen nodded, turned, and walked away. Jonet stood in the doorway and watched. Her friend's head was bowed, her steps slow, steady, resolute. As she walked, she became gradually less distinct in the darkness until Jonet could barely see where she had gone. The woman had simply slipped away. Her own hand rested on her unborn child. She had aye been at home in this world, taking so much for granted, but now everything felt hostile.

*

Helen's journey from Calder through the spreading light was wearisome but uneventful. She walked for long miles, the hills of home spread out to her right, the grim outline of the Castle ahead of her. Her main concern was passing through the West Port under the scrutiny of the guards, but she fell in with a kindly older couple just a mile or so outside the city walls. They were eagerly travelling to see their newborn grandson for the first time, and Helen walked unnoticed through the gate alongside them, breathing a silent prayer of gratitude for the provision of these unwitting angels. They parted outside the White Hart Inn at the west end of the Grassmarket, and Helen looked around. She remembered standing here with James, the mist swirling around and the gallows looming dark above them. There were no gallows erected today, at least, and the small patch of sky she could see above the towering buildings was a bright, chilly blue. She felt the familiar unease at the clamour, the stink, the malevolence of the city, but it did not overwhelm her as it had done before. Whatever the danger, whatever the evil, she was here. Somewhere in this city, James Renwick languished in a prison cell. Where else could she be?

Her route carried her past the site where he had been arrested just a few days earlier. She heard again her husband's hollow voice recounting the terrible events of that day. Ahead was the dark mouth of the Cowgate, where Nathaniel had escaped to safety, where Mr Renwick might have escaped too, had he not been injured by the guard's attack. She reached the foot of the West Bow and turned up, walking between tall, leaning houses. Lines of clean washing hung above her in the grimy air, put out in the unlikely hope that the weak February sun might somehow dry them. She was making for John Lockup's house. She knew it was risky, but where else could she go? She was desperate to find out if James and Sandy were safe, and to know all that there was to know.

Her plans changed when she reached the top of the West Bow. Some sort of disturbance was taking place. She saw a woman and man hurrying past, a group of children dancing along, pushing and pulling at one another. A man from the town guard was trying unsuccessfully to control the flow of people. They were all making for the High Street – to the High Kirk, perhaps? She quickened her steps and joined the crowd, which was slowing, thickening. It wasn't the entrance to the kirk, but to the Tolbooth – Edinburgh's prison. Helen tried to work her way through the tightly packed crowd, her body tense at the unpleasant sensation of being close to so many people. She drew in her breath sharply to see some poor man attached to the wall of the Tolbooth by jougs, his clothes soaked and stained with glaur and eggs, yet despite a few jeers he was not the one holding the crowd's attention. Outside the Tolbooth entrance stood three men, and by dint of weaving to and fro she caught a glimpse of each of them. One was a servant waiting behind, but side by side were the brightly dressed herald of the court, trumpet in hand, and a solemn faced lawyer robed in black. As she watched, the herald lifted his trumpet to his lips and proceeded to blow out a shrill fanfare. The tumult died away to a low rumble.

What new horror was coming?

The herald spoke first in legal language, declaring the absolute sovereignty of the king. Aye, no room for question or disagreement in this Scotland now. In front of her a large man in a wig kept moving and blocking her view. Voices cried out from the crowd: 'Get on with it!' 'Hang the rebels!' 'Shame on you!' 'Renwick for Archbishop!'

She clenched her fingers tightly and waited.

'You, the said Mr James Renwick, having shaken off all fear of God ...'

She shook her head. How could they say such a thing? She knew no one else who lived life in such complete fear of God, no one. That was the reason for it all.

'... having entered yourself into the society of some rebels of most damnable and pernicious principles and disloyal practices, you took upon you to be a preacher to those traitors ...'

Dear God, they were calling good evil and evil good, and

no one even thought it strange.

'... became so desperate a villain that you did openly and frequently preach in the fields, declaiming against the authority and government of our sovereign lord the king ... to make war against his Majesty ...'

In the fields. Such blessing she had known in the fields, when the cloud of God's glory had descended upon them. How desperately she needed to hold onto those moments of blessing, of knowledge, of communion now.

'... requiring your hearers to provide arms, and to come armed to these rendezvouses of rebellion ...'

A woman was crying, a little way to her left.

'... with your hand you wrote down in a book, found upon you when you were taken, the heads of these treasonable sermons, with the dates and places where you had preached the same.'

So they had evidence. Dates. Places.

'And being apprehended within the city of Edinburgh, ye did desperately fire upon the officers that came to take you.'

If he fired upon them, how was it not one of them was injured?

'Being brought to the Viscount of Tarbart's lodging, ye did there, in the presence of the lord chancellor, and several other counsellors, avowedly and traitorously declare, that ye could not in your conscience acknowledge the king to be your sovereign, and that the lineal succession did not give a right to govern.'

Oh James. But she lifted her head, proud of him.

'Wherethrough ye the said James Renwick has committed and is guilty of the crimes of high treason above specified; which being found by an assize, you ought to be punished with forfeiture of life, lands and goods, to the terror and

example of others to commit the like hereafter.'

Guilty. Of the crime of high treason. Forfeiture of life.

The herald sounded his trumpet once more and read out a list of names, those from whom the jury would be selected. Helen heard none of them. High treason. The herald and the lawyer disappeared through the door of the Tolbooth, presumably to deliver the indictment to the prisoner's face. She pictured him in chains and in filth. Dear God, may he hold his head high.

Guilty. High treason.

Forfeiture of life.

And the crowd was surging about her now, the moment of drama over, but Helen could not move. *I have feared this moment for so very, very long – and it is here.* And then a hand took her elbow, a voice spoke her name. She turned. Sandy was standing there beside her, his hat low over his face. Had she ever seen him look so weary? 'You came,' he said.

'Aye. Kirstie and Bel are safe. Beatrix is in Calder, but I had to come. And my husband?'

'He's fine,' Sandy said at once. 'He is with friends. We should go there now.'

'Go where?'

Sandy had his hand under her arm and was leading her away from the Tolbooth. She cast a desperate glance back at the dark building inside which, somewhere, James Renwick was even now facing down his accusers. It was surely a betrayal to walk away. Sandy caught her look.

'There's much we can tell you, but no here. There is some danger, of course, but they ken where we are, and so far they seem content to let us be. I think there's enough to fash them as they work out what to do with Mr Renwick.'

'Is it not all too clear what they will do with him?'

Sandy shook his head. 'We canna speak of it here. Come.'

He told her as they walked that they were not staying

in John Lockup's house, but in lodgings offered by a sympathiser in a close further down the High Street, nearer the Netherbow Port. 'They returned to John's house later that day and ransacked it. It's best we stay away. John has fled south to Newcastle.'

Helen was sorry. She had liked the rotund merchant with his warm, welcoming manner. Still, at least he was safe. It was a serious crime to have harboured a wanted traitor. Meantime, Sandy led her to their lodgings. They entered a close so dark she could not see where it was safe to place her feet, and the stench caught her throat and made her gag. At the end of the close was a drab little courtyard. Through an opening in the rear wall she could see that the houses here were built up over a steep drop, with the ground behind falling away far below.

Sandy opened a door and guided her down some steps, and through another door. The room they entered was far humbler than John Lockup's genteel apartment, and her immediate impression was that it was full of people. The walls were rough stone with no timber panelling. One grimy window looked out over the void she had noticed from the courtyard, and the other, with shutters closed, faced onto the courtyard itself. There was little furniture – a table, a couple of creepie stools and settles, and some blankets on the floor to serve as beds. A small fire burned in the centre of the room, and the atmosphere was thick with smoke which made her eyes sting. Heads turned as they entered, and her husband immediately heaved himself to his feet and came towards her. They embraced.

I have hardly thought of him these last hours, Helen realised with a twinge of shame, and yet I am so very relieved and comforted to see him.

She began to remove her cloak. An older woman, who was seated on one of the few proper armchairs, gave a slight laugh. 'You may prefer to wait a while, dearie. This place isna ower warm.'

She was right. It was not so much cold as damp, a chilling dampness which penetrated the bones. Then she turned at the sound of the door opening. A young woman slipped in and made immediately for the older woman, bending to kiss her. Helen recognised the newcomer as the girl who had been crying quietly while the indictment was read. She looked to her husband, questioning.

'Helen, these are Mistress Elizabeth Corsane and Meg Renwick – Mr Renwick's mother and sister. And you remember Nat.'

Until now she had not noticed Nathaniel in the room, but it didn't escape her attention that Renwick's sister, having greeted her mother, sat down close to his side and began to tell him quietly of her experiences, her eyes never leaving his face. But at that moment it was Renwick's mother who interested Helen most. The woman who had nurtured him, who surely, in part, had made him what he became. Gnarled hands which had nursed him. A slight, grey-haired lady with a presence beyond her stature, she smiled warmly at Helen. 'Welcome, my dear,' she said. 'You gave my son shelter. Thank you for your care of him.'

'It's been my privilege,' Helen replied honestly. Sandy meantime had been exchanging a few words with her husband, but now he turned to address the gathered company. 'It's done,' he said abruptly. 'He is indicted for high treason.'

A murmur passed round the room, and Elizabeth Corsane shook her head in distress. As Sandy repeated many details of the indictment, Helen drew James to one side and told him about the raid on their home. He, in turn, recounted how he had returned to find the house on Castlehill ransacked. He had retrieved Moss but many of his goods had been stolen. She was barely listening. 'What word have you of Mr Renwick?' she asked. 'Have they harmed him?'

191

Her voice was too loud; it had reached his mother. Elizabeth Corsane raised her head, and the dark shadows under her watery eyes betrayed the horror she was enduring. 'We think not,' she said. 'We can only pray that the Lord stays their hand. I have asked to see him; please God, they will allow it.'

It was on the tip of Helen's tongue to ask to come too – but how could she? She had only just met this woman; she had no right, no claim on James Renwick, not as his family had.

And yet there was that one evening.

'So what happens next?' she asked instead.

'They select the jurors,' said Sandy, 'and then hold a trial. And it sickens my soul, but did you notice that James Boyle's name was among the list of witnesses? They say he's taken the oath and renounced the Covenants to save his skin. Much guid may it do him in eternity.'

'Surely he wouldna testify against Mr Renwick!' exclaimed Helen. Just a short time ago Boyle had been prominent among them, even leading the praise at some of Renwick's field preachings.

'If a man will renounce his God, then no doubt he will renounce his friends.'

'Well, we must pray that it isna so,' said Elizabeth Corsane. 'Come, friends. Let us pray for a miracle in our ain time – and then let us eat. There are difficult days ahead of us yet.'

Chapter Thirteen

Sunday 5th February 1688

The twelfth Sabbath of Jonet Gothskirk's public appearance in Sackcloth.

Mr Mackenzie leaned over the edge of his pulpit above her, to make his announcement.

'Jonet Gothskirk has presented a petition requesting that, by reason of the nearness of her time of delivery, the next Sabbath may be her day of receiving. The kirk session will meet this Tuesday at the regular hour to consider the matter.'

It was the first she had heard of the reason they had given in the petition presented 'on her behalf', as Davy had put it. Thankfully she was not as near as all that yet – Mam reckoned she still had another two months to go. But dear God, where would she be when those two months were ended, and her bairn pushed its way into the world? There was no place for her here in Calder. Would she be in Inverness? Gripping the edges of the stool, she thought again of her last hushed conversation with Helen. She had almost believed, with Helen's cool gaze holding hers, that she could stand firm and refuse to marry him. But today in the kirk, as the minister announced the procedure by which she would be released from one sentence into the next, she could see again just how helpless she was. Like those wee dried up leaf boats at the mercy of the stream, her fate was determined by forces far beyond her control. The kirk, the law of the land, even her own family. No one could be strong enough to resist. No one.

Having intimated the meeting, Mr Mackenzie at least paid her no further notice today, preferring instead to focus his triumphant attention on the capture of the wicked James Renwick. Weary, Jonet tried not to listen but could not quite shut out his jubilant exultation over the agonising death which now awaited the traitor.

Such darkness had descended.

The darkness remained close over the next couple of days as they waited to see how events would unfold. Beatrix was still with them, quiet and watchful as ever. On Wednesday morning, a representative of the kirk session came to the cottage. Mam called her from the tub at the back of the house where she and Beatrix were busy washing clothes. Dear God, this must be it. Jonet rubbed her soapy hands dry on her apron and came inside. Thank God, it was Tam Sime the session clerk who awaited her, not the minister himself. Tam was a good man and had been a friend of her father's. She could mind the two of them working together in the fields, and how they would pause for a bit of a chat and a laugh when Mam sent her to bring their piece and ale to them. Such different days. But he was here to bring judgement, for all that. She gripped her skirts and waited.

'As ye ken, lass, kirk session considered your petition last night. We agreed that Mr Mackenzie will confer with you on Tuesday next at six in the evening. The purpose of the meeting is to discover your sense of sorrow for your sin, and so to consider whether to grant your petition. You needna appear in sackcloth while your petition is under consideration.' He paused and looked right at her, and his eyes were kind. 'Listen to me, lass, the minister is minded to grant your petition, but only if you show your shame and sorrow and hold your tongue to all else. Make sure you do, and you will be released.'

She nodded, numb, and watched him go. Mam was smiling, a rare thing. 'It's near ower, Jonet, lass,' she said. 'You heard Tam tell you exactly what you must do. Oh, thank God, at last it is near ower.'

Aye, near ower for Mam. Near ower for Davy. Near ower for all of them, all but her. That same aching loneliness that she'd known at Kirstie's threatened to smother the life from her once more. A grey and brutal inevitability. She shook her head, unable to rejoice with Mam but not quite able to argue either. 'I'll get back to the washing,' she said, and returned to where Beatrix was still up to her elbows in soapy water.

Beatrix had been with them nearly a week now, and in that time no word had come from Edinburgh. The girl said little, but the shadows under her dark eyes seemed to become more pronounced in her white face each day that passed, and Jonet had noticed that she had bitten her fingernails to the quick. Now she glanced up at Jonet. 'Are you freed, then?'

Jonet hesitated. She had said little to Beatrix about her Sabbaths in sackcloth, but of course the younger girl knew all about it. This was Helen's daughter, after all. Suddenly needing to share her horror, she helped the girl lift and wring the water from a shift. 'It seems I may soon be restored by the kirk, in order to be wed.'

Beatrix pulled the shift towards her. 'I was listening,' she admitted. And then, seemingly unconnected, she added, 'I've decided to go to Edinburgh the morn.'

'But your Mam wanted you to return to Pentland if she didna come for you.'

'Aye, but what's the use of that? She may be in prison for all we ken. If I go to Pentland, they will keep me there, and I'll ken nothing of what's going on. No, I have decided. I am going to Edinburgh at first light.' She paused. 'Come with me?'

Come with me? Jonet was about to protest, but then she remembered what Tam Sime had said: 'You needna appear in sackcloth while your petition is under consideration.' In theory she was now free until her meeting with the minister next Tuesday. *Come with me?* She had lifted another item from the tub and stood motionless, heedless of the water pouring from the sodden garment onto her feet. It was lunacy, of course – to go and join the supporters of the captured James Renwick in the very city where he was held. But what was there for her here? Nothing.

Come with me.

'I dinna ken if I can walk that far,' she said, gesturing towards her pregnant belly.

'You can if you want to.' Beatrix spoke with certainty, and Jonet heard the echo of the girl's mother in her tone. She took a breath and felt something stir amid the deadness inside.

'I'll come.'

*

In Edinburgh, those who had chosen to walk with the fair-haired young preacher were waiting out those same long days of his imprisonment. Each day, one or two of their number would venture onto the streets for news, gleaning stories which leaked out from behind locked doors.

They say that when the Captain of the Guard first saw him, he laughed aloud and asked, 'Is this boy *the Renwick that the nation has been so troubled with?'*

What did they think they were hunting? Some violent monster? The deil incarnate?

Aye, and the Earl of Perth – a Papist himself, mind you – found his answers so full of integrity and reason that he cried him a true Presbyterian, of old Knox's principles.

There were plenty men in that room who claim to be Presbyterians – I hope they were shamed, though I doubt it.

Helen clasped and unclasped her hands, walking over to the door for the fifth time in the last half hour. She opened it a fraction to look out. 'Dear God, I hope it was not a trap.'

No one answered. They had all been astonished when Elizabeth's request to visit her son in the Tolbooth was granted. Astonished, and not a little wary. She had brushed their concerns aside, hurriedly wrapping her cloak around her shoulders. *What mother would turn down the chance to comfort her son?* For all that, she did not allow Meg to join her, no matter the girl's protests and tears. As a compromise, Nathaniel had offered to walk them both the short distance to the Tolbooth, where he would stay outside with Meg while her mother entered. That had been over an hour ago, and those left behind in the room could do nothing but wait and pray.

I to the hills will lift mine eyes.
From whence doth come mine aid?
My safety cometh from the Lord,
who heaven and earth hath made.

As they sang quietly together, Helen leaned against her husband. The shutter was half open to let in some air, and she could see the dark shapes of the other buildings in the courtyard. Oh, to be back in the hills, in the fresh clean air, with the sky arching above them, more glorious than any cathedral roof. There they had sung these familiar words in the company not just of James Renwick but of the great communion of saints. And they had looked to the hills and listened for the soldiers coming, but the danger had always remained just one step away. Now here they were in the heart of a hostile city, with malevolent hordes surrounding them on all sides, while their dearest friend and leader was held in the jaws of Leviathan.

The moon by night thee shall not smite,
nor yet the sun by day

And as they were praying, the door creaked. Helen watched, heavy with dread, as Meg entered first. Behind her came Elizabeth, leaning on Nathaniel's arm, more bowed and fragile than ever. They were safe then. But what news, what news? Suppressing the desire to rush forward, to throw herself at Elizabeth's feet and beg for answers, she instead hurried to help them remove their outer layers and to provide

197

them with ale. They gathered round the low fire. 'He is well,' said his mother.

Her face was grey and strained, but there was a light in her eyes which had not been there this morning. Reflected glory? Oh God, what had they done? What did she mean, *well?*

'Have they harmed him?' James asked. Helen was grateful, even as her body tensed in readiness for the answer. She could not have spoken the query aloud herself, but she had thought of nothing else since she had first heard he was taken. The boot. The thumbscrews. His precious flesh ripped, his bones splintered. Blood oozing slowly onto the floor. His dear face, twisted in agony, screaming. His greatest fear, and hers.

Elizabeth shook her head. 'They have not, and he is certain they will not.' She took a long drink. 'Friends, my son is ready for all that will be asked of him. I was feart at first that his faith had faltered, for he said he couldna pray. But he laughed at me – aye, he can laugh yet – and said he could hardly pray for being so filled with the joy of the Lord.' Beside her Meg was greeting and leaning against Nathaniel, but James Renwick's mother did not cry.

'He is whole and unharmed, and they have made no move to torture him. And yet, my heart has been tormented with fear – the fear of walking through these city ports and seeing his bonny head, his beloved hands, sliced from his body and put on display to be devoured by the corbies. How does any mother ever bear such things?'

Helen, whose dreams were haunted by the prospect of that sight, closed her eyes.

'I hadna meant to grieve him, but he saw my trouble as aye he does, and he spake words to me which I believe we all need to hear, if we are to find our way through these wicked days.'

Helen looked up to find that Elizabeth was watching her.

198

Their gaze locked.

'He has offered his life to the Lord and has sought that He will bind them to do nae mair. He is sure they shall not be permitted to torture his body, nor touch one hair of his head further.'

He has offered his life to the Lord.

Aye, she had known the ending almost from the beginning. He had sensed it too, long since. But how, dear God *how*, were they meant to continue without him? A dry sob escaped from her mouth. His mother reached out with hands which had nursed him and raised him, clasping Helen's own. 'He is right sad to be leaving his beloved flock, but he is certain that only this last testimony will bring people to understand the truth he has spoken all these years.'

Helen nodded. She couldn't speak. Her husband had his head in his hands, and Meg was still weeping. And yet his mother, so calm in her heartbreak, so proud and so loyal, continued. 'He kens we are gathered here and he is sustained by our prayers. His trial will be Wednesday. Afore that, Helen, he would like to see you.'

Merciful Lord. Something was struggling to burst open inside her. Naked and unashamed.

'It is, of course, dangerous,' Elizabeth continued, looking quickly towards James Currie. 'He would understand if you choose not to enter the Tolbooth – though the guards were civil enough to me.'

'Helen?' It was her husband's voice, questioning, uncertain. Dear James, so steadfast. She raised her head, dark eyes burning in a chalk white face.

'Of course I will go.'

That night Helen lay awake, with her husband's body pressed against her amid the heap of blankets which served as their bed. Tomorrow she would see him. He was going to die – there could be little doubt about that, though there was aye

199

room for a miracle. But right now, she was able to push the dread of his trial and murder into the distance and to focus on this moment. In the midst of her searing grief there was a tiny throb of joy. He had asked for her.

Tomorrow, she would be with him, she would speak with him, she would drink him in. She had not believed she would have the chance again.

Such precious moments they had spent together in the past, as they stood firm together for the Lord and the Covenant in Scotland. A sacred bond that surely could never be broken. She remembered again that day when her friend had come to the Canongate Tolbooth, and first mentioned the lad Renwick returning from Holland to preach. She had thought then that she would not live to set eyes upon him. And even when he was first among them, she like many others had her doubts. There were whispers about his ordination, his beliefs, his practices. All that began to change as she met the man himself, as she had explained to Jonet. First, she heard him as a preacher, then she knew him as a friend. The rumours and the lies fell away like chaff from gathered grain. What life he breathed into their trembling hearts! He pointed them to the Lord and gave them such understanding of these times in which they lived. Aye, it was hard now not to fear what would become of them without his wisdom, his guidance, his presence among them. And yet, all he had taught them lived on. If this last sacrifice was required of him, then those who were left must stand firm and continue his work.

She knew all that in her head, but in the darkness of the night-time in a cold, damp Edinburgh hiding place, barbed pain dragged across her heart and the tears dripped silently down her face and onto the blankets. If he had just been a preacher she admired, she could have found the strength to face this. They had lost many godly men and women to the scaffold before now, and some she had known well and admired. But James Renwick was so very different. No other preacher had walked right in and claimed a place in her heart. She thought back again to those nights when she was a widow, and she had these men stay in her house while the children lay asleep. Folk gossiped, at first, but when had she ever cared what folk thought? And so she and James Renwick grew closer, sitting together as the shadows from the fire flickered around the walls, as the shutters creaked, and the bairns made noises in their sleep. Even at the time she had known these were moments to be treasured, and she had stored up each conversation with care. And now, lying here in the stale Edinburgh air, she reached in and unwrapped each memory, reliving the way he had very gradually revealed his heart to her. How privileged she had been to share in his grief over the state of the kirk in Scotland, and his concern for those who remained faithful in these dark times. She had listened to the pain in his voice as he spoke of his betrayal by his fellow students in Holland, and then his bewilderment at coming home to the slander of those who should have supported him. She remembered barely breathing as he revealed his own struggles with doubt, and with the very existence of the God he nevertheless served. And into that darkness, unable to see his face, she found herself in turn speaking of things she had never thought to say aloud – the difficulties of life with her first husband, the horror of those long weeks in prison, her fears for her bairns. For long years she had known a forlorn loneliness at following God's call when no one else seemed to hear it. In James Renwick's company she at last caught its echo.

And they were alone in the house, and the bairns were fast asleep. The danger was outside, but they were sheltered within, and it was before she was wed, when she barely knew James Currie. There would have been nothing wrong with it, nothing at all. And so they clung to each other in that one precious, fierce embrace.

But his calling was not to marriage.

And when he was gone, Helen lay and sobbed as her lonely body yearned with frustration for the moment that had slipped away – yet even in her grief she knew they had chosen wisely. The cause in which they both believed was too great a thing to be deflected. How terrible, to be the temptation which might distract James Renwick from the gospel. He sensed it too, she knew he did, and for a while he stayed away.

What did any of it mean? Sometimes she could almost persuade herself that it had simply been an instinctive response to shared sorrow and loneliness, an evening which meant nothing and should just be forgotten. Perhaps he had forgotten already.

But then she would see him again and feel once more that heightened awareness in his presence, catch the warm smile in his glance. She came to know James Currie and accepted his marriage proposal. Stood before James Renwick as his blessing sealed their union, and knew she was right in the centre of the will of God.

A sacrifice which in one sense was no sacrifice at all – and yet cost her nearly everything she had.

A love which would surely remain with her long after the breath had been squeezed from James Renwick's earthly body.

There was a greater call on both their lives than human love – but dear God, it hurt.

There were no tears, next morning, as she prepared to visit the Tolbooth. Elizabeth pressed some writing materials into her hands. 'He asked for these. He's anxious to write some letters and to record his testimony. It's a lot to ask, but do you think you could get them to him? They didna search me.'

Helen slipped them inside her cloak. Today she was

practical, efficient. Yes, she would take some food and drink for him, and money for the guard. No, it was better that her husband did not accompany her. Only a few days ago they had been searching for him, and it would do no one any good if he were also imprisoned. She listened to their many messages, repeated them, bowed her head under Elizabeth's whispered blessing, and slipped out into the courtyard. Through the dark, slimy close, picking her way over the filth, she stepped out onto the High Street. On a Monday morning all was activity. Her own life seemed suspended in unreality, as she walked past the street traders and merchants and on through an ordinary Edinburgh morning, with all that was *ordinary* rapidly crumbling around her.

The Tolbooth stood in the centre of the High Street, in front of the High Kirk. She explained her business to the guard on the door and was led into the lower level of the prison. She was completely unprepared for the surge of bile which heaved within her as she followed him along the first dark corridor, lit by flickering torches on the wall. This was not the building in which she had been held, but every sound, every smell, every sensation was so horribly familiar. The moans and curses from behind closed doors. The creak of a hinge, the scrape of a chain across the ground. The sound of sharp footsteps echoing on the stone floor. The stench of human waste, the streaming damp. For a moment Helen stopped, blind, and reached out a hand to the clammy wall. She was standing once more in the darkest place in her life. Her heart was racing, her legs were in danger of giving way, and the awful sensation of being confined for week after week after endless week was smothering the breath from her. Then she took a quick gulp of the putrid air and lifted her head. This was for Mr Renwick.

As she followed the guard up a turnpike stair, the panic at her surroundings began to subside and was overtaken by a new fear. What would it be like, to see him held in this place rather than free on the hills? She had seen good people broken by this torment before now. And would she be able to control her own weakness? The tears she had wept unseen last night, they *must not* return in daylight. The purpose of her visit was to offer him strength and comfort, and to glory in his presence once more. Nothing should reveal the depth of her distress.

Easy to say.

As the guard led her along a narrow, airless corridor, the door ahead of them opened. The man who emerged was dressed in the gown of a curate. He gave his head a little shake as he left the room and then stalked past them, scowling. Helen paid him little attention. Across the small room, seated at a table, was James Renwick. Were it not for the heavy chain dragging across the floor, he could almost have been at leisure. There was a new hollowness about his face, but warmth in his smile as he saw her come into the room. 'Helen, thank God! I thought you were another of the endless stream of priests and curates that they send to try to change my mind.'

The guard had taken the basket of food and was looking through it, extracting a few items for himself. Now he placed it on the table with a quick nod and held out a hand which was lined with grime. Helen placed the coins in his outstretched palm and then, as he turned aside to pull out a leather pouch, she deftly slipped the writing materials into the basket, moving a loaf of bread on top of them. The guard had checked the basket once; he would be unlikely to check it again. She walked forward and clasped Mr Renwick's thin, icy hands. 'James.'

She would not cry.

These were sacred moments which would never come again.

Perhaps it's the mercy of God that makes such eternal notions hard to grasp. Instead she focused on the reality of his presence, the normality of speaking with him – no matter that the surroundings were anything but normal – and she drew comfort. She could push away just for a while the terrible prospect of the next few days. He asked about his mother and Meg, and then about James and the children. She told him all she could. They were still holding hands. She felt his thin grip tighten on her wrist and there was more urgency in his tone.

'Helen, I asked you to come here because I need you to explain to the others why these things must happen. Only my death, if God wills it, can prove the truth of all my words ower these past years. I'm praying that God will use my death to bring about a great change here in Scotland. So dinna grieve for me. Soon I will be released from the lies that break my heart.'

She nodded, not quite able to speak. His voice was so familiar, so reassuring, and yet his words so dreadful. They had little time. She concentrated on etching his words into her mind, holding on to this moment, this reality, for all time to come.

They shared the bread and salted fish she had brought, though Helen ate very little. They spoke about mutual friends, about the impact of his arrest on the Society people, about the folk who were dear to him and were on his heart. In many ways it was the same conversation she could have had with him at any point over the last few precarious years, gathered in a sympathetic house or perhaps out in the hills.

But then the guard told her to leave.

A look was held between them then, and it was a taut, helpless, wordless look of love. Helen took a deep breath – for all the air was fetid and dank – and walked towards the door. Then she turned. The words in her head were the words the Lord had given to her when she herself was in prison, in fear of her life. 'You will get the white robes.'

And in the intensity of his gaze she knew he was seeing

through the crack in time to the splendour too. 'Aye, and palms in my hands.'

He was smiling.

She turned then, blinded by tears, and left him.

His trial took place two days later, on Wednesday. Nathaniel led Helen, Elizabeth and Meg through the surging crowds in Parliament Close to the grand Parliament House, where the Justiciary Court would meet. The wicked, idolatrous Charles Stuart looked down on them proudly from his horse, and though it was only a statue, Helen averted her eyes. Her husband was not with them. They all agreed it was still wiser for him to keep a low profile, so he headed down to Leith to pursue some business.

They squeezed onto the packed public benches in a great, cold, high-ceilinged room lit through tall windows which offered a glimpse to the High Kirk outside. She caught her breath, and Elizabeth's hand, as they led the prisoner in. *I have a greater Judge to go afore, the Judge of all the earth* – that's what she'd told the guard on the day of her own appearance before the Lord Chancellor all those years ago. But this was a full trial, and its outcome a foregone conclusion.

The presiding judge, bedecked in crimson and white, was an elderly, jowly man with a round, red face. 'Linlithgow, the most senior judge in Scotland, and a real enemy of the Covenant,' whispered Nathaniel, who was scribbling notes in a pocketbook throughout. 'See that judge there, that's Hog of Harcarse. Interesting, I've heard rumours about him. He might no be quite the government man they take him to be. That could be in our favour.'

Helen glanced across at the third of the four judges seated on a raised wooden platform and saw a man with dark eyes set in a pale face above a long nose. His mouth looked rather feminine. But Nathaniel had moved on. 'It's the Advocate, of course, who brings the case. That's John Dalrymple of Stair. There's a turncoat if ever you saw one. He was imprisoned himsel, you ken, for sheltering Covenanters on his faither's land, yet now he's cast all principle aside for the robes of office. We canna hope for much from him.'

Helen shook her head. She was barely listening, and looked at the slight, grey figure of James Renwick as he stood before these portentous authorities. Nathaniel didn't seem to realise that the allegiances and opinions of the bewigged judges were just debris. Inconsequential. *For we wrestle not against flesh and blood, but against principalities, against powers, against the rulers of the darkness of this world, against spiritual wickedness in high places.*

But proceedings were beginning with the reading of the indictment she had heard outside the Tolbooth on Saturday, when she had first arrived in Edinburgh. James Renwick was challenged to answer whether he still held to all he had admitted before the Privy Council. Helen pressed her fingers together tightly. *Dear God, give him strength, give him boldness, give him all he needs.*

He lifted his head and spoke as clearly and authoritatively as ever he had spoken on hillside or in byre. 'I acknowledge all but where it says I have shaken off all fear of God; that I deny. It is because I fear to offend God and violate the law that I am standing ready to be condemned.'

There were murmurs from the public benches. The judges looked at one another, then apparently agreed to ignore this troublesome statement. Dalrymple went on to detail the three charges which would be brought against the defendant: denying the king's authority, declaring the payment of cess unlawful, and encouraging the carrying of arms. Each charge, Helen knew, was something which Mr Renwick would freely acknowledge, and each charge could lead only to the foot of the scaffold.

She was willing him to look her way, but his eyes were on

the Advocate, as he gave his full attention to the proceedings taking place. She could see the concentration on his face, the small frown on his forehead. Next came the selection of a jury. Nathaniel leaned towards her. 'Watch now, they will choose some who once sided with us, just to test them.' From the forty-five names, fifteen were chosen. Sure enough, Helen recognised one or two as men who had previously supported their cause, but who had fallen away since the Toleration. James Renwick was listening closely. He had the right to object to any of the jurors, should he be able to give good reason. He shook his head, but then turned towards the jury, looking straight at them. 'For your ain sakes, I trust none of you professes Protestant or Presbyterian principles, or adheres to the covenanted work of Reformation.'

The silence in the courtroom, long and charged, was broken by a disturbance from among the jurors. One young man scrambled to his feet, his face deathly white. 'I canna, may God help me, I canna be part of this wickedness,' he cried out, as he turned and ran from the court. There were whoops and cheers from the rabble in the public benches, but to her left, Helen heard Elizabeth whisper, 'God guard and keep that saint.' Helen nodded, sombre. No doubt the man would be in trouble with the authorities, but at least there was still some goodness left in the hearts of Scotsmen.

All this had taken some considerable time, but now the interrogation proper would begin. Dalrymple stepped forward. Helen remained focused on Mr Renwick. His brown eyes seemed to have sunk deeper into his thin, colourless face, and her heart ached at the strain she could see on him. Yet his concentration was absolute, and he answered Dalrymple's questions in the clear voice which had commended the Gospel from a rock in the Pentlands. The usurper might be the late king's brother, but by the Word of God and the ancient laws of this kingdom, he had no right to rule. As for the cess, it was a tax used specifically to suppress the Gospel and so it could not possibly be lawful.

Helen's fingernails dug into her flesh as she listened to him freely explaining his position. She had heard these arguments often. She wondered how his hearers could be anything other than moved by them – and yet, in her heart she knew that every word he spoke simply confirmed his death sentence. She kept her eyes fixed upon him, rarely glancing aside to the other figures in the courtroom but watching, praying, and longing through the sheer power of her gaze to convey her silent support to him. But then Dalrymple made such a dramatic gesture that she turned. Tall and superior looking, with fleshy cheeks and a pronounced nose, he produced a small pocketbook and waved it around the courtroom with a flourish. Helen, who had seen that pocketbook before, glanced quickly back at the prisoner and then closed her eyes. What exactly was written in there?

Dalrymple was leafing through the little book, looking at it with undisguised relish. 'Interesting, aye, surely this is interesting,' he murmured. 'Names, or at least initials. Sermon notes of the most treasonable kind. Very, very interesting.' He looked up swiftly and his tone was incisive. 'Do you hold to the sentiments expressed in this pocketbook, sentiments upon which I believe you expanded at a recent unlawful gathering at the Braid Hills?'

As he clutched the rail, Mr Renwick's fingers were white, but he spoke evenly. 'If you have added nothing, I will own it. What's more, I am ready to seal all the truths contained in that book with my blood.'

Beside her, Elizabeth gave a moan. Helen laid her own hand over the older woman's bony fingers. But now one of the judges, whose name Helen had forgotten, walked across the room and laid a document before Mr Renwick. 'It'll be a summary of the interrogations and his answers,' Nathaniel whispered.

James Renwick took the document and read it through

slowly. Then he lifted his head. 'I canna sign this. To do so would be to acknowledge the authority of this Court, which I will never do.'

Another murmur ran around the court. The judges conferred together, and then Dalrymple, looking irritated, stepped forward. 'You accept that this document is a true record of your words?'

'I couldna have written a better one mysel, and I thank you for it,' replied Mr Renwick, to a ripple of laughter in the room. 'I am heartened to know that my words have been understood! But I dinna acknowledge your authority.'

'Damn the fanatic!' the Earl of Linlithgow spluttered at this. 'Condemn him and be done!'

But Dalrymple took a step back, and it seemed to Helen that a shadow of some kind passed over his face. This man was once a supporter of the Covenanters. He understood how they thought. The advocate's tone was measured as he said, 'I would expect you to be keen to have such a clear statement of your position publicly available, in that case.'

'Sly dog,' breathed Nathaniel. But Mr Renwick looked at him steadily for a moment and then held out his hand for the quill.

'Very well. I will sign the paper as my testimony, but no in obedience to you.' He scribbled his name quickly, whereupon Linlithgow snatched the document and scrawled his own signature. Two witnesses were then called, who briefly asserted that the prisoner had expressed similar sentiments on his first, private examination by the committee of the Privy Council. And then the jury was asked to retire.

As they filed out, Elizabeth asked Nathaniel how long it would take. He shook his head, unsure. Helen took a deep breath, then bent her head and buried her face in her hands. If ever she had needed to pray, then surely now was the time. And yet words would not come. Dear God, dear God. Oh, sweet Jesus. Dear God.

Preserve him.

And yet …

I am ready to seal these truths with my blood.

You will get the white robes.

Footsteps on flagstones and a long creak. The heavy door opened and the jury re-entered, their spokesman at the head. He was a small, grey-haired, ordinary looking man with a kindly face. Surely such a man could not condemn the good to die? 'Bannatyne of Kames,' Nathaniel whispered, scribbling in his pocketbook. 'He is an elder in the kirk in Bute.'

Bannatyne cleared his throat nervously and then, not lifting his eyes from the paper in front of him, began to read. His voice was soft, west coast, and the language was legal, and the blood was thundering inside Helen's head.

But one phrase was quite clear.

'–the said Mr James Renwick is guilty of the crimes libelled.'

Guilty.

Only then did Bannatyne lift his mild head and glance once, quickly, apologetically, towards the prisoner who stood, impassive.

Guilty.

It was nearly over. Someone else rose now. 'The dempster. He will pronounce sentence,' murmured Nathaniel. And there was, of course, no doubt about that sentence. The mutterings and murmurings from the public benches fell silent, the foot shuffling, the coughing. The judges and the jury, in their turn, were still. In the cold silence the people were waiting and, it seemed suddenly to Helen, even heaven itself was waiting.

'Forasmuch as it is found that Mr James Renwick, preacher, is guilty of the treasonable crimes mentioned … the said Mr James Renwick is to be taken upon Friday next, the tenth of February, betwixt two and four o'clock in the afternoon, to the Grassmarket of Edinburgh, and there to be hanged on a gibbet till he be dead; and all his lands, heritages, goods and gear whatsoever to be forfeited and escheat to his Majesty's use, which is pronounced for doom.'

Her eyes were closed now, against these self-satisfied men in their robes and wigs, and against this awful, wicked Scotland of theirs which would take one so gentle, so steadfast, so true – and hang him on a gibbet till he be dead. Dimly she heard the judge ask if he wanted more time. And around her the floor, the walls, the very room lurched, and she opened her eyes to steady herself within it, and she was looking right at him. His head was held high and all the strain had been smoothed away. He smiled as he answered, 'Long or short, it is all one to me. My Master's time is best.' Then he turned and he looked at them – at Helen, at Nathaniel, at his mother and his sister – and he nodded. Just once, but unmistakably. And then they took him, and he was gone.

*

It had seemed such a good idea in the daylight.

Now, as Jonet and Beatrix made their way along the unfamiliar track towards Edinburgh in the gloom, the elder girl was far less sure. The early morning world was not so much dark as deep blue, as blue as the paint on Mam's treasured Dutch plate, which had been given to her by her mistress on her marriage and stored high out of the reach of small hands ever since. An owl hooted repeatedly somewhere, and Beatrix's fingers tightened on her arm. As they walked on, the blue began to lighten, shot through with ghostly glimmers of day, until it gradually faded to reveal a thawing landscape.

Jonet had never been to Edinburgh before, and to travel there with little idea of where she was headed, with only a thirteen-year-old lass for company, was beginning to seem unwise to say the least. She had journeyed with Beatrix once before, through the hills to Pentland, but that was a familiar route on which there were few travellers. Here, even at this early hour, they met a surprising number of others on the road. There was the hawker selling fish 'fresh frae the Forth' whose stink lingered long after he was out of sight. There was a minister dressed in black whose route crossed theirs; he interrogated them, clearly disapproving, but eventually went on his way. And most alarming of all were the soldiers, three of them riding at speed, but, thank God, they didn't slow up at all and were gone in a filthy splattering of mud. Jonet sensed threat at every turn, but beyond the odd lewd remark thrown their way, no one interfered with their progress.

Weary and footsore, they passed through the West Port a little before midday and entered a city in ferment. By this time, Jonet was lightheaded with exhaustion and unsure which way to turn. 'You need something to eat,' Beatrix said. 'Come, let's find a shop. I have the coins my mother gave me.'

It was not a shop but a streetseller they found, a scrawny wee lass about the same age as Beatrix with a huge basket of freshly baked bread strapped to her front. They made their purchases and Jonet moved aside, but Beatrix lingered. Jonet broke a piece off the loaf she had bought. It smelled good and tasted even better. Just a short distance above her head, a woman was hanging out of a window, bellowing for her child to come home.

Beatrix came alongside. 'What were you doing?' Jonet asked.

The younger girl's dark eyes were clouded. 'I asked her about Mr Renwick.' Jonet glanced round nervously, but Beatrix shook her head. 'You dinna need fash. She says the entire town is speaking of him. The trial was yesterday. He is to hang the morn.'

The bread in her mouth was suddenly dry and coarse. 'Hang,' she whispered.

'Aye. But like I say, the entire town is in uproar about it.

She says there are protests taking place outside the Tolbooth. That's where we must go. That's where my mother will surely be. It's this way, so she says.' Beatrix's voice was trembling, but she moved forward with determination, pushing aside the offer of bread. Jonet followed. He was to hang, then. It was what they had expected since they first heard he had been taken, but she had not thought she would be here when it occurred. Would Beatrix and Helen want her to go and watch? She couldn't imagine anything more horrible. She might only have known him a short time, but she would never forget that he had spoken to her with tenderness and respect when all others had offered nothing but scorn and condemnation. She remembered the clean, sharp summons of his words and the honesty of his gaze. She had expected to meet a vengeful fanatic and had found instead a young man who, under enormous pressure, brought encouragement to his people. And that day among the hills, his words had somehow broken through her hopelessness, promising something as free as the wind which carried the music of the ancient psalms. She might not think of herself as one of his followers, but she couldn't bear to watch him die.

Beatrix was hurrying up the curve of the street ahead of her. Already weary after their journey, Jonet struggled to keep up. She slowed to a more comfortable pace and began to pay more attention to the sights and sounds of the city around her. Despite everything, she was surprised by a faint excitement stirring in her heart. The death of James Renwick was a tragedy, but Edinburgh was a grand place to be for all that. The people rushing about, the noise and laughter and singing and shouting, even the patchwork of smells – how invigorating it was after the oppressive atmosphere of Calder, where everyone watched you constantly. She had escaped once before, to the dairy loft, but Will's treachery had dragged her home amid grime and sackcloth. Now that was nearly over. Maybe she could leave Calder and hide in

214

the city, amid its life and its energy and its noise. Here in Edinburgh, could she possibly be free at last?

They had reached the Lawnmarket, and the thoroughfare outside the Tolbooth was, as they had been told, surging with protesters. She lost sight of Beatrix almost at once, the girl darting into the heart of the noisy throng of people. Jonet stood on the edge and watched, leaning against a wall and resting a hand on her bairn. The crowd was made up almost completely of women, and some were weeping while others were chanting, calling for the release of James Renwick. Members of the city guard stood on the fringes, evidently unwilling to get involved. Close to her stood two older women, arm in arm. 'Sic a bonny young man,' one said. 'It's a shame, that's what it is.'

'He's a fanatic though, Kate.'

'Well I ken that, but he's just a lad, and a bonny one an a,' said Kate, wiping tears away with the edge of her shawl. 'What's the world coming to. It's right what they say, this king willna rest until he's done awa with all who oppose him and handed Scotland ower to Rome. I dinna like it, Jenny. I dinna like it.'

Suddenly Beatrix was in front of her. She hadn't seen her coming among the crowds, and Jonet thought what a perfect place this was to hide, right enough. 'The folks we seek havena come here,' the younger girl said with care. 'But someone has told me where to find them. Come with me. It's this way.'

As they continued down the High Street, Beatrix was almost skipping, brimful of energy. 'I dinna believe they will hang him. How can they, with the whole city in uproar about it? We must just keep praying that they will let him go free – just as they freed my mother when my friends and I prayed for her. God will save him, and then all the judges and the ministers and all these other people will ken that Mr Renwick has been right all along. About everything.'

Jonet said nothing. The authorities had been hunting for James Renwick for months, years even. Now they had him, there was not a puppy's chance in the dog pit of them letting him go free. Beatrix's words, her renewed hope, reminded Jonet how young she was. She slipped an arm round the girl's thin waist. 'You're cauld. Let's find your Mam.'

All at once the energy went out of the younger girl. Her voice was so quiet that Jonet nearly missed what she said. 'I thought he would marry her.'

'Who?'

'James Renwick. I thought he would marry my Mam.' There was an unevenness in her voice now. 'He used to bide with us, and I'd be lying awake in bed and I would listen to them. They were speaking quietly, but I could hear them. And then sometimes they werena speaking, they were just quiet. I thought he loved her. And I'm sure Mam loved him. So why did they no wed? I like my stepfaither well enough, but she should have married Mr Renwick.'

Jonet felt a chill inside at the younger girl's words and turned to face her. Beatrix must be stopped from saying any more. A boy running behind them nearly crashed into them and cursed. She pulled Beatrix aside to the shelter of the nearest building. The girl was trembling, in reaction maybe. Jonet remembered all that had remained unsaid, but implied, on that snowy day in the shieling. She had guessed then that Helen held Mr Renwick very dear. But Helen had a husband, and no one knew better than Jonet the cost of even a whisper of adultery.

What *was* adultery, anyway?

To lie with a man when you didn't know he had a wife?

Or to be married to one man, and give your heart to another?

'I wouldna say these things to anyone else, Beatrix,' she said carefully. 'It could make things gey hard for your Mam. People might no understand.'

216

'But you do.'

The girl was holding back tears. For her mother? For the condemned man she wanted to be her father? Poor, poor bairn. There was noise coming from behind them, more shouting and lots of cheering. Jonet ignored it and pulled Beatrix close to her in a quick hug. 'I think I do,' she said.

They arrived at the dark entrance to the close at the same time as Sandy. He hardly took in that they were there, just bundled them along and into the chilly room before announcing, 'It's been postponed! The execution willna take place tomorrow after all!'

The next few moments were bewildering. Amid the tears and exclamations, Beatrix was seized by her mother, who hugged her close. Jonet stood to one side, unsure what to do. This room was full of people, and she only knew some of them. She felt a heat rise to her cheeks as she noticed Nathaniel deep in conversation with Sandy. She hadn't realised he would be here. She stepped forward to join them, but before she could, a pretty young girl that she had never seen before caught hold of his arm. She was laughing and crying at the same time, and Nathaniel returned her embrace. Jonet looked away quickly and moved over to Helen, who smiled and greeted her. 'Thank you for taking care of Beatrix,' she said. Her face was thin and lined, and all the strength in her dark eyes could not hide her torment. Jonet thought again of Beatrix's words, and of the infinite pain of losing something which was never yours to begin with.

'She took just as much care of me,' Jonet replied, looking round for somewhere to sit down. Helen noticed.

'You're pale – you must be worn out from the journey. Here, have a seat, I'll get you a drink.'

Jonet followed her direction, thankful. Between physical weariness and the contrasting emotions of the last few hours, she was exhausted. She sipped the ale and glanced across the room. Nathaniel and the girl were still in conversation. Helen followed her gaze. 'That's James Renwick's sister Meg,' she said quietly.

But Sandy was now speaking to the whole group. 'I think they would prefer not to hang him,' he said, when they were all seated around the fire, some on stools and some on blankets and cushions on the floor. 'He is so steadfast, so sure, they're afraid of the effect on the people. We saw the protests in the streets today. They're doing all they can to persuade him to back down. Only he never will.'

'His friends are no longer allowed to see him, in case we strengthen his resolve – as if his strength comes from us!' Helen said with scorn. 'Only Elizabeth and Meg may see him now. Meantime, they send anyone they can think of who might change his mind.'

'He is patient with them all,' said his mother quietly. 'That is, all but one group of priests who keep coming to argue with him. He told them to be gone, for he will live and die a Presbyterian Protestant.'

'I swear they never thought it would come to this,' Sandy continued. 'They judged him by their ain character and thought he would give way to save his life. Now they're shamed, for the whole world can see they lied about him. We heard this morning that even the King's Advocate himsel, John Dalrymple of Stair, has tried to persuade him to acknowledge the king's authority. Like Pilate, washing his hands. No doubt that man is tormented in his soul, for not only has he turned his back on the Lord's Covenant, he will have the blood of the Lord's servant on his hands.'

'So is there hope, then, if they are feart to go through with it?' Jonet asked.

Helen lifted her head, and though she looked at Jonet, she was staring into a place Jonet could not see. When she spoke it might have been to herself.

'Dear God, how I wish that could be true. But I have

looked into his eyes, and he already has one foot on the ladder that reaches to heaven.'

Jonet spent three nights with them in that damp, smoky room, relishing her freedom. During that time people came and went and the story remained the same – the authorities were afraid to execute James Renwick and were doing all they could to persuade him to back down, but he remained steadfast. On the Sabbath some others sidled into their hiding place to join them for worship, with the praise led once more by Nathaniel. Jonet watched him. Three days she had been living in this room with him, and although there had never been a repeat of that disconcerting moment of intimacy at Helen's house, she was enjoying being in his company. He had set up a little corner of the room as his workspace, two upturned crates with a single candle serving as a desk. Last night, she had stood watching him as he covered sheet upon sheet with words, marvelling at the fluency with which the ink flowed over parchment, an unexpected longing stirring in her heart at the mysterious sight of the writing she could not read. Mam had taught her to shape the letters of her name but had had neither time nor ability to do much more, and there had only been schooling for Davy. Nathaniel sensed her presence and looked up. He had a smudge of ink across his forehead and his black hair was even wilder than usual.

'You spend every evening at your papers,' Jonet said. 'What do you plan to do with all this writing?'

He held up an inky finger and kept writing furiously, then laid down his quill. 'I want to gather as much direct testimony as I can from those who have shared in our struggle for the Covenant.'

'But surely that's dangerous.'

Nathaniel nodded. 'That's why in all my notes I use cipher. But Mr Renwick is sure that the time will come when this story can be told – when it *must* be told. And so

I'm writing down all I can recall from those I met in the stinkhole of Dunnottar, and all that's happened since. Later, God willing, I'll travel our land seeking out stories of the ministry of saints like Donald Cargill, Sandy Peden, Richard Cameron. One day the world will read my book and will understand why they died.'

She found herself unaccountably moved. 'That's such a grand ambition to have. I envy you. I can write little more than my own name for only my brother attended the school, and that for just a year or two.'

He smiled then, and she felt the floor shift slightly. 'I'm sure that's no fault of yours. There's a generation in Scotland which has been robbed of the learning it deserves. It was the dream of the Reformers that each bairn in Scotland would be taught to read and write. Boy and girl, rich and poor. Pray God that one day this strife will be ower and we'll be free to make that happen.' He paused. 'Meantime, I could teach you, a wee bit?' Then, perhaps seeing the confusion on her face, 'I'm sorry, I dinna mean to offend.'

Dear God. To learn to write. Possibility upon possibility seemed to be opening up to her here in Edinburgh! But still Calder awaited her. Always Calder, pulling her back, tightening the cords around her. She took a deep breath. 'Why would I be offended? It was I who mentioned it. But although it's right kind of you, I think' – she hesitated and twisted her fingers together tightly – 'I think I willna be here lang enough to take up your offer. But thank you.'

He shook his head. 'I mean it. If things change, then I would be glad to help you. It would grieve me to think that my wee Sarah could be deprived of the chance to learn to read and write, and if that's true for her then it's true for all girls and boys alike. Pray God for peace in our land to allow it to be so.'

'Where is Sarah?' Jonet asked.

'With my sister.' His soft dark eyes were troubled. 'But

she has five bairns of her ain and little time to look to another. I worry about her, but I need to be here.'

She left him to his papers then, but she noticed Helen watching as she turned away. And although there was regret at having to turn down his offer, she glowed that he had even thought of it. She hadn't had much conversation with him since. He wasn't often in the house, spending most of his time out in Edinburgh meeting with other supporters, but when he was here, she couldn't help but notice that he paid a good deal of attention to Meg, who hung about him, as well as to James Renwick's mother.

Nathaniel led them that Sabbath in worship which was particularly heartfelt. They prayed fervently for the miracle of release, almost seeming to convince themselves that there was hope. Jonet watched and listened to them, her spirits low. She didn't for one moment believe that the authorities would let Mr Renwick go free. Later, the little group dispersed. Elizabeth and Meg went once more to visit him, while Helen and Beatrix began to prepare some mutton stew for the evening.

It was a wet day, and Sandy and Nathaniel were pulling on their outdoor clothes to venture out when there came a loud rattle of the tirling pin, followed by urgent hammering on the outer door. They looked at one another with the usual wariness, and Sandy opened the door. There was astonishment in his voice. 'Davy!'

'Where is she? Get out of my way.'

'Easy, man!' Sandy laid a hand on his good-brother's arm, but Davy shook him off.

'Where is she?'

Jonet had been standing at the table, chopping carrots for Helen's stew. Her fingers tightened on the knife and she turned to him across the smoky room. 'Are you looking for me?'

'Well of course I am, you daft bitch.' Davy was rain-soaked and trembling with fury.

Sandy, taller and broader, moved right in front of him. 'Enough of that. Show some courtesy,' he said. Davy tried to move round him, but Sandy continued to block him. 'Just you calm down, and then you can tell us why you're here.'

'I ken why he's here,' said Jonet, working hard to keep her voice steady. 'You'll have come to take me hame to meet with the minister, aye? Kind of you.'

Davy ignored the sarcasm. 'What did you think you were doing, running awa here? It took me lang enough to find you. And what kind of a fool are you, anyway, lodging with traitors to the king?'

Nathaniel had paused in the act of strapping his boots, and now he stepped forward. 'I dinna ken you, chiel, but I dinna like your tone. You either do as this guid man says and calm yoursel down, or you leave.'

Davy looked between the two of them, furious but helpless. Jonet watched as he tried to gain control of himself, and she was reminded of the wee lad Davy in a rage. He ignored the men and spoke directly to Jonet. 'I have a horse outside which will bear us baith. Gather your gear, we are leaving for Calder.'

Jonet turned aside. Of course, she had known she would have to return – and yet, each anonymous day in the city had fanned a little more life into the tiny flame, and had strengthened her hope that there might be another way. Now an icy draught of panic threatened to snuff it out completely. 'Has he returned?'

'No, but think if he had! How would it have looked if you werena hame yet again? Thank God I returned when I did and found you gone. Come with me now and there will be no harm done. You'll meet the minister on Tuesday and naebody will ever ken.'

'And if she doesna choose to?' This was Helen, speaking for the first time. Davy glared at her.

'What business of yours is that? But she will, else she'll be in sackcloth all her days. That right, Jonet?'

She tried her best to rekindle that wee blaze of hope. 'I dinna care what you think of me, Davy, no, nor the folks in Calder either. I'll bide here in the city and make a life for mysel.' But she could hear for herself that her retort sounded as childish as Davy's had done earlier. Why did speaking to her brother aye strip the years from her? He laughed his scorn in her face.

'And what kind of a life might that be – the life of a whore perhaps? For make no mistake, Jonet, this is the only chance for you and your bairn to have a respectable life. Dinna lose it.'

Her brother must really hate her, to want her gone so much. This room, this Edinburgh life, was moving out of focus. Inverness. She gripped the edge of the table to keep herself steady. Then Helen's arm slipped round her, a solid, reassuring buttress.

'Jonet kens she can stay here with me.'

'Aye, and what a lot you have to offer her!' retorted Davy, waving his arm scornfully around the room. 'A pigsty would gie more comfort! As if I would leave her in this den of thieves and vipers. My sister is coming hame with me.'

If he scorned and hated her as much as he did, why did he care what happened to her? Surely if she chose to take her chance in the teeming heart of Edinburgh without a certificate of good conduct from the kirk, he could just wash his hands of her? This was Davy. She had known him forever. Helen's support and Davy's riddles combined to clear the haze, and she began to see what she must do. 'I willna marry him,' she said.

'But you must.'

'Why must I, Davy? Why does it matter to you? What's in it for you?'

He glared at her. 'What do you think? I want to save Mam

the shame of a bastard grandchild. If you had any thought to her, you would do the same.' But he did not quite meet her eye.

She nodded slowly, still with that new clarity of thought, and gently laid down the knife and moved away from Helen. 'I will come with you, I will meet the minister, and I will be restored to the congregation. But I'm warning you, I willna marry him.'

His shoulders relaxed. She was coming with him, and no doubt he was confident he could bully her into marriage once she was there. But the man she was meant to wed was not yet in Calder. She would take this opportunity to have her sentence lifted, and then return to Edinburgh with a kirk certificate. This was where her future lay, this vibrant city of life and opportunity. This was where she would be free. She smiled at Helen, her friend. 'Thank you,' she said. 'I'll be back soon.'

*

Sandy said he would accompany them to the town walls. Helen and Nathaniel watched them go. 'I hope she is strong enough to keep to what she has said, but I fear for her,' said Helen, returning to stir the stew. His earlier plans forgotten, Nathaniel pulled a seat up close to her and watched.

'Would marriage be such a bad thing?' he asked.

'In this case I believe it would be. This man will take her far from everyone she kens, and she's but a young lass who was wronged and has paid dearly. I dinna believe she should pay further, but I dinna trust that brother of hers.'

'But there is to be a bairn. What does this Highlander want with her?'

Helen laughed without humour. 'What do most men want in a woman, Nat, especially one so much younger? Someone to keep his house and warm his bed for free. But och, I've grown fond of the lass. I fear for her.'

Nathaniel was silent. His long white fingers fidgeted

224

absently with a frayed thread on his sleeve as he stared at the steam rising from the pot. For a while Helen was silent too, and then, not looking at him, she said, 'You could do worse.'

'What?'

'Jonet. You could do worse. She's a guid lass, and you could do with someone to care for Sarah. And she likes you, any fool can see that.'

'Heaven save us, Helen!' Nathaniel exclaimed. 'You're worse than my mother!'

She laughed. 'Ach Nat, I wouldna suggest it if I hadna seen the way she looks at you. I ken you're still grieving, but grief doesna keep a house nor mind a bairn.'

He looked set to argue, then all at once covered his face with his hands. When he looked up again, she felt a twinge of remorse. 'How can you even be speaking of this when James is condemned to die?' he asked quietly, and his pain echoed her own sorrow.

Helen swallowed. 'Aye, Nat, but he wants us to carry on. And he wants you to travel the land, gathering the testimonies of those who have held faithful, and to publish them for all the world to read. A wife would be a grand help to you in that, especially to ensure Sarah is well cared for.'

He pulled the thread free. 'I had wondered–' He stopped and got to his feet. 'That's enough. I willna speak of this again, and I would ask you no to either. I'm awa to see what news there is out there.'

She didn't argue but watched him go. There was a slight smile on her face, but it soon passed. She was burdened for Jonet, but there was only so much room in her heart for anxiety, and soon James Renwick filled her thoughts once more.

*

Jonet sat alone in the cottage in Calder waiting for the minister.

Davy had omitted to mention that he was bringing her

225

home to an empty house. 'Mam and Mary have gone to stay with Kirstie,' he said as he helped her dismount in the darkness. 'Mam was fretting, what with Kirstie's man being caught up in all that business in Edinburgh.' Davy himself slept in the house but was gone at daybreak. It was so strange to be here alone. This was the home of her childhood, its nooks and its beams still redolent with memories of her father. She carried out the daily tasks, cleaning and washing, preparing food and seeing to the hens, but never in all her days had the home she grew up in been without the laughter and activity and inconsequential squabbles of family life. It was an absence which felt bleak, and yet another reminder that her future lay elsewhere.

By the time the light was fading on Tuesday she had been far too long with her own thoughts and could settle to nothing. She sat by the fire with her needlework barely touched on her lap, waiting for the minister to chap the door. The wind was bending round the house, creaking the cruck frame and whistling under the thatch, rustling memories and doubts out from every corner. She tried to summon the spirit of Helen, the clarity and support she had known with Helen's strong arm around her waist, but there was nothing. Instead, thoughts of Helen prompted only fear for the fate of her Edinburgh friends. Nathaniel, with his long fingers and his untidy sweep of hair, who had offered to teach her to write. Even now, he could have been arrested, and where was she? Sitting in an empty house waiting for the minister to come so that she could beg forgiveness for her shame. How could she even have thought Nathaniel could look kindly on a disgraced woman like her? No, her fate surely lay elsewhere.

She shivered. She still held to her decision to refuse to be married against her will, but her fingers shook as she pulled the needle through the hem of a dress for the bairn, stitching fear into her soul as she worked. What if it was not the minister who appeared at the door? What if it was the man from Inverness? What would she do then, alone in this house? She had seen the way he looked at her, had felt the heat in his grasp. Aye, her declaration that she wouldn't have him would be futile if he came this way while she was here alone. In his eyes she knew she was already his, and he would make it so.

She would never have come if she'd known Mam was from home. So many times over these two days she had nearly turned and fled back to Edinburgh. Yet she clung to the unexpected clarity she had experienced when Davy confronted her. Freedom from her sentence was within reach, and she must grasp it.

A knock sounded on the door.

Jonet started, jabbed herself with the needle, and dropped her work on the floor. As she bent to pick it up, the door scraped open. *Please God, please God.* It was the minister who entered with a rush of cold air, and she was weak with relief, for all her heart beat ever faster.

There he stood before her, Norman Mackenzie, dressed in the black garb and white bands of his position. The man who gloried in her misery week after week from his pulpit. He removed his hat, and she thought that the yellowing hair on top of his head made him look like a chicken. The thought pleased her and stilled her fear a little.

'You are alone, Jonet?' he asked.

'Aye, sir.' Helen had told her that Mr Renwick refused to use the titles of those judges who interrogated him, as to do so would be to acknowledge their authority. Now she was facing her own trial.

He sat down on Mam's chair. 'Where's your mother?'

'She's with my sister in Pentland this week.'

Norman Mackenzie nodded his head slowly. 'Pentland,' he said thoughtfully. 'Now there's an uncanny chance. I was hearing of Pentland just earlier this day, in connection with that rogue Renwick. You ken, I suppose, that he is in custody awaiting death? A friend of mine tells me some of his evil tracts were found in a house in Pentland, no less.'

Her finger was bleeding where she had jabbed it with the needle. She hadn't noticed until now. She wiped it on her gown, not wanting to suck the blood away under his eyes.

'My friend tells me,' Mackenzie continued, 'that the dog Renwick has named those who conspired with him in producing and distributing the tracts, in order to save his skin. He will die anyway of course. Best place for that vagabond is swinging on the end of a rope, aye, and then his head and hands on display as a warning to all. Our Scots kirk would be peaceful in these days were it no for the likes of him. But now he has loosened his tongue we can be rid of many of his fanatical associates too.' He looked directly at Jonet. 'Pentland, eh?'

Her mouth was dry, her hands were clammy. Why was he saying all this to her? Could it be true that Mr Renwick had given in, had named his supporters? What would that mean for Helen and Nathaniel and perhaps for Kirstie and Sandy too? Mam and Mary were there right now. She must warn them. How could she warn them? And all the time this unpleasant man was looking at her closely, a little smile on his face, and something knowing in his small, cold eyes. 'Pentland,' he said again.

Aye, he knew.

'So, Jonet,' he said, suddenly changing direction. 'You have presented a petition to the kirk session.'

She nodded. She couldn't speak. There were too many thoughts birling round her head.

'You wish to be received into the communion of the kirk once more.'

She nodded again. He leaned forward. His face was very close to hers. She could smell onion on his breath. 'Answer me,' he whispered.

'Aye, sir.'

'And on what grounds should I recommend you be received?'

She took a deep breath. This was the little speech she had prepared. Her remorse, her realisation of her sin, her repentance. 'I–' she began.

'Go on.'

But the room was full of him, the black-robed man with the tiny gloating eyes. Maybe if she closed her eyes, she could say it. Shut him out. Imagine you're speaking not to this man but to Mr Renwick. *Swinging on the end of a rope.* It swam round her head, the smell of the minister, the sense of him, the thought of Mr Renwick, of Helen, of Kirstie. Bile rose sharp in her throat and she shook her head, unable to speak.

Abruptly, he got to his feet, shoving Mam's chair back. 'You waste my time, Jonet Gothskirk. You are naught but a foolish harlot with no sense of shame. You will appear afore the congregation in sackcloth once again this coming Sabbath and see if that brings you to your senses. And you will remain right here in Calder until that time, hear me? Angus and your brother must just wait a wee bittie longer to get their wish. The discipline of the kirk willna be rushed.' He turned as if to go and then stopped. Mixed with his anger there was something else, something almost like distress. 'I ministered in Carsphairn afore I came here, Jonet.'

She stared at him bewildered.

'Carsphairn. Have you heard of Carsphairn, Jonet?'

Carsphairn. It was familiar, yet the swirling fog wouldn't reveal her thoughts quickly enough to work out what he was saying. She was rigid.

'Carsphairn was my first kirk. It was dear to me, though even then there were rebels who would harass the guid folk who came to hear me. Aye, but I had a near escape, Jonet, for the murderous disciples of that traitor Renwick shot the curate who came after me. Shot him and left him to die in a pool of blood on the threshold I had crossed each day. These Society people are violent rebels against the king and against God, and you would do well to renounce their false teaching.'

His face was scarlet. He glared at her, and slammed the door shut behind him so that the little house shook. Jonet watched him go, then slid to her knees. She hadn't understood much of what he had said, but she knew this much: her sentence was to go on and on, and she was to remain here in Calder. The darkness of it engulfed her.

Angus and your brother must just wait a wee bittie longer to get their wish.

Her head was pounding with his voice, with her own feebleness, and with bewilderment.

Swinging on the end of a rope.

There was no end to it, no end at all. The sound of keening echoed in her ears, and it came from her own mouth. She clasped the swelling of her bairn. Where would it end, dear God, where would this all end?

*

'Where will this all end?'

Nathaniel brought the news that they had dragged Mr Renwick from his cell to be interrogated once more. His mother was fragile tonight. 'Twenty-six years ago this day, I gave birth to him,' she whispered, brushing tears from failing eyes which still saw not just infant James but the other bairns she had borne before him and Meg, every one of them dying. 'Was he preserved for this?'

They had confronted him with the copies of the paper from Helen's house. He freely acknowledged his own part in its production but refused to name any others. According to Nathaniel's reliable source – a guard in the Tolbooth – they threatened him with torture. 'He laughed at them, for even they wouldna dare torture a man already condemned

230

to die. It goes against all the laws of our kingdom. They promised him his life in exchange for just a few names, but he wouldna oblige them.'

These were long, difficult days, but they were hurrying towards their terrible conclusion. Although his friends could no longer visit him, his mother had managed to smuggle out a couple of letters written on the paper Helen had given him. She unfolded one to read aloud, as they gathered round. 'My dear friends in Christ,' she began, and faltered. 'I'm sorry. I canna. Nat, would you?' She held the letter out, her hand trembling.

Nathaniel breathed in as he took it, steadying himself. 'My dear friends in Christ,' he read aloud. 'It has pleased the Lord to deliver me up into the hands of men, and I think fit to send you this salutation, which I expect will be the last.'

Helen closed her eyes, caring nothing for her own tears. It wasn't Nat's voice but the dear voice of James Renwick. She wanted to remember every phrase.

'Since I came to prison, the Lord has been wonderfully kind. I praise the Lord for His enabling me to be plain and positive in all my confessions. I would exhort every one of you to make sure your particular reconciliation with God in Christ, and to be careful in keeping your Societies, to be frequent and fervent in prayer, to read much the written Word of God, and to examine yourselves by it. Beware of the ministers that have accepted this Toleration. Do not fear that the Lord will cast off Scotland, for He will certainly return and show Himself glorious in our land. But watch and pray.' He paused, 'There is nothing in this world I am sorry to leave but you; but I go unto better company. Farewell.'

Later, when the letters had been passed around and read and reread, Nathaniel took them away. Helen watched him, sitting in his corner by the light of one candle, scribbling furiously. She needed no such copy. One phrase in particular was already seared into her memory for as long as she had left on this earth.

There is nothing in this world I am sorry to leave but you. *He wrote those words to me.*

*

Jonet was seated at the table kneading dough when Davy arrived, apoplectic at the news that she would not be received after all this Sabbath. 'But you must!'

'Take it up with the minister then.'

'And I will do that. But you planned this, you stupid bitch, did you not? You planned it to thwart me.'

'To *thwart* you? Forgive me, Davy but it is my marriage that is thwarted and not yours.'

'That's what you think.'

She stopped then, pushing her knuckles into the dough. This was what she had been grasping for, what she had sensed in Edinburgh, the reason behind it all. 'What do you mean?'

He glared at her and then, all of a sudden, the fight leaked out of him. He sat down on the bench by the table and picked at the edge of the dough with his filthy fingers. She refrained from slapping his hand away as Mam would have done. They were on the edge of something far too important. 'Ach, you would ken one day anyway,' he said. 'It so happens that Angus owes your man from Inverness a great deal of money. He has promised to cancel the debt on your marriage.'

She stared at him. 'You are *selling* me?'

'No, I am rescuing you.'

Inside her, a bubble of laughter was rising up. She understood, at last she understood, and it meant there was no need to marry this man from Inverness. None at all. It was all for the sake of Angus the blacksmith, a man she barely knew and cared nothing for. She could make her repentance, shake the dust of Calder from her feet, and set out for Edinburgh and a new life. It was over. Her foolish, foolish brother had created a web which had almost entrapped her, but she was

232

free.

'Ach Davy, I dinna need rescuing. Angus must just find another way to settle his debt, for I am not a part of it. It's nothing to me, nor to you either.'

But her brother's face was grey, and he was looking down at the table. 'That's where you're wrong.'

She looked at him sharply. She had never seen him look this way, weary and beaten. 'Tell me,' she said.

'There is another man who would have Elspet, a goldsmith frae Edinburgh with far greater wealth than I can offer. She doesna want him. But if Angus canna settle the debt another way, he has said that the goldsmith must have her.'

'And you thought to sacrifice your sister for the sake of your own happiness?' she whispered.

'Ach, it wasna like that,' said Davy. 'You were in trouble, and Angus offered a solution. I thought it would be for the best all round. No other man would have you, after all. You would be saved from shame and Elspet would be free to become my wife. And he might have been a guid man.'

He might have been. Jonet thought of the leering eyes, the hanging belly, and shivered. She faced her brother, the dough forgotten in front of her. The depth of his lies and betrayal horrified her, and the 'no other man would have you' still had the power to sting. And yet, somewhere in the midst of it all, she sensed that she was not the only victim. What of Elspet, promised to her brother but to be offered up to another to pay her father's debts? And Davy, for all his bluster, was powerless. What world was this? What cruelty? She reached out and covered her brother's hand with her own, wondering how many years it was since they had last held hands. 'I willna marry him, Davy.'

'Aye.'

'Will you write to him and tell him?'

Davy looked at her. 'It might be too late. He may already be on his way.'

'But you can try.'

'He will call in the debt then.'

Jonet nodded. 'But it's Angus's debt, no yours. You must fight for Elspet, as I have had to fight to escape the fate you planned for me.'

He pulled his hand free. 'All I want is to be free to marry my woman and to begin the life we had planned together.' He swung his legs round and got to his feet. 'I must find Elspet. It's a mess, right enough.'

'A mess,' she agreed, and watched him go.

*

Friday dawned, and this time they all knew there could be no reprieve. They spent the morning together in prayer. The authorities continued to leave them alone; Renwick's sentence was already causing enough trouble on the streets. Nevertheless, they all started when there came a loud and insistent rattle of the tirling pin and a rough voice shouting, 'Open up!'

Sandy and Nat together went to the door. Before them stood two men dressed in the scarlet garb of the town guard. 'The prisoner Renwick has asked for his mother and sister. We will escort you to the Tolbooth.'

With a quick cry, Elizabeth was on her feet. 'Praise be to God.' They had not expected to be allowed to see him today and had taken their leave of him on their last visit. 'Hurry!' cried Meg, but her mother delayed.

'We must take food. Here, what have we, this oatcake, and the apples Sandy brought in. We shall share a last meal with him, at least.'

Helen watched, and envy was a cold snake slithering up her spine. Oh, to have the right to be by his side in these last hours. To have the right to be summoned, the right to break bread with him. Instead she must feed on that last exchange – *you will get white robes* – and the words of his final letter, which he knew would be read in her presence.

There is nothing in this world I am sorry to leave but you.

When later they left their dark little sanctuary – for such it had become over these days – Edinburgh was simmering with macabre excitement. Every execution was a performance to be relished, but the burgh folks had not seen the hanging of such a bonny, young, eloquent preacher for some years. And what sport with the body afterwards? There was sure to be blood and gore to follow. As the little group of Renwick's supporters passed along the close and out into the High Street, they could taste with revulsion the anticipation in the air. Last week's protests had so easily transformed into today's festival. They paused where the waves of people swept round the Tolbooth and looked at one another, a tight little huddle. Here they had agreed to part. Soon the drums would begin to beat, and members of the guard would lead Renwick from the Tolbooth firstly to the town council house and then down to the Grassmarket itself. Sandy was among those who would go straight to the Grassmarket and take up a position as near to the scaffold as possible, for it was sure to be busy. Others, including Helen, James and Nathaniel, would follow the procession from the prison itself. 'Even if he doesna see me, I'll be right beside him every step,' said Helen, no longer caring what others thought.

Already the streets were seething, and Sandy was lost in the throng almost at once. Helen was grateful for the strength of her husband's arm around her as she tried to stand firm against the crowds. Beatrix was not with them. After a stormy scene, the girl had reluctantly agreed to stay in the house with two or three other supporters and pray. Helen was glad. She had no space in her heart today to spare for her daughter's needs.

And then the drums began to beat an ominous rhythm into her head which would echo there for the rest of her life.

Such frustration, trying to see through the crowds. The

door had opened, here they were bringing him out, and yet she could catch no more than a glimpse. There were Elizabeth and Meg, an embrace, and now he was being led away. Oh, how his mother was wailing, now that he had passed from her arms for the last time. She could barely stand upright. The dignified woman was broken and old, and Helen regretted the slither of envy.

Still they beat the drums. They pushed back the crowds, led him forward, and now she could see him, really see him, for the first time. His head was held high and his lips were moving, but she could not hear a word above the insistent beat. Nathaniel was ducking and diving among the crowd, and now he returned to walk beside them. 'What did he say?' Helen demanded.

Nathaniel took his time, collected his thoughts. 'He answered them from Jeremiah: *Know ye for certain, that if ye put me to death, ye shall surely bring innocent blood upon yourselves, and upon this city, and upon the inhabitants thereof.*'

'True,' said her husband, shaking his head.

'Aye, but they close their ears and their minds to the truth he speaks,' said Helen. 'Edinburgh's streets are long since soaked in martyrs' blood. The evil done in this city today shall haunt its closes, aye and its kirks also, for all time to come.'

'Would you believe they offered him one of their tolerated ministers to attend him? He laughed at them and pointed out that, if he would have had one of *them* as a comforter, he wouldna be here this day.'

Still they beat the drums. Moving at the heart of a great mass of people, they followed the route down the Bow, past the nailed-up windows of Major Weir's godforsaken house, and into the Grassmarket, black as it was with the expectant multitude.

Still they beat the drums.

Somewhere here would be Sandy and the others, but it was no use to look for them. Nathaniel, with his mission to document everything in detail, was determined to find his way to the foot of the scaffold. By clinging to his cloak, Helen stuck close to him, and her husband followed behind her. Something very near to panic threatened to choke her, as the stench and the sounds and the great shifting mass of humanity pressed all around. She struggled to suppress it, pushing her way between people, ignoring the curses, shouts and blows that came her way, thinking only of getting as close as possible to the place where he would take his last breath.

To be cheated of the chance to hear his final precious words? Not while she walked free.

They fought their way almost to the front of the crowd, just a short distance from the little huddle of people at the heart of which must be James Renwick, although they couldn't yet see him. And then one of the town guards broke away and came towards them. Alarmed, Helen gripped James tightly by the hand.

'Are you Nathaniel Walker?'

'Aye, that I am,' answered Nat, and if she hadn't come to know him well, she would never have heard the slight tremor in his voice.

'You have permission to accompany the prisoner on the scaffold.'

In the clamour surrounding them, Helen wasn't sure she had heard correctly. Nathaniel threw her a look of bewildered astonishment and then, giving a little shrug, followed the soldier. Helen turned. 'James?'

Her husband shook his head. 'God's ways are mysterious.'

'But is it a trap?'

James slipped an arm around her. 'It may not be. Perhaps he has asked for a friend and has been permitted. And you ken Mr Renwick wants Nat to record everything. This way his words will be remembered, no matter how desperate they are to drown them out.'

And still the drums beat on.

And then he was there. James Renwick, mounting the platform. Fair, slight. Exhausted. Resolute. He turned, he looked out over them all, and Helen couldn't help but let out a gasp. Her hand covered her mouth. Around her the crowd gave a drawn-out sigh, gratified to see him clearly at last. He stood there, his Bible firm in his hand. If he hadn't been dressed in the prisoner's shirt, he could almost have been standing on that rock in the Pentland Hills.

How will we ever manage without him? How can this possibly be the last time? *Strengthen him.*

'Mr Renwick, own our king and we shall pray for you!'

The call came from right behind her. Helen swung round, ready to rebuke, but Renwick responded in a clear, strong voice, 'I will have nane of your prayers; I am here to bear my testimony against you, and all such as you.'

The man beside her wasn't done. 'Own our king and pray for him, whatever you say against us.'

'I'll discourse nae mair with you,' Renwick answered. 'I am soon to appear afore Him who is King of Kings and Lord of Lords, who shall pour shame, contempt and confusion upon all the kings of the earth that havena ruled for Him.'

This provoked cries of 'shame!' and 'treason!' but also another long, gentle *ooh,* as those near the front of the crowd absorbed his words. But James Renwick had already dismissed the heckler from his mind. Even as the drums beat on, he calmly raised his head and began to sing. Helen strained to listen through that awful, endless clamour. With a little thrill she recognised Psalm 103; she knew it well and joined in. Beside her, her husband also picked up the words, and then around them, here and there, she heard one voice after another join together.

O thou my soul, bless God the Lord;

238

and all that in me is
Be stirred up his holy name
to magnify and bless.

The Grassmarket was heaving with a crowd that was mostly gleeful or hostile, the wicked scaffold loomed over them, the air reeked with cattle shit and sweat, and the clamour of the drums beat on. And yet, as the words of the psalm drifted out, tremulous at first and then growing in volume, and as her husband gripped her hand, Helen felt her body tingle with a sense of holiness. Here, in these moments, she would swear the angels themselves were joining James Renwick in his worship.

But unto them that do him fear
God's mercy never ends;
And to their children's children still
His righteousness extends.

The drums beat on, and the authorities waited. They would soon have their prize. He opened his Bible and began to read, as was his right. Again, it was hard to hear, but by straining she could catch some of the 19th chapter of Revelation. She knew the tears were flowing now and did nothing to stop them.

'And after these things I heard a great voice of much people in heaven, saying, Alleluia; Salvation, and glory, and honour, and power, unto the Lord our God.'

And it was so *commonplace*, to have him there before her, reading the familiar words in his voice which carried in it the grace and authority of Scripture; so commonplace, and yet so hideous, so completely grotesque.

And still the drums beat on.

He prayed to his Lord and then turned to the people. She could hardly breathe. He was looking her way.

There is nothing in this world that I am sorry to leave but you.

He told them plainly that he was laying down his life for holding to truths for which he was neither afraid nor ashamed to suffer. He explained his position, the principles she had heard many times. The drums still beat, the crowd still called out, and Nathaniel stood beside him and scribbled in his pocketbook. He was giving up his life as a testimony against a king who thought he could claim and abuse authority which belonged only to God.

They didn't like that. He was ordered to stop. He said, 'I have near done.' He had a long way to go yet.

'You that are the people of God, do not weary, for there is a storm coming that shall try your foundations.'

Aye, that I know. It's all I can do to keep my feet.

'Scotland must be rid of Scotland afore the delivery come.'

They had had enough. They told him to climb the ladder. He did so, and she was no longer breathing. Then he stopped and prayed in a voice as loud as any he had yet used. The drums beat on, but the crowd had fallen strangely still as the moment approached. Helen could hear more clearly.

'Lord, I die in the faith that You willna leave Scotland, but that You will make the blood of Your witnesses the seed of Your Church; and return again, and be glorious in our land. And now, Lord, I am ready.'

Beside her, her husband made a sound she had never dreamed to hear from him, a strangled, smothered howl of grief. She watched them move towards Renwick, ready to tie the blindfold about his face. He pulled back. She gasped. Surely now, at the very end, he would not give way? No, he would not. He turned – not to the crowd, not to the hooded hangman, but to look down at Nathaniel, who still stood below him on the platform. 'As to the remnant I leave,' he called out urgently. 'Tell them from me no to be discouraged. Keep your ground and the Lord will provide you teachers and ministers. And when He comes, He will make these despised truths glorious on the earth.'

So his last thought was for them, his friends, his flock. *Keep your ground.* 'We will,' she said aloud. Reaching into a future she could not yet know and depositing his words for when she was sure to need them.

The Lord will provide.

The hangman moved forward. She saw James Renwick's lips move, then the cloth was tied over his face and she could no longer tell what he was saying. No matter; those last words were surely for his Lord alone. She thought, not for the first time that day, of Mary the mother of Jesus standing at the foot of the cross, watching, faithful and heartbroken, as her beloved son sweated, twisted, bled and died in agony. *Even if he doesna see me, I will be beside him every step.* She would not turn away, she would not close her eyes. She would not miss a second of the time his soul had left on this earth, not even to wipe away the tears. And so she watched intently as the noose was lowered over his slim neck, and as he was turned over the ladder. She watched in horror the seemingly endless struggle, as his beautiful body twisted and kicked and jerked. She watched, until he swung still.

Our River Jordan is very deep but it isna very wide.

And she stood there amid the chaos of the Grassmarket, the jeers and the tears, the screams and the sighs, and she heard none of it. For as his body emptied and his spirit soared, Helen Alexander glimpsed glory through her tears. Her heart had shattered into a thousand pieces and she would mourn the young preacher for the rest of her days, but in that precious moment she sensed they were part of something so much bigger and brighter and more powerful than death or distance or time, something which no human power would ever be able to control. Always there, rarely seen, but for just a second the curtain had twitched back, and it was radiant. The edge of eternity.

Someone tugged her arm. It was Meg, her face swollen

with crying, Nathaniel by her side. Dazed, she couldn't for a moment focus on what they were saying, but Meg thrust something into her arms and turned. And then Nathaniel was pulling her forwards, towards the platform where his lifeless body still hung. 'They say we may take him,' said Nat. 'But we must be quick, lest they change their minds.'

And then she realised that the bundle she now held was a winding sheet.

Meg hurried away. Elizabeth, who had intended to perform this last service, had collapsed with the strain, and her distraught daughter was taking her to safety. The mass of the crowd began to disperse, reluctantly accepting that there would be no ghoulish aftershow, and Renwick's little band of followers made their way tentatively towards the scaffold. Helen took a quick breath. This final task was unexpected, but praise God his own prophecy had been fulfilled, and they had not mutilated his body. She lifted her head. It would be an honour and a privilege.

Two of the guardsmen had cut him down and he lay, a crumpled, disfigured, soiled heap. 'Aye, tak him for burial, but be quick about it,' one said. Helen glanced round. She had prepared bodies for burial many times, of course, at home in Pentland. But where? Surely not here, amid the onlookers and the scoffers. *Lord, where?*

Her husband stepped forward, placed a hand gently on her shoulder. 'I will carry him up to Greyfriars Kirkyard. They have opened the common grave.'

The common grave. For criminals. Dear God.

'We will need water. And light.' The afternoon gloom was closing in all around them. 'Is there nowhere else we can go?'

'We have prepared some for burial in the Chapel of the Hammermen in the Cowgate,' Nathaniel said. 'But I think we should go direct to Greyfriars today, else darkness will owertake us.'

There was sense in this. A young lass stepped forward. Helen had never seen her before, but her red-rimmed eyes spoke of her grief. 'I can bring a lantern frae hame, mistress, in nae mair than five minutes.'

'And I will bring water frae the well,' said another.

Her heart was tight with horror, yet she felt an unexpected surge of warmth at the steadfastness, the commitment, of the little group surrounding her. And then her husband, dear James, stooped and lifted him. Helen felt a sob rise in her throat as she watched him take the young preacher in his arms, holding him as carefully as a sleeping bairn. Nathaniel placed a hand on his shoulder and walked alongside, ready to share the burden. Down from the platform they came, the little procession, with James and Nathaniel carrying the lifeless body in front, and the others following on. Behind them the soldiers wasted no time in dismantling the gallows. There was a crash, a curse, a guffaw. Their task was near done; the tavern awaited. Helen and her friends crossed the Grassmarket and climbed the steep path towards the kirkyard. The young lass with her lantern had joined them, breathless. They entered the kirkyard, the solid mass of the kirk with its square tower looming above them. Shifting shadows hinted at things unseen.

She would not go close to the common grave. She touched James on the arm. 'Here.'

They spread the winding cloth out on the damp ground and laid his lifeless body gently down. It was a task for women. Her husband held the lantern close, and its flame lit up the gleaming tears on his face. Tenderly, so tenderly, Helen and the other women undressed him and wiped away the filth. They worked in silence and without tears, grateful for the privilege of performing this last service. Swiftly his broken nakedness was wound within the white shroud, and then his face was covered for all time. Helen laid her hand on the cloth, tracing its folds, caressing the texture of the

243

weave with fingertips which had known more of his body now than they ever had in life. This intimacy was what she had given up. And as she touched the cloth, she saw white linen spread out across the hillside, wine and bread laid out. *This is the new covenant in my blood.*

All at once she knew that this moment, here in the quiet stillness of the kirkyard, this was her parting. She had done all she could for him. 'Take him,' she said quickly. 'My part is played.'

So they lifted him, James at one end and Nathaniel at the other, and carried his shrouded corpse over to the ground laid aside for criminals. She watched the wavering light of the lantern move between the graves, saw the shadowy figures of the waiting gravediggers, hats removed, surprisingly respectful. The February sky had darkened quickly, and there was a damp smell of rotting leaves and sodden grass tinged with decay which seeped from the open grave. She turned her head to look up at the dark bulk of the kirk itself. Aye, this was where it had all begun. Fifty years ago to this very month, almost to this very day, Scots men and women had gathered in this kirk and kirkyard and had taken it upon themselves to sign a public contract with God on behalf of their nation. The blood and the tears had been flowing ever since. Now, half a century later, they were laying in the ground the one who had been the very best and brightest of them all. Surely there was no hope left.

But the dream which had stubbornly persisted through the decades, the Scotland he believed in and had tried to show them, it still shone faintly through the tears, the blood and the grime.

Scotland must be rid of Scotland afore the delivery come.

Chapter Fourteen

Sunday 19th February 1688

This is the thirteenth Sabbath of Jonet Gothskirk's public appearance in Sackcloth for her Adultery, who at that time should have been received, as she had petitioned: but because of her stupidity, and that she could discover no sense or feeling of her sin, nor sorrow for the same, she was ordained to continue in the place appointed for public repentance.

Such scorn Mr Mackenzie heaped upon her that morning, just a few days after his visit to her home. Such contempt.

Yet it was not his venom towards her, but his gleeful recounting of the execution of James Renwick, which shattered her protective shell.

Nathaniel had brought the news from Edinburgh, arriving on horseback yesterday. She was outside at the time and looked up in alarm when she heard him approaching. After all, Davy's letter to Inverness might not have arrived in time. There could yet be a reckoning to come. But the wild black hair and the shabby overcoat were unmistakable, and a pinprick of light shone through the blanket of her fear as she ushered him into the house.

His face was drawn, and his dark eyes were dull, clouded with the horrors they had seen. 'It's done. They hanged him yesterday.'

She had been expecting it, of course, and yet the words still fell into the silence of the cottage with a hideous, discordant, echoing clang. She reached out a hand towards him, but he didn't notice. 'The others are on their way back to Pentland now,' he said, his voice harsh and brittle. 'I am travelling to my sister's to collect Sarah, but I said I'd come by your place. Helen wanted you to know and wanted to be sure you were safe.'

'I am safe.' She hesitated. How she longed to tell him what had happened since that confrontation with Davy in Edinburgh, and what it all meant for her future. But his shoulders were bowed, and his face was haggard. He was consumed by grief for his friend. Now was not the time.

He nodded his head briefly. 'Grand.' He glanced round. 'No, I willna take a drink, thank you. I must be on my way. Fare well, Jonet.'

So distant, and barely even looking at her.

'Fare well.'

And then he was gone, and it was over. Mr Renwick was dead, and it was over. This wicked world had choked the life out of the person who had first offered her hope. She had been drawn to James Renwick against her initial judgement, despite herself, but now that he was gone, she had nowhere left to turn. This must surely be the end for his little group of supporters who had welcomed her when all others shunned her. They would be broken and they would scatter. Whatever it had been, it was over.

She sat alone in the gloom of the cottage, her face in her hands, and wondered why the tears did not come.

Tears came the next day, as she perched on the stool in the gown of shame and heard Mr Mackenzie's words raining around her ears. She could barely remember the conversation they had had in her mother's house earlier in the week. Possibly he had warned her that her failure to show suitable repentance would bring yet another public rebuke. Her fingers picked at the filthy sackcloth, but she saw only a white winding cloth. She cared nothing for this gown now; nothing for her shame. She cared nothing for the shallow stares of the congregation, not even Davy and his foolish schemes. She perched, head bowed, before the congregation, and his words assaulted her. Stupidity. No feeling of her sin. No sorrow for the same.

No sorrow?

She could feel the tears falling, but this sorrow was in no way for her sin. Four long months she had sat here, determined to show no emotion, but today she had no will, no strength, no resistance. She sat before the minister and the congregation and listened to the rain battering against the windows and his words battering against her soul, and the tears leaked out of her.

If there was a gleam of satisfaction in his eyes, she did not see it. He expounded on her shame, and he gloried in the final triumph over the rebellious traitor Renwick two days earlier, well knowing that every word would wound her. And she sat there, head bowed, tears running, nose dripping, all reserves gone, her grief a deep well fed by such a bitter stream. Aye, she wept now for all that had happened over the past months, for the betrayal which had brought her to her knees and the cruel men who were intent on keeping her there; for her Mam's weary love and the treacherous web her brother had spun. She wept for the innocent bairn she would bring into this ruthless world, already soiled in the eyes of the kirk. She wept for Helen, whose heart had surely been wrapped in a shroud in a bleak Edinburgh kirkyard. And most of all she wept for the preacher on the hillside whose eyes had seen into her soul, and who now lay discarded amid the bones of Edinburgh's thieves and murderers.

And then it was over, and it seemed it might be over forever. Was this what the minister had wanted all along – to see her resistance crumble? To bring her to her knees? Was it all those in power ever wanted?

'Present your petition once more,' he said to her as they left, 'and I believe it will now be received.'

*

247

Back in Pentland they moved around one another in stunned silence.

No deid bell rang for him. No lykewake, no kisting. He had gone to his Maker with a prayer on his lips and had no need of superstition. Nevertheless, familiar customs bring comfort to the living not the dead. But here in Pentland there was no comfort to be found.

His death had created a great noise throughout the kingdom, and utter silence among those who loved him most.

They cleared out of their grimy Edinburgh room and scattered to their homes. Too soon to make plans. Too soon to know whether the authorities would now be satisfied or would continue to hunt them down.

Too soon for anything but wordless grief.

Chapter Fifteen

Sunday 26th February 1688

This day Jonet Gothskirk was received, having showed greater signs of the sense she had of her Adultery with William Murdoch, and declared in Sackcloth her sorrow and repentance for the same sin.

A week later she stepped out of the kirk into the sharpness of the late February air. She had been received into the communion of the kirk once more. The winter was over. She would never have to pull that foul sackcloth over her rounded body again and, God willing, by the time her bairn was born she would be far from this place and its kirk and its people.

As for sorrow, as for repentance? She had known both and was a prisoner to neither.

Today the sun was shining, with just a touch of warmth hinting that spring would soon come again. She would hurry home as fast as she could, rip off the gown and scrub, scrub, scrub, until not a trace of its stench and its feel and its power over her remained. She would rejoice with Mam and Mary, who had returned from Pentland during the week. She would

—

She stopped. The low sun obscured her vision, but the man walking slowly towards her was unmistakable. Davy's letter had not reached Inverness in time, then.

She glanced round. The other kirkgoers were far behind, for she had rushed off at such a pace, and not many came this way anyway. Mam and Mary were at home in the cottage. Davy had sauntered off with Elspet after the service. She was alone.

He was walking towards her, hands deep in the pockets of his coat, not hurrying, but nevertheless she felt the sinister intent as each measured stride brought him closer. She clenched her fists. This was it then. Time to tell him. Foolishly, she wished she could be properly dressed for this meeting – anything but this awful gown. But that meant nothing. Nothing.

'Still in sackcloth, then?' He walked up close to her, far too close, and she remembered the sour smell of his breath. She paused. Perhaps it would favour her if he thought she had not yet been restored.

'Aye.'

He caught hold of her wrist, held it tight. 'I have waited long enough. We leave for Inverness tonight, kirk or no kirk.'

'I would rather die first.'

His grip tightened and he looked down at her, his steely eyes boring into her. 'Is that right, now? Well, die you might, lass, but I'll be having what I'm owed first. You and that fool of a brother of yours have played me long enough. Now come, gather your things, and we'll be off.'

She struggled to pull her hand free, but his fingers were an iron shackle. 'What you're owed is frae Angus, and has nothing to do with me. I'm sorry your journey is wasted but I will never marry you, so let me go.'

He grinned at her then, and in his grin was the leering arrogance of a man accustomed to getting whatever he wanted. 'I dinna think so, my lass. That brother of yours has signed you away. You are mine, you and your bastard both. We can be doing this the hard way or the easy way, but you are coming to Inverness with me.' He yanked her arm, twisting it behind her so that it seared in agony, and he began to push her ahead of him along the path. She tried to struggle, but finding it hurt all the more, she stopped.

'That's better,' he said, letting her arm fall more naturally to her side, but never for a second relaxing the grip which felt as though it would snap her wrist in two. 'This way, aye?'

He was walking her towards her house. Tears of pain half blinded her, but she no longer fought him. She tried to calm herself, to think. There was no way he could force her to go with him, no way at all. Thank God Mam and Mary were back from Pentland; they would summon Davy or the neighbours to help. She walked the last few feet to the open door and stepped in. 'Mam?'

The house was empty.

He slammed the door shut behind her and leaned against it, grinning at her. 'Did I not say? Your Mam and your wee sister went to fetch your brother and Aonghas, to sort this all out once and for all they said. But my horse is saddled and ready to go. We'll be long gone afore they get here.'

And then she was truly frightened for the first time. Her heart was beating loudly, but still she held herself tall. 'I'm going nowhere with you,' she said. Thank God her voice still sounded firm.

The force of the blow across her face caught her completely by surprise. 'Bitch!' he snarled, as she staggered against the table. 'Filthy whore!' He hit her again and she was on the floor, curled in on herself, her arms protectively wrapped round her stomach. 'Do you know how much silver it is I have wasted, coming up and down this road for you? By God, I wouldn't have you as wife now if they were paying me to take you, but I'll have what I'm owed, you whore, I will have you.'

She knew she was screaming, she knew she was fighting, but then there was a hand over her mouth and another wrenching at the gown, tearing the sackcloth apart. She tried to bite on his hand, but he was pushing so hard she could barely breathe, and the back of her head was being driven into the damp earthen ground. She could feel the strength of him as he thrust himself against her, his breeks ripped open, and she flailed about with her free arm for something, anything, with which to hit him. She found nothing at all; there was no way she could fight him off, no way she could survive this. She gasped again for breath, for help, for life – and above his frantic grunting she heard Helen's voice, as clear as could be. *Be strong, Jonet. Resist.*

Resist. She tried again with that free arm. Reaching up and taking hold of those greasy, greying curls, she gripped them and yanked his hair with all the strength she could muster. He loosened his grip just a little, enough for her to bite down hard on his hand. He swore in pain but shifted his hand from her mouth to her throat. He was pushing down now, squeezing, the air was no longer reaching her lungs, the world was losing focus, she could no longer scream, she could no longer fight, she could no longer breathe …

The crash, when it came, was distant, and even when the hands were released from her neck and the weight of him from her body, she hardly knew it. She curled in on herself once more and lay on the ground, eyes closed, painfully gasping for the slightest breath. There were distant sounds of shouting and the crashing of furniture overturning, but the pounding inside her skull was far, far louder. Then a hand on her temple, gentle, a voice. 'Jonet?'

She opened her eyes. Still caught in that terrifying whirlwind of what was real and what was not, she thought it was Helen. A touch on her skin, a face in front of hers, but dancing black pinpricks obscured the features. Gradually the concerned face came into focus. Nathaniel. She struggled to lift herself from the floor. He took her arm and helped her to move slowly into a sitting position. Everything hurt and it was hard to breathe. The floor was shifting. Nathaniel. She turned towards him, leaned forwards, and was sick. All over him.

Maybe an hour later, calm had been restored. The

furniture had been put to rights, and Jonet was seated by the fire with a blanket round her shoulders and a mug of warm spiced wine in her hands. She was still shivering, she ached all over, and occasional sharp pains in her stomach made her fear for the bairn, but she was safe. Nathaniel too had changed his clothes, squeezing into Davy's shirt and breeks in place of the ones now covered in Jonet's vomit. Mam had been fussing round, getting drinks and clean clothes for them all, but even she had been persuaded by Davy to sit.

Jonet had told her story – how he had been waiting for her after the kirk, how he had threatened her and hit her and tried to rape her. White-faced, Davy explained how he had come running as soon as Mam told him of the Highlander's return. He had met Nathaniel riding through and persuaded him to come too. Together, they had entered the house just in time. 'He'll be well on his way to Inverness now, and he won't be back,' said Nathaniel. There was a smear of blood across his cheek. 'We saw to that. Angus'll have nae mair trouble with him either.'

'But what were you doing here in the first place?' Jonet asked Nathaniel. A slight colour spread up his neck.

'I've been in Pentland the last couple of days. Helen's no doing so well. I thought as it might do her good to see you, if you would be willing to come.'

Jonet took a sip. She could feel the warmth beginning to spread through her body, but she was still shivering and every movement hurt. 'I think I maybe need a day or two, but aye, I would be glad to see her. How is she?'

Nathaniel shook his head. 'No well at all. She has taken his loss right hard. If you can come, I have a horse you can ride.'

Jonet looked round the room. 'I thought she was here. I heard her voice.'

'That would be me,' said Mam. 'I should think they heard me in Edinburgh.'

Jonet took another drink. She knew it hadn't been Mam. She made up her mind. 'Helen has been a guid friend to me. I'll sleep here the night and then I'll come the morn. There's nothing to keep me here now. Nothing at all.'

Nothing at all.

After all that had gone before, there was something extraordinarily comforting about riding over the familiar route to Pentland with Nathaniel walking beside her, leading the horse. The pains in her stomach had eased, but she kept an arm cradled protectively around her belly, as though holding the babe in place. By silent agreement, they did not speak about the traumatic events of the day before. Instead, Jonet asked Nathaniel about his friendship with James Renwick and his involvement with the Society people. He spoke of the dark days when he had been chained with over a hundred men and women in the foul dungeon at Dunnottar Castle. He and some others had managed to escape, climbing down the steep, slippery cliff, although two of them had lost their grip and fallen to their deaths amid the crashing waves below. He told her too of his childhood sweetheart who had died giving birth to Sarah. 'She was as committed to the cause as I was,' he said. 'When she was gone, I was near mad with grief, and for a while I became so reckless it's a miracle I wasna taken a second time. When Sarah was tiny, I paid her little enough attention. But then she grew, and she began to smile and to take an interest, and it was James Renwick who reminded me of my duties towards her. For many can fight for the cause but only I can be faither to Sarah.'

'And now?' asked Jonet.

'Now that we have no preacher, I dinna ken what will become of us. But on the scaffold, he promised the Lord would bring us new ministers, and we must just be faithful, and pray and wait, as we have done so many times afore.' There was a break in his voice as he spoke. Without thinking she placed a hand on the hand with which he held the leading rein. He looked up at her, and smiled, and didn't pull his hand away, instead letting his long fingers interlock with hers.

The hint of spring in the air had slipped away, and this landscape was asleep, still shrouded in winter. She heard a repeated sound above and looked up. 'Look,' she said to him in wonder, and they both paused to watch the arrowhead of geese flying high overhead. 'They believe spring is on its way, anyhow,' said Nathaniel. For many more miles they travelled in a companionable silence. The short afternoon was disappearing into darkness as they arrived in Pentland, and Jonet was thinking of nothing so much as the pot of nourishing soup which would surely be hanging over Kirstie's fire. Nathaniel helped her down. She pushed open Kirstie's door, but the house was empty and the fire smoored to a faint red glow.

'They're no here,' she said.

'I'll stable the horse beside Sandy's, and then we'll go round to see Helen and James. That's where they will be.'

Despite herself, Jonet felt the fear stirring once more as they approached Helen's house. It was a very short time since the authorities had been here and ransacked the place. Would they now have turned their attentions towards Mr Renwick's friends and supporters? Those last days in Edinburgh had left no secrets; every one of them was marked out to all who cared to notice. And yet, when she thought of the horror and grief of the events which had played out in the Grassmarket, and their likely impact on Helen, she knew she must draw alongside her dear friend. For such, somewhere along the line, had this woman become.

Inside they were all at prayer, so Nathaniel and Jonet slipped in quietly and sat at one side, close together. Kirstie caught her sister's hand and gave it a tight squeeze, but said nothing. James Currie was reading from Scripture.

'And it came to pass, when they were gone over, that Elijah said unto Elisha, Ask what I shall do for thee, before I be taken away from thee. And Elisha said, I pray thee, let a double portion of thy spirit be upon me.'

As he read, Jonet found herself watching Helen. The older woman sat at the table, rigid and morose. Her face was grey in the dim light of the cruisie lamp which flickered between them. Her eyes were swollen, and as her husband read the words, more tears began to slide down the crevices of her face. Jonet looked at the children. Jamie was staring at the floor, shuffling his feet in the straw and determined not to look at his mother. Charlie looked scared. But Beatrix was watching her mother, and her big dark eyes glowed in her white face with their strange intensity. Jonet shivered.

'Our hearts are sair,' said James, 'but the Lord is aye faithful. We have lost our leader, but we havena lost the spirit of Almighty God.'

Helen lowered her head to rest on her arms on the table, and her body shook with sobs. Jonet had rarely seen a woman so bereft, no, not even Mam when their father died, and her own eyes pricked with tears. Helen had always been so strong, so certain, so full of determination. Jonet stood up and moved round behind Helen, placing both hands gently on her shoulders. 'James, I fear your wife isna well,' she said. 'She needs bed rest. Let me help her prepare.'

'Please do, please do help her,' said James Currie at once, his round face creased with bewildered sadness. Jonet led Helen beyond the curtain and helped her to undress. Helen was as compliant as a child, and silent too. It was only when Jonet was combing out her long hair that she spoke.

'I canna believe he's gone.'

'I know. But he–'

Helen caught Jonet's hand and stopped her. 'I still think he's out there somewhere, speaking for liberty, speaking for Christ. For so long I have prayed for him, day and night.

256

There wasna a night these last few years that I didna go to bed believing he might chap our door in the darkness. I'm listening out for him still. And then I close my eyes, and I see him hanging on that rope, his beautiful face blackened, and I think I will never sleep again.' She began to cry again. Jonet held her and said nothing, just stroking the long dark hair threaded with grey. Gradually Helen's breathing began to calm. Jonet helped her to lie down and sat beside her, rubbing her back as she would for wee Mary after a nightmare. She could hear the low murmur of voices from beyond the curtain. When Helen's breathing became more even and she had slipped into sleep, Jonet returned to the room, her heart weighed down with her friend's grief. Kirstie and Sandy had already left. Nathaniel was standing by the fireside. 'How is she?'

'Sleeping.' Jonet shook her head. 'I'm weary. James, I will leave you for now.'

'I'll come with you,' said Nathaniel. She glanced at him and then nodded quickly. They stepped out into the inky darkness and walked arm in arm the short distance to Kirstie's house, where light now flickered from a candle left in the window for them. Inside, the sisters embraced. 'Helen is broken,' said Jonet.

Kirstie nodded, her eyes widening as Nathaniel pulled Jonet down to sit on the bench beside him and held her close. 'She has made hersel fevered,' she said. 'The same thing happened after she was in prison, though that was afore I came to Pentland. She feels things right sair. But I trust her strength and her faith will lead her through this dark time.'

'She loved him.'

Kirstie threw her a quick look. 'Aye, I believe that she did. But she loves James Currie also. Pray in God's mercy they will be blessed with bairns of their ain, for she is in sair need of comfort.'

Jonet laid her hand on her own stomach and leaned back

257

against Nathaniel's arm, watching as Kirstie prodded the fire into life. There was a sadness hanging heavy over them all, as they grieved for James Renwick and for the horror of the world that had murdered him, and as they waited in dread to see how events would now unfold. And yet, even in the sadness and the fear, she was aware of the tiniest stirring of joy in her own heart. She was done with the sackcloth and done too with Inverness and with men who sought to control and abuse her. Nat's arm lay warm and comforting across her shoulders, and although it was too soon to say what that might mean, it felt good. The new kindling caught, and flames flickered upwards, sending shadows dancing around the walls. Winter was nearly over. This land into which her bairn would be born remained harsh and unrelenting, but she had walked through the worst of it and she had kept her footing.

Today, that was enough.

Chapter Sixteen

1706

The leaves still cling to the trees in Greyfriars Kirkyard, but their greens are fading to yellows and browns. Helen stands beneath the spread of one such tree, at a distance from the small group of dark-clad men. Her heart is thudding in her breast and her stomach tight with nausea. Yet there is nothing whatsoever to fear.

She clasps her gloved hands tightly together. Today's ceremony will be formal, orderly, honourable. She could stand with them if she chose – James urged her to – but she prefers it this way. She has not been back to Greyfriars Kirkyard in eighteen years, and the memories of that godforsaken February afternoon when they wound his lifeless body might well drown her. Better to be alone.

She breathes in. That smell again. Damp leaves, wet grass, and raw, screaming pain.

The slope down to the Grassmarket is steeper than she remembers, the spires and rooftops appearing through dense smoke far below. She has only been back to Edinburgh a handful of times in all these years. It is not a place which does her good. She still loathes the clamour, the chaos and the greed, the streets running with filth, the oppressively tall buildings looming above dark, narrow closes. The airlessness. And at each turn, each corner, another memory waits to skewer her heart afresh. Even now she cannot fathom how Nat and Jonet could bear to set up home in this evil place, to raise their children here.

But she has come today, because today is the culmination of a great deal of prayer and planning. Today, at last, the city of Edinburgh will unveil a fitting memorial to James Renwick, and to all the other saints who were martyred for the Covenant and discarded among the murderers and thieves in the common grave in Greyfriars Kirkyard.

History will record that the memorial was designed and paid for by James Currie, merchant in Pentland. History will not record the power of a wife's persuasion. None of these robed and wigged men standing here remember, if ever they knew, that those who paid to erect this stone are the very same family who, hunted and hounded, gathered his lifeless body into their arms eighteen years earlier. And if they do know, if they do remember, they will not understand, because not one of them has ever paid the cost of such faithfulness.

She watches as the words are spoken, as one of their black-frocked ministers says a prayer. She feels the familiar twist of bitterness. And then they are finished and they are walking back towards her, James dragging his bad leg behind him along the muddy path. It's so much worse these days. He stops and lifts his elbow for her to take his arm, and for them to walk together to join Jonet and Nat who are waiting by the kirkyard gate. She shakes her head. 'Just give me a wee minute.'

He understands. He has always understood, her dear, faithful husband, and she still marvels at it. But today her thoughts are for her long dead leader, her love. She waits until they have moved away and then walks quickly to stand in front of the stone. A simple block closely inscribed with the words she and James worked on together, and – the part which thrills her heart – at the foot an open Bible, carved with words from the Book of Revelation, words of her choosing. Her finger reaches out, tracing the fresh lettering.

And white robes were given to every one of them.

She sees herself again, her younger, slimmer self, standing in the damp darkness of his prison cell, blinded by tears, and telling him, 'You will get the white robes.' His reply, 'and palms in my hands'. Eighteen years later, a sob of grief rises from her heart once more.

Even now, she cannot often bring herself to revisit the horror and wickedness of the days and weeks surrounding his murder. Her horizons closed in on that day, and her world became a place of utter black despair. Only the care of her husband and her friends, and the dawning knowledge of the growing life within her, slowly lifted her out of that pit. And when she raised her eyes to the world around her once more, she discovered that things had begun to spin and change at an alarming pace. Destabilising. For the first time in her life, Helen found it impossible to know in which direction she should be facing. Scotland threw out the bishops and became a Presbyterian country once again. The tyrant King James fled to the continent, taking with him that infant son whose conception had been heralded with bonfires up and down the country just a few months earlier. The curates were roughly hounded out of their kirks and their manses by the covenanting folks, among them Norman Mackenzie of Calder who had made her friend Jonet's life such a misery. He became a brewer, and never returned to the pulpit.

People she had trusted became enemies; people who had been enemies she was urged to welcome as friends. It was utterly bewildering, and how she longed for Mr Renwick to help her navigate such unfamiliar territory.

Some say that Mr Renwick's death hastened the end of the corrupt regime. It might be true. She is not sure. Mr Lining and Mr Shields, who took over the leadership of the Society people, were in undue haste to reunite with the state-sanctioned Church of Scotland. Many of the faithful followed them, among them Nathaniel, who tried to persuade her that Mr Renwick would have done likewise. How quickly people presume to appropriate the opinions of the dead. Kirstie and Sandy, living next door and raising their bairns, also returned to the kirk with relief. But Helen was uncertain, and so she and James stayed out.

Why?

There were theological arguments, of course, particularly the failure to reaffirm the Covenants, but when it came down to it, she knew she could not bring herself to accept that those who had smiled upon his murder could possibly be of God. She could not forgive. Why, Hew Kennedy became their first Moderator, and John Dalrymple of Stair, who had strutted across the stage at the trial, was also a supporter of the new king and new kirk. These men had his precious blood on their hands, and she and her family would have nothing to do with them.

Ever.

Sorrowing that so few of her friends remained in the remnant, she found comfort in remembering that James Renwick had also grieved over those who no longer stood by his side.

And so the struggle continued, but the danger waned. No one hunted them down now. No one cared. And she and James had their own trials to contend with – God was not finished with them yet. Their beloved first child was conceived in that darkest of times, within a few weeks of James Renwick's death. He seemed a gift of unimaginable tenderness, the one shaft of light breaking through her torment. He was born in November, their little James – what else could they possibly have called him? And for twelve years he danced through their lives, sprinkling laughter, a child of grace.

And then he was gone, taken from them by the fever in one cruel night of sweat, vomit and agony.

And that was to be the tortuous pattern. Three children she bore James Currie, and none of them surviving, each of them taken by the childhood illnesses which her first family had weathered easily. Grief was a tombstone in the heart of their home, a shadow on the hearth and an emptiness in the beds.

She watched with gratitude as Beatrix, Jamie and Charlie

grew to adulthood, and each in turn found a good and godly partner. They were a blessing to her. And she did not speak it aloud, for it would pierce her husband's heart even further, but deep within she knew that her first family, and not her second, had been blessed and prayed over by the godly James Renwick. The Lord honoured his prayers.

And today she will honour him.

She takes a step back, to better view the whole memorial. It is well done. Those who stroll idly by on an afternoon promenade will find a testament in stone to the sacrifice of these brave men and women. They will not be forgotten. And yet, there is an anger still smouldering within her heart, the reason she kept her distance from those self-satisfied men from Edinburgh's establishment. It suits them *now* to claim the honour of the ordinary people who endured the very worst for their faith – but where were they twenty years ago? Some in exile perhaps, hiding in Holland, but many of them were too busy looking after their own skins to think of standing for truth. And now they dare to claim him as their own, to twist his deeds to their own ends. The times they live in now, they are no less evil, but the malevolence is surely more subtle, more beguiling.

And people will believe them, and Mr Renwick's name will be misused, and they will not understand.

They dare to call this freedom.

The tears in her eyes are tears not of grief but of frustration. She thought that today would bring a sense of peace, of completion, but it is not so. The memorial is good, but the memorial is not enough. Already, this day, she has seen how it will be misused. No, what is needed is something more intimate, something which tells the whole story from the point of view of those who lived through it. Mr Shields wrote an account of their struggles in the immediate aftermath of James Renwick's death, but at that time he was dismissed as a fanatic. And Mr Shields can write no more, having perished under the hot sun on that disastrous expedition to establish a Scots colony at Darien. A clear judgement of God on their wicked nation, like the harsh years of famine which followed Mr Renwick's killing. And now there is this foolish new plan to relinquish the last of Scotland's freedom to England in the Treaty of Union. And still the people do not understand. Does she alone hear the thunderous warnings of heaven?

As for Nathaniel, he is still scribbling, still gathering notes, and becoming increasingly eccentric by the day. She has begun to doubt if he will ever finish his life's work.

It leaves only one answer. She lays her hand briefly on the carved Bible once more. She will not let them twist his life to their own ends. The only way to determine which version of this story will prevail is to tell it herself. Her life will reveal his. A woman's story, from her childhood until today, including all the years of their suffering. There is more than one way to write the history of this land.

She walks between tombstones in the shadow of the kirk, her feet brushing fallen leaves, to where her husband and friends stand waiting for her.

The cold stone of memory ever at her back.

Fact or fiction?

This book is a work of fiction, but Helen Alexander and Jonet Gothskirk are both real women who lived in the harsh and turbulent society of late-17th century Scotland.

Helen Alexander recorded her story in an extraordinary memoir written near the end of her life, which was published alongside her husband James Currie's memories in *Passages in the Lives of Helen Alexander and James Currie.* Hers is a rare female voice from the male-dominated Covenanting wars. Helen's account is supported in places by other sources and reveals just how deeply she was involved in the major political events of the day. It was when I read her simple yet intensely moving account of winding the body of James Renwick in Greyfriars Kirkyard that I wanted to explore her story further. Many of the events and characters in her story are therefore based on historical facts.

Jonet Gothskirk's story is very different. The sackcloth gown she was condemned to wear is displayed in the National Museum of Scotland in Edinburgh. As a researcher employed in the creation of the displays, I went to the archives to look for evidence of how this gown was used. In the minutes of West Calder Kirk Session, I uncovered the story of Jonet Gothskirk, sentenced to appear before the congregation week after week for adultery with William Murdoch.

Millions of visitors to the museum have seen the gown and read Jonet's name since the display opened in 1998. She is remembered only for her 'sin'; no other definitive evidence of her life exists. That's not unusual – the lives of many women and men of her status went unrecorded unless they came up against authority in some way. But there must have been much more to Jonet, and so I have given her a story.

Jonet and Helen would never actually have met. The extracts from the minute book at the start of each chapter record word for word what happened to Jonet, but her sentence took place in 1677, not 1687, and in the parish of West Calder. Norman MacKenzie was the minister of the neighbouring parish of Midcalder, and so was not the minister in the pulpit overseeing Jonet's penance. For the purpose of the book I chose to merge the two parishes into the imaginary village of Calder. The character of Nathaniel is loosely based on Patrick Walker, who was imprisoned in Dunnottar and later compiled stories of the Covenanters in *Six Saints of the Covenant*. The other characters in Jonet's story are all fictitious.

Acknowledgements

The Covenanters by Hugh MacDiarmid (Complete Poems Vol 1, 2017) is reprinted by kind permission of Carcanet Press, Manchester, UK.

I would like also to thank all those who have contributed to the very long journey of making this book a reality. Scotland's creative writing centre, Moniack Mhor, is a wonderful place. The people I met there and shared good times and good conversations with during two different courses really helped me to have confidence in myself as a fiction writer, and to understand the book I was trying to write. I am grateful to all of them.

Thank you too to Sandy Jamieson, Rachel Imrie, Hannah Lee, Anna Jones, Sara Roberts and the whole team at Ringwood for believing in *What You Call Free* and helping to make it the book it is today. Particular thanks to Nicola Campbell, Cover Designer, for her inspired work in producing such a striking cover.

Most of all, thanks go to my family, particularly to Mary and Peter, my parents, and to David, Elizabeth and Alastair, whose support and love is everything.

About the author

'But always, it's the stories of the people which intrigue me the most. Writing fiction allows me to explore their lives in a different way' – Flora Johnston.

Flora Johnston is a writer and researcher of all things Scottish. She has written various works of non-fiction, including *St Cuthbert: The Life of a Saint, Faith in a Crisis: Famine, Eviction and The Church in North and South Uist*, and many other nuanced titles that explore education, architecture and religious histories.

Flora has spent many years researching and writing about Scotland's fascinating history in exhibitions, books and digital media, following on from her degree in Scottish History from the University of St. Andrews.

Alongside her literary endeavours, Flora worked for the National Museum of Scotland on the creation of the Museum of Scotland. Whilst researching material for these exhibitions she unearthed some remarkable stories, one of which had a particularly profound impact on her, and whose protagonist, Jonet, became the muse for her debut work of fiction.

More from Ringwood

Some titles from the Ringwood, available from the website in both print and ebook format, as well as usual outlets.
www.ringwoodpublishing.com
mail@ringwoodpublishing.com

There's a Problem with Dad

Carlos Alba

George Lovelace has always done everything by the book – a steady job, wife and children, so why has he felt out of step with those around him?
His sharp, analytical mind only got him so far in his career because he couldn't relate to his workmates. He never managed to make friends, and relations with his wife and children were strained and unpredictable. Now a widower in his 70s, he stands alone against a world that feels as alien as ever – where feelings and intuition always seem more important than cold logic.

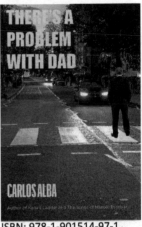

ISBN: 978-1-901514-97-1
£9.99

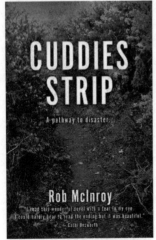

ISBN: 978-1901514-88-9 £9.99

Cuddies Strip

Rob McInroy

Cuddies Strip is based on a true crime and faithfully follows the investigation and subsequent trial but it also examines the mores of the times and the insensitive treatment of women in a male-dominated society.
It is a highly absorbing period piece from 1930s Scotland, with strong contemporary resonances: both about the nature and responsiveness of police services and the ingrained misogyny of the whole criminal justice system.

Memoirs of a Feminist Mother

Carol Fox

As a committed feminist, Carol Fox has achieved success for very many women, but her greatest battle described in this book was very personal. Following serious fertility problems, Carol made the positive decision to become a single parent by choice, to have a child while she still could. Refused access to fertility treatment in Scotland she had no choice but to move to London. Through sheer determination and tenacity, Carol obtained treatment in England in the early 1990s and her daughter was born in 1992, following extensive fertility treatment and battles against judgemental attitudes which appear almost vindictive to us 25 years later. Her story has attracted media coverage, sparking debates on motherhood and the right to be a single parent in the UK.

ISBN: 978-1-901514-21-6   £9.99

In the Shadow of the Crane

John Keeman

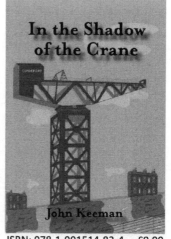

John is born into a Glasgow in flux. Post-WWII, circumstances seem to be improving for the poorest amongst the population.

Yet, as John struggles to gain and maintain a sense of financial and employment stability, he watches as the country around him changes again and his beloved city is decimated by Thatcherism.

He finds his passion in the law, and represents some of the most vulnerable in his battle against injustices.

ISBN: 978-1-901514-83-4   £9.99

Not the Life Imagined

Anne Pettigrew

A darkly humorous, thought-provoking story of Scottish medical students in the sixties, a time of changing social and sexual mores.

Beth Slater is shocked at how few female medical students there are and that some people, think they shouldn't be there at all. Devastated by a close friend's suicide, Beth uncovers a revealing diary and vows to find the person responsible for her death.

Beth charts the students' changing, often stormy, relationships over two decades. In time, indiscretions surface with dire consequences for some.

ISBN: 978-1-901514-70-4   £9.99

Murder at the Mela

Leela Soma

Newly appointed as Glasgow's first Asian DI, Alok Patel's first assignment is the investigation of the brutal murder of Nadia, an Asian woman. Her body was discovered in the aftermath of the Mela festival in Kelvingrove Park. During the Mela, a small fight erupted between a BNP group and an Asian gang, but was quickly quelled by police.

This novel peels away the layers of Glasgow's Asian communities, while exploring the complicated relationships between Asian people and the city.

ISBN: 978-1-901514-90-2
£9.99